"It's c⸱⸱⸱⸱⸱⸱⸱⸱⸱⸱⸱⸱⸱⸱ The atta⸱⸱⸱⸱⸱⸱⸱.⸱"

"What a⸱⸱⸱⸱⸱⸱⸱⸱⸱⸱⸱⸱⸱⸱⸱⸱s he lifted the han⸱⸱⸱⸱⸱⸱⸱⸱⸱⸱ess.

"She's made it back to her security team," Price told him. "They're headed for the ground floor."

The Executioner judged the wind, hefted the hang glider and sprinted across the hotel's roof toward the front of the building. Full-throated autofire erupted behind him, bullets ripping through the HVAC units and throwing swarms of sparks in all directions.

Without hesitation, Bolan kept sprinting, driving himself over the roof until the edge fell away and gravity reached up to claim him. He dropped, hurtling down the side of the building.

MACK BOLAN ®
The Executioner

DON PENDLETON'S
THE EXECUTIONER®
FINAL PLAY

The Moon Shadow Trilogy
Book III

A GOLD EAGLE BOOK FROM
WORLDWIDE®

TORONTO • NEW YORK • LONDON
AMSTERDAM • PARIS • SYDNEY • HAMBURG
STOCKHOLM • ATHENS • TOKYO • MILAN
MADRID • WARSAW • BUDAPEST • AUCKLAND

First edition September 2003
ISBN 0-373-64298-9

Special thanks and acknowledgment to
Mel Odom for his contribution to this work.

FINAL PLAY

I would be true, for there are those who trust me;
I would be pure, for there are those who care;
I would be strong, for there is much to suffer;
I would be brave, for there is much to dare.

—Howard Arnold Walter
1883–1918

The saying goes that the enemy of my enemy is
my friend. And from time to time that rings true.
But trust is hard earned. A wise man watches his
back—always.

—Mack Bolan

THE
MACK BOLAN®
LEGEND

Nothing less than a war could have fashioned the destiny of the man called Mack Bolan. Bolan earned the Executioner title in the jungle hell of Vietnam.

But this soldier also wore another name—Sergeant Mercy. He was so tagged because of the compassion he showed to wounded comrades-in-arms and Vietnamese civilians.

Mack Bolan's second tour of duty ended prematurely when he was given emergency leave to return home and bury his family, victims of the Mob. Then he declared a one-man war against the Mafia.

He confronted the Families head-on from coast to coast, and soon a hope of victory began to appear. But Bolan had broken society's every rule. That same society started gunning for this elusive warrior—to no avail.

So Bolan was offered amnesty to work within the system against terrorism. This time, as an employee of Uncle Sam, Bolan became Colonel John Phoenix. With a command center at Stony Man Farm in Virginia, he and his new allies—Able Team and Phoenix Force—waged relentless war on a new adversary: the KGB.

But when his one true love, April Rose, died at the hands of the Soviet terror machine, Bolan severed all ties with Establishment authority.

Now, after a lengthy lone-wolf struggle and much soul-searching, the Executioner has agreed to enter an "arm's-length" alliance with his government once more, reserving the right to pursue personal missions in his Everlasting War.

Prologue

Shanghai, China, 1929

"You are killing yourself, brother."

Irritably, Jik-Chang Zhao refused to open his eyes and look upon the speaker. He contented himself swimming within the lax and beautiful dream that the opium smoke brought to him. Only fragments of the dream darted through his thoughts, none of them complete, but he was convinced that he had been happy while under the powerful drug's seduction.

"Your enemies are gathering, Jik-Chang." There was no way to know if the announcement came on the heels of the first or if hours had passed. The opium had that kind of effect when Jik-Chang allowed himself to become fully submersed. The light from the scented candle burning nearby limned his eyelids more strongly.

Lying on the thick pillows piled atop the cushioned bed in one of the most expensive rooms in the opium den, Jik-Chang slid his left hand beneath his robe. He was left-handed. Most people watching him in the shadows of the room would have kept watch on his right hand resting lightly on his chest. He curled his left hand around the butt of the pistol he had hidden there.

The pistol was big and solid, reassuring. It was one of the .45 Colt Model 1911s that the American Army had used during the Moro Insurrection in the Philippines only a few years earlier. He kept the safety off and a live round under the hammer.

The Colt .45 was the most powerful handgun Jik-Chang had ever used. During his tenure as master of the Moon Shadows, the triad crime family he headed, he had experienced many occasions to use weapons against enemies. At twenty-eight, one of the youngest of the present triad crime lords, he had become a master of killing.

Jik-Chang kept his breathing shallow. A trace of the opium smoke lingered in his nostrils, burned within his lungs and left a taste at the back of his throat. He heard other voices now. All of them were farther away. A phonograph crackled and spit as the needle worked its way through an American big band song.

"If Guo and Xian only learned patience," the calm voice went on, "they would know that you will accomplish your own death in short order without any help from them."

No longer able to hang on to the fleeting caress of the smoke that had filled his lungs, Jik-Chang opened his eyes. Even the dim candlelight thrust needles into his brain. He cursed, which triggered a coughing fit.

"Your body rejects the poison that you stubbornly fill it with, brother. If you will not listen to me, then you should at least listen to your own body."

"Shut up," Jik-Chang snarled, then coughed more violently. Crimson lightning slashed through his mind.

"Why do you use the opium, brother?"

Jik-Chang wheezed and thought he would never again regain his breath. This time, he felt certain, he had pushed his body too far and he would never regain himself or his mind. The thought didn't scare him, but neither did he find the possibility restful.

Death waited for him every day. Every step he took to further the empire he built, every move he made to protect that empire from those who would take power or wealth from his organization, steeped him that much more in death.

When at last the coughing fit passed and he could breathe again, Jik-Chang cursed and commanded, "Go away from me, Pheng-Kiat. Go away from me if you value your life."

"Brother," Pheng-Kiat stated quietly, "I value my life as I value all things. I value your life, as well. That is why I have come here from the temple."

"You should have stayed at the temple to ring your prayer bells."

Pheng-Kiat was quiet for a time, or perhaps the opium smoke still in Jik-Chang's lungs and mind only made the time seem long.

"When I heard that you were worse, brother," Pheng-Kiat said, "that you were spending more and more time in these accursed dens, I knew I had to come to Shanghai to see you. And to once more attempt to reason with you."

"You are the unreasonable one." Gathering his strength, Jik-Chang sat up on the bed. He brought his legs up under him and held the .45 in one fist. "You insist on spending your whole life in that monastery believing that you will be safe from all of the world."

"The monastery will stand," Pheng-Kiat insisted.

"With the enmity the Shaolin temples have earned from the warlords running China these days, the monastery won't stand long."

"Brother, we carry the bedrock of the monastery within us." Pheng-Kiat sat lotus fashion in the corner of the room near the pitcher and washbasin. He was thin and dressed in orange saffron robes. Candlelight gleamed from his freshly shaved scalp. "That building may be torn down, scattered to the four winds, but the Shaolin will exist forever."

Jik-Chang snorted bitterly. "And you accuse me of spending my days wrapped in dreams."

"Dreams are a natural state. In fact, there has been much discussion about whether a man lives his life or only thinks he does."

The room felt cold. Tapestries from myth covered the windowless walls, filled with dragons and tigers and warriors armed with spears, swords, shields and bows. Other tapestries showed fireworks bursting in the air and ships sailing across endless seas. Gray smoke eddied around the single tea candle floating in a small bowl of perfumed water and rose petals. Hanging drapes covered the doorway.

Jik-Chang pulled a heavy blanket more tightly around his shoulders. He looked at his brother and wondered again how a miraculous birth of twins could leave two brothers so far apart in life. Legend and superstition always stated that twins were powerful, full of portent and possibilities.

But since their earliest days, Jik-Chang and Pheng-Kiat had been as different as night and day, as different as yin and yang. Where Jik-Chang had always been a man of rapacious appetites for wine and women and danger, Pheng-Kiat had always sought out the quiet places in life and had always turned his own thinking inward.

Sixteen years ago, when Boon-Siong—who had been eldest son of Mushu Zhao, who had brought the Moon Shadows to prominence among the crime families in Shanghai—had given the older twin to the monastery, people had thought it was to keep the two boys from fighting for the right to command the Moon Shadows. Instead, Boon-Siong had chosen to hide his weaker son away where the Moon Shadow triad's enemies couldn't use him as a hostage against the triad.

The Zhao family still contributed to the monastery on a regular basis as Boon-Siong had ordained. Everyone knew that the monastery protected their own with a fierceness that belied their gentle teachings. The Shaolin priests and initiates had learned harsh lessons from past abuses at the hands of emperors, foreigners and the various warlords.

And, Jik-Chang knew, the Shaolin temples were not completely clear of crime themselves. The Boxer Rebellion at the turn of the twentieth century had been helped along by many of the temples that preached a benevolent way of life. The Europeans, Americans and Japanese who had invaded China in the previous years had sought to dominate the country for their own profits. The English had fought two wars for the express purpose of protecting their opium markets.

"Perhaps then," Jik-Chang said, "I only dream you, brother, and have dreams of poisoning myself with the English opium."

Pheng-Kiat's brow wrinkled. Evidently the conundrum the priests had posed to him during his learning in the temple had never actually touched his life.

Regaining his strength as the last of the opium trailed out of his body, Jik-Chang opened the small box beside the bed and took out his pocket watch. The time was almost three-thirty. He guessed that it was in the afternoon because the opium smoke had never lasted an unexpected twelve hours.

Jik-Chang exchanged his robes for the white European suit he wore as regular dress. Despite their wars and reluctance to continue doing business with the English, French and Americans, most of Shanghai had adopted the foreigners' ways and their dress. The Moon Shadow warlord shrugged into a double shoulder holster rig. He shoved the .45 he had slept with into the other holster of the matched pair.

"So many guns, brother." Pheng-Kiat shook his head as if in sadness. "You will die by the gun."

"Only if that happens before munitions makers invent one of those beam pistols like the heroes in those pulp magazines you read." Not all of Pheng-Kiat's reading was limited to the ancient texts the monks ascribed to. One of their younger brothers often sent American pulp magazines up the Whangpoo River to the monastery with the monthly tribute.

Pheng-Kiat grinned with the same boyish embarrassment he had always had. "A guilty pleasure, brother."

"One the monks would understand?"

"Sadly, no. Although my master has found my small cache of pulps and turned a blind eye to them."

Jik-Chang knotted his tie with only a little difficulty. "Then perhaps these monks of yours are even less perfect than you think if they promote such dissention and a lack of discipline within their ranks."

"They are not perfect," Pheng-Kiat protested. "They only strive toward perfection. As must every man."

Jik-Chang's temples pounded with the familiar headache that filled his skull. "I have no time and no attention for this argument." He pulled on his coat on and started for the door.

Fluid and seemingly without effort, Pheng-Kiat rose to his feet. His orange robe straightened and fell to his ankles without a sound. He walked at Jik-Chang's side with the same lack of noise.

"Good," Pheng-Kiat said. "I don't care to be defending myself."

"Nor do I," Jik-Chang said.

Pheng-Kiat sighed deeply as they passed through the drapes that covered the doorway. "Brother, I am only concerned about your health."

"Why? When I die, the shipments to the monastery will continue. Unless, of course, one of the triads that war with us manages to take over our territories."

The argument was an old one, and Jik-Chang didn't want to get into it again. Pheng-Kiat always sought him out in one of the opium dens he frequented. Although the establishments weren't supposed to allow anyone in to see him, his brother always managed to slip through.

Monks were supposed to have abilities that made them stronger and faster than normal men, but Jik-Chang had seen plenty of them die when they crossed the wrong warlord. He secretly guessed that it was because Pheng-Kiat was a favorite of many in Shanghai, especially the women who worked in the opium dens and in the singsong houses. His brother had a broad knowledge of medicine and often tended the women, as well as their children. Pheng-Kiat was more involved with everyday people than most monks tended to be.

They walked through the narrow hallway down three flights of stairs. As they went down, the opium den became less and less opulent. Blankets strung from twine partitioned several rooms. Men moaned and cursed and dreamed on cots on the floor that were the same size as caskets.

"Do you ever see this?" Pheng-Kiat asked quietly as they walked toward the vestibule.

"No." At the time that Jik-Chang entered the opium den, the only thing he was truly aware of was the clamoring need for the smoke in his lungs.

"The smoke takes you to your death, brother."

"Every day takes me to my death," Jik-Chang said.

The guards posted at the doors wore traditional Chinese coolie uniforms, but the triad leader knew that they kept pistols concealed within that clothing and rifles and shotguns close to hand. The Moon Shadows protected the opium house, and Jik-Chang never questioned their loyalty.

"The smoke makes you vulnerable in more ways than one," Pheng-Kiat stated.

Jik-Chang stepped through the vestibule and out into the harsh afternoon sunlight that shone down over Shanghai. The city had changed even during the years that Jik-Chang had been alive, growing and evolving as more and more trade centered there. Diverse nations cast envious eyes on the city, and the profits—legal, as well as illegal—were divided by a number of groups willing to kill for them.

"Your enemies know of your weakness," Pheng-Kiat said as they went down the wooden stairs in front of the building. The opium den was sandwiched between a theater and a restaurant. The alley contained a singsong house and small warehouses that held smuggled goods as well as stolen and illegal ones.

The stench from the Whangpoo River only a dozen blocks away was heavy and fetid still in September. Boats and ships plied the waters, and ships' mates and crew yelled at each other in a dozen different languages.

"I know of the weaknesses of my enemies," Jik-Chang said. "It keeps us balanced."

"That balance changed a few days ago. Guo and Xian have united."

Jik-Chang halted at the bottom of the stairs, not wanting to venture out into the muddy street the recent rains had left. Despite the fact that the streets were stone, mud washed out from the flats that surrounded the city. Several times when the Whangpoo flooded, the lower parts of Shanghai flooded, as well.

"How do you know Guo and Xian united?" Jik-Chang demanded.

"The monastery is the center of much news, brother," Pheng-Kiat answered. "We offer a protected marketplace for many who live in the city, as well as those tribes who come down from the hills. While there, people speak of things that trouble them." He paused. "Much of what troubles them is the constant warring between the triads."

"The triads will always make war," Jik-Chang said. He stared at the surrounding buildings and felt cold again. "Only by being willing to spill the blood of others, as well as ourselves, can our business grow." He waved at his driver, parked in the alley on the other side of the street. The man waved back and attempted to start the engine.

Pheng-Kiat shook his head. "That is only here. There are other places where such a life is not necessary."

"You don't know what you're talking about." Sickness twisted Jik-Chang's head. He banked the anger he felt at his brother. The argument had always been there between them since the Black Swans had killed their father.

"Hong Kong is more peaceful than Shanghai."

"The damn English are still there, and they are still in control." Jik-Chang dug in his pockets and produced a pack of American cigarettes. The Moon Shadows handled a lot in the way of contraband.

"The English maintain a firmer control in Hong Kong," Pheng-Kiat replied. "The legitimate trade there is more important, and a family that is smart and quick and willing to work hard can do a lot for themselves."

Jik-Chang lit his cigarette and stared at his brother. "This is an old argument. Our father didn't listen when you talked to him of this."

"I keep hoping that you will."

"No. Our place is here."

"Here?" Pheng-Kiat waved to indicate the city spread around them. "This city is filled only with harshness and crime."

"Those are your names for it. I call it opportunity."

Pheng-Kiat stared at Jik-Chang. "We are dying here, brother," the monk said. "You know that yourself. More and more of our young cousins die during the bitter feuds between the triads, or trying to keep control of businesses the British and the Japanese desire. Even the Americans and the French see us only as vassals that provide goods, markets and services they want to expand their own resources."

"They teach economy at the monastery, priest?"

"Yes."

That surprised Jik-Chang.

"A history of a people is often a history of its trade," Pheng-Kiat replied. "If you were more enlightened, you would know these things. That's how I am also able to say that Hong Kong would be a good place for the Moon Shadows."

"I'm not leaving this place." Jik-Chang shook his head angrily. "Our father died here to protect our investments and holdings. I can do no less."

"Our father will still be dead. But there are other people you can save if you but will."

"I am working on saving them. I've allied the Moon Shadows with the Green Gang Society, and I have curried favor with Chiang Kai-shek. He controls the Kuomintang, and he has taken a stand against the Chinese Communists and rejected further aid from the Russians. Soon, we will banish all the foreigners from our lands."

"Not for a very long time. Besides the Western armies that protect the trade those countries have here, the Japanese lie in wait and are already fortifying their positions in Manchuria. The Japanese are still trying to recover from the Great Kanto Earthquake that leveled Tokyo. And there is much unrest in the outside world after the Great War ended. My teachers predict another war before too long. They believe that such a war will give Japan all the excuse she needs to try to seize lands within China. Hong Kong is farther south, and the British will strive to hold those lands."

A Ford motorcar trundled from the alleyway. The narrow tires slipped and jerked through the rutted mud covering the paving stones.

"A new life can be made for our family in Hong Kong." Pheng-Kiat reached inside his robe sleeve and took out a rolled parchment. "It is time we gave up our criminal ways, brother."

"Those are the only ways left to us," Jik-Chang said. "You know the history of our family. When Chi-Kan Zhao first became a pirate in those long-ago days, he marked his descendants and their descendants with the bad luck that plagues us."

"Chi-Kan was a strong man," Pheng-Kiat said. "He did what he had to do so that his family might survive at the time. But the times have changed. It will take a strong man to change the course of that luck."

Wearily, Jik-Chang shook his head. "I am not that man. You know that yourself. You told me you know of my weakness."

"Opium."

"Yes."

"That weakness has been defeated by others," Pheng-Kiat said in a serious tone. "I have helped them. You are strong as any of them. Jik-Chang, you are the strongest man I have ever known."

For an instant, Jik-Chang felt embarrassed. Kind words flowed easily from his brother, but he had seldom returned them over the years. Sometimes he felt there was no kindness left in him. "I don't wish to. The opium is the only thing that lets me dream." He looked at his brother. "I weary of the constant fear and responsibility. They eat at a man like locusts until nothing is left, not even the bones."

Pheng-Kiat placed his hands upon his brother's shoulders. His hazel eyes shone in the sun. "You can make a difference, Jik-Chang. You have the hearts of our family in a way that our father never did. He did not have your ability to inspire them, nor did he have your drive to progress beyond what the family already held."

All of what Pheng-Kiat said was true. Jik-Chang knew that. But he didn't want to think about everything his brother said. His head felt still too muddled by the opium. He could think clearly, but it was only with effort.

The car pulled in front of the stairs.

"I have these papers," Pheng-Kiat said. "I have gone over them many times." He held the rolled parchment. "I have drawn up plans for businesses in Hong Kong. Legitimate businesses that our family can buy or build or take part in down in Hong Kong. I've been promised."

"Legitimate businesses." Jik-Chang snorted. "Do you know how little profits are involved in legitimate businesses?"

"People can get by on little," Pheng-Kiat said. "As long as they feel safe. This place will never be safe for us. Perhaps we will never truly find homes in China."

A curse ripped from Jik-Chang's throat. "Where then should

we go, brother? To Gold Mountain?" Gold Mountain was what the Chinese had called California back in the 1850s. "I've been told the Americans have built all the railroads they need and that there is no more room for laundries. Chinese whores are not treated well there, and the Italian Mafia controls most of the crime. There is no place for us there."

"Please," Pheng-Kiat said. "Look at these papers."

Jik-Chang willed his heart to be hard and cold, but as he looked at his twin, he felt the bond between them. No matter the differences between them, the love still remained.

Then Jik-Chang saw the driver of his car bring up a .455 Webley pistol and point the weapon at him. As the sights centered on him, Jik-Chang realized the man was not his driver at all.

"Look out!" Jik-Chang shouted, reaching for the .45 holstered under his left arm while throwing himself at Pheng-Kiat. He collided with his twin as he brought up the .45 and squeezed off rounds.

The massive .455 slug cut the air where Jik-Chang had been standing. In the next heartbeat, one of his .45 rounds slapped through the car's windshield. The following round caught the assassin full in the face and snapped his head back.

Four other men came from the surrounding buildings, all of them carrying pistols, shotguns and rifles. Jik-Chang cataloged the men with the skills he had honed while staying alive at his father's side through dozens of firefights. A flash of orange saffron robe told him that Pheng-Kiat was already in motion, as well.

A bullet caught Jik-Chang above his left hip and spun him. He pulled his other .45 and turned with the force of the blow, lifting both pistols and firing into the center of the man to his left. Even as the man went down, another raised a shotgun.

Jik-Chang threw himself forward, sliding through the mud under the car. The shotgun exploded behind him, striking the car's rear tire and shredding the rubber. A few stray pellets struck Jik-Chang's left thigh. A blazing trail of fire ignited along his leg.

Crawling on his elbows and knees, Jik-Chang turned and fired at the man with the shotgun. The bullets knocked the man's legs from under him. Then, with blood streaming down his side, Jik-Chang crawled from the back of the car, stood and ran to the wounded man as he tried to bring his shotgun back up. The Moon Shadow leader pointed his left-hand pistol at the man's head and squeezed the trigger, emptying the assassin's skull in a crimson rush.

The third man tried to stand his ground. He carried a long-barreled .38 revolver many of the American sailors favored as hideout guns. The assassin sighted carefully and fired.

Jik-Chang felt the bullet slam into his ribs on the right side. He brought up both his own pistols and fired at the center of the man. The man fell backward and sprawled across the mud and the paving stones.

One man was left.

Fear and the leftover effects of the opium smoke hammered Jik-Chang's frantic thoughts. He raced back to the car, taking the shelter the vehicle afforded. He stood with his back to the car, his knees bent to drop his head below the window line, and listened.

Footsteps sounded on the other side of the car.

Rising, fear and rage screaming inside his head, Jik-Chang turned and darted forward with both pistols raised. He fired at the figure in front of him on the other side of the car, never noticing the orange robes until it was too late.

The bullets hit Pheng-Kiat dead center in the chest and drove him back a step. He released his hold on the man beside him whom he had taken captive. It had been Pheng-Kiat's prisoner that Jik-Chang had heard.

And he had shot his brother.

The assassin, freed of the monk's hold, raced away.

Stunned, Jik-Chang crossed to the other side of the car. Scarlet blossoms stained the front of Pheng-Kiat's robe. His eyes looked feverish, glassy.

Jik-Chang dropped to his knees, laid his pistols at his sides and took his brother into his arms. "Pheng-Kiat!"

His brother reached up to him. Blood leaked from the corner of his mouth.

Holding his brother tightly, feeling the hot tears burn his eyes, Jik-Chang tried to speak and couldn't.

"Not you," Pheng-Kiat wheezed. "Our family's...bad luck." Blood bubbled and burst at his mouth, then ran down his chin. "Chi-Kan's legacy...you must...break it, brother." He lifted the parchment he had offered earlier.

With a shaking hand, mind screaming for the opium to dull his senses, Jik-Chang took the parchment.

"Only way," Pheng-Kiat whispered. "All...other paths...only... death. You must...promise."

"I do, brother. I swear to you." And Jik-Chang held his brother until Pheng-Kiat died, their blood mixing in the street.

British Columbia, Canada

Bright afternoon sun lanced the scattered puffy clouds that floated above Vancouver's international airport. A departing DC-10 raked thunder over the surrounding area, heeling westward and catching the gleaming sun for an instant.

Mack Bolan stood in the United States arrival area of the airport near the florist shop on the second level. He wore a green, brushed denim shirt, khakis, running shoes and a brown lightweight jacket. Clear-lensed glasses, a false beard and an Atlanta Braves ball cap made him look like a college professor on vacation. A book bag carried in one hand enhanced that appearance.

With all the new security involved at the airports, the Executioner hadn't tried to bring a weapon on-site. He doubted that Saengkeo Zhao and her entourage brought weapons into the airport either.

She and Johnny Kwan, as well as two dozen other "employees," stayed grouped together, a phalanx that moved through the arrivals line. The entourage elicited notice from the surrounding groups there to meet family members or business associates.

Men and women in plainclothes and jackets stood grouped loosely around the area. Earbuds snaked up the sides of their necks and poked into ear canals. Bolan figured them at once for police officers.

Reaching inside his jacket, Bolan took out a slimline cell phone. He flipped the bottom open and used the speed-dial function.

"Yeah," Jack Grimaldi answered on the first ring.

"Show time," Bolan said.

"I'll have the car around front," the pilot responded, " and see if I notice any conspicuous limousines."

"Do that," Bolan suggested, and broke the connection. Grimaldi was there to keep an eye on the perimeter.

The Executioner felt edgy and tired despite the three hours' sleep he'd managed during the early hours of the morning. The mission he'd taken onto his own plate in New York had led him to Arizona following the trail of a mystery woman who had turned out to be Pei-Ling Bao. Pei-Ling Bao was a friend of Saengkeo Zhao, who had become the leader of the Moon Shadows triad after her brother, Syn-Tek, had been found murdered little more than a week before.

The Moon Shadow triad dated back hundreds of years to the early days of piracy in China's history. Saengkeo Zhao had been active with her father and brother in managing the crime organization's affairs, and had stepped in immediately to lead the Moon Shadows after her brother's death.

A deadly trail had led Bolan to the woman in the cold, harsh waters of the Indian Ocean. Whispers had slipped through the shadows of crime syndicates about the three nuclear weapons that had gone missing when the Russian submarine *Kursk* had been raised from her watery grave. The Executioner had tracked those weapons down to New York City, where the *mafiya* had been arranging a buy-back of one of the weapons from a Chinese triad called the Green Ghosts.

Joining forces with Leo Turrin and Don De Luca's American mafia while masquerading as a Black Ace, Bolan had managed to capture one of the Russians. During the later interrogation, Bolan had learned what had become of *Kursk*'s missing arsenal after the salvage.

Those weapons had ended up in the hands of Russian *mafiya*, which had lost them to a group that was suspected of being Chinese pirates. One of those weapons had been recovered off the coast of China, obviously lost during the battle aboard *Jadviga*, the Russian freighter that had been transporting the illegal and dangerous cargo.

Before Bolan could further interrogate the prisoner, a hit team made up of ex-CIA agents had broken into the hiding area and killed him. Bolan and Turrin had barely managed to escape. But they had learned about Pei-Ling Bao. Barbara Price, mission controller for Stony Man Farm, the ultrasecret hardsite in Virginia that provided support and equipment to Able Team and Phoenix Force, had offered Bolan help in the form of intelligence and communications.

The CIA had turned down Harold Brognola's offer of assistance, and the President had agreed to that. Phoenix Force and Able Team were off the board, but Bolan had chosen to pursue the matter. That was one of the reasons he maintained his arm's-length relationship with Stony Man Farm in spite of the friendships he had with those people.

Outside of Scottsdale, Arizona, the Executioner had taken out the Chinese snakeheads transporting illegal Chinese aliens from Mexico. He had found Pei-Ling Bao, whom the Soaring Dragons had intended to sell to one of the hot-mattress brothels where women were kept as virtual slaves for sex. Pei-Ling Bao's friendship with Zhao had pointed Bolan in the direction of the Moon Shadows.

Leo Turrin had kept working in New York, following up leads on the *mafiya*. He'd turned up the lead about the nuclear weapon aboard *Charity's Smile* in the Indian Ocean. Bolan had gone there with Jack Grimaldi, Stony Man Farm's ace pilot, and had confronted the *mafiya* team transporting the weapon. He'd also confronted Saengkeo Zhao, who had obviously been there to take the nuclear weapon by force.

The confrontation had ended in a stalemate. Bolan had sunk the freighter and sent the warhead down into the brine, where it was later recovered by a U.S. Navy salvage team. No mention had been made about the missing nuclear weapons.

After breaking the engagement in the Indian Ocean, Bolan had targeted the Moon Shadows. He'd moved into the Vancouver, British Columbia area, tracking down Eric Barnes, one of the big movers and shakers in trafficking illegal arms and drugs. The Executioner had ripped through the crime-related holdings of the Moon Shadows all night, hoping to draw Saengkeo Zhao out into the open. Evidently, the attacks had been successful.

Saengkeo Zhao had flown to Vancouver under her own name rather than an alias. According to Price's intel, Zhao's point of departure had been Los Angeles. That was where Pei-Ling Bao had been released to the Moon Shadow lawyers after the Stony Man mission controller had arranged for her to be turned over to the Immigration and Naturalization Services. Pei-Ling Bao had also been scheduled to leave L.A. that evening.

The Moon Shadow triad leader strode through the airport with Kwan at her side. She wore a short-waisted blue tweed jacket over a white blouse and pale blue suede jeans. At first glance, Saengkeo Zhao looked demure.

The image clashed sharply with the memory Bolan had of her

aboard *Charity's Smile*. Aboard the Russian freighter, Saengkeo had been a black-clad angel of death. She'd fought viciously, cutting a swath through the Russian *mafiya*.

Johnny Kwan, the head of the security for the Moon Shadows, walked at Saengkeo Zhao's side with a security team. He and his men wore tailored black suits.

A female police officer in plainclothes led two men on an interception course, stopping Saengkeo and chatting briefly. At the end of it, Saengkeo nodded and accompanied the police from the airport.

Bolan watched them go. The cell phone buzzed for attention in his jacket and he pulled it out. "Yeah."

"The Vancouver police just took Zhao in for questioning," Price said.

"I know." Bolan watched the group disappear through the glass doors that led outside the airport. Unmarked police cars swept into the loading area like vultures descending on defenseless prey. "What do they have on her?"

"Nothing," Price replied. "They'll make her life miserable for a little while, then they'll have to cut her loose. She didn't have to go with them now."

"Except that if she didn't, the police department could make things harder for her while she's here."

"They may do that anyway," Price pointed out.

"Yeah," Bolan said, trailing along in the wake of the Moon Shadows and Vancouver police. "But she's also getting to know who's going to be swinging the weight on her."

"There's that," Price agreed. "But she's leaving herself terribly open."

"That's the message she's sending. Come get her if they think they can. It's a gutsy move." The warrior respected that.

"If it doesn't get her killed."

Bolan silently watched Saengkeo decline the invitation to sit in one of the unmarked police vehicles. One of the police constables reluctantly accepted the offer of a ride in one of the limousines waiting for the Moon Shadows. The move was all about respect, and Bolan knew that.

"I found out who the people were that took Jack last night," Price said. During the attack on the Moon Shadow connections in Vancouver, an unidentified group that had come across as American agents had taken prisoner Grimaldi briefly.

"Who were they?"

"I'd rather go into it back at the next safehouse."

Bolan accepted that. He and Grimaldi had spent the remainder of the night and part of the morning regrouping and catching a few hours of sleep in a houseboat out on Burrard Inlet. The warrior executioner watched as Saengkeo Zhao's limousine glided away from the curb, melding with the traffic.

"Can you keep her in view?" Bolan asked.

"Yes. We made the confirmation outside the airport. If nobody does anything too radical, we're good here." Stony Man Farm had access to a LEO, a low-Earth-orbit geosynchronous satellite with video tracking capability. If Saengkeo Zhao didn't try to move too quickly across too much distance or get lost in a crowd, they could monitor her.

"If you had a nuclear weapon," Bolan asked, "would you come to a city where you were going to be the target of an unknown enemy?"

"I would," Price countered, "if I wanted to make sure that the unknown enemy got killed quickly."

"That's something to keep in mind," Bolan agreed.

"CONSTABLE SIMONS," Saengkeo Zhao said, trying not to show any of the angry frustration that struggled desperately to break loose inside her, "at this point you're wasting my time and running the risk of insulting me."

Paul Simons had a youthful appearance, but gray tinted his blond temples and hair. His skin complexion was pasty, the color of a man who rarely got outside or who worked primarily nights. Most people would have underestimated him, underestimated the drive that he possessed. He had taken his blue blazer off within minutes of arriving at the conference room where Saengkeo had been kept in relative comfort since being brought in to the main department at 2120 Cambie Street. He still wore his blue tie over a starched white shirt with sharp creases.

"Inspector Simons," Simons corrected automatically.

"Inspector." Saengkeo nodded. The man's immediate claiming of his title told her what she needed to know about what drove him. The skillful way he'd posed his questions in the interview room had proved that he had plenty of experience, and let her know that his superiors stood behind the one-way glass that filled the wall to her left.

Simons made a show of relaxing. He reached for the coffee cup at his side and took a sip. Saengkeo hadn't touched her tea, which had been brought shortly after she'd been shown to the room. The brand was one of her favorites, proving that they knew something of her, but the knowledge wasn't anything that two minutes' time spent with a server at a restaurant in Vancouver that she frequented wouldn't have told them.

"I don't feel that the time has been a waste," Simons said. "As a matter of fact, I feel that—"

"Perhaps," Saengkeo interrupted, "you have the time to repeat questions in different manners only to hear me say again and again that I know nothing of what happened last night. I don't know who committed terrorist actions against businesses my family owned and operated, or had investments with." She had to phrase the last carefully, knowing she was leaving records that her attorneys would have to deal with at some point. "I would, however, like very much to find out who did this so that the Vancouver Police Department can arrest the individual or individuals responsible for the murder of my family's employees. I will have to face the families of those men and tell them that I feel confident in the Vancouver Police Department's ability to find that murderer. I will have to tell them that I feel confident in your ability."

Simons's face hardened a little. "Miss Zhao, perhaps you fail to realize your position of culpability in these matters. The Carnation Building enterprise—"

"Was perfectly legal," Saengkeo said.

"Not if there was prostitution taking place on those premises."

"Was there? If so, feel free to talk to my attorneys about the matter."

"There was gambling going on at the Sports Fan Bar & Grill," Simons said, not missing a beat.

"If so," Saengkeo said, "I didn't know about it. My family was only a silent partner in the restaurant. Again, if you have proof of that, talk to my attorneys. Not me."

"A court may find your family guilty."

"If so, we will be forced to pay a fine." And that was the strongest charge that could be brought against her and her family. Even then, the government might not want to do even that. The Moon Shadow triad's legitimate businesses paid a hefty amount of taxes every year. Losing that much of the tax base, plus risking an unfavorable reaction from the Asian community of the city, might not be something the city chose to do.

Simons opened an aluminum flight attaché case on the conference table. He took out a folder, then spread 8X10 color photographs across the tabletop. The photographs showed dead men and wrecked cars. Soot stained the cars, left from the gasoline-fed fires that had consumed them.

The inspector tapped pictures that held images of the dead men. "Do you know these men?"

Saengkeo looked at the pictures. "No."

"You don't know any of these men?" Suspicious disbelief rang in Simons's words.

"No," Saengkeo said, lifting her eyes to the inspector's.

"I was told that they worked for you."

"No."

"Your family has a large number of holdings in this city," Simons said good-naturedly. "Perhaps you don't know everyone that works for you."

"You can check through my employee records," Saengkeo said. "I'm sure my attorneys will insist on a court order, though."

Simons frowned. "We're trying to keep the attorneys clear of these matters."

"So am I."

Simons started to say something, then chose not to.

"What business were they supposed to work for me in?" Saengkeo needed to know how strong the case against her and her family might be.

"They were money collectors."

"You believe they worked for one of the finance agencies that my family owns?"

"Not exactly."

"Then what exactly?" Saengkeo said.

"These men were reported enforcers," Simons said, "who collected monies from illegal businesses that the Moon Shadows were involved in."

"Careful, Inspector," Saengkeo warned gently. "You're treading very close to slander here." She reached into her purse and took out the microcassette recorder she'd been using to secretly tape the conversation. She didn't bother to reveal the transmitter built into her purse that relayed the conversation to an audio recording studio in one of the other Moon Shadow businesses.

"They were men who were allegedly involved in collecting monies from illegal businesses that the Moon Shadows allegedly controlled," Simons said.

"Were they such enforcers?"

Simons hesitated, cut his gaze to the microcassette recorder, then back to Saengkeo. "We are still building the case regarding that."

"You're building the case against these murdered men, hoping to somehow disenfranchise my business, my family, and yet you don't pursue the man who did this." Saengkeo edged her words with venomous sarcasm. "Should that be the message I take back to those grieving families?"

A nervous tic fluttered to life around Simons's left eye. "Miss Zhao—"

"Men my family employed," Saengkeo said, then tapped the pictures of the dead men on the tabletop, "and men you presume were employed by my family were murdered tonight, Inspector Simons. You have work to do already without implicating my family or me in this matter."

Simons leaned back in his chair. "Why do you think this man—or men—attacked the Zhao family businesses?"

"I don't know. When you find this man, you should ask him."

"Do you know who he is?"

"No."

"Do any of your people?"

"None that I have talked to."

"We're having trouble talking to your employees, Miss Zhao. They all seem more than a little reticent to volunteer information about the situations."

"My employees," Saengkeo said, "will be more than happy to give you any information about the murders."

Simons started to say something.

Saengkeo cut the inspector off. "My employees will not, however, tolerate questioning about my family's business."

Leaning forward, placing his elbows on the table, Simons said, "They aren't going to talk to us because you've told them not to?"

"They're not going to talk to you," Saengkeo replied, "because they have learned not to trust anyone outside the family. They have been betrayed several times in their dealings with government agents and entities. If I did not intercede on your behalf in this matter, they would not talk to you at all."

Simons knew that was the truth. Saengkeo could tell that the man knew that by the small slump of defeat that showed in his shoulders. Transplanted Asian communities were notorious for not talking to law enforcement even when they were victims.

"No one knows who that man was," Simons said. "The detectives on the case feel that your people know but aren't telling us."

"They're wrong."

"Is that right, Miss Zhao?" Simons stared at her with intent earnestness. "Would you tell us if you knew? Would you tell me?"

Saengkeo took a folder from her own valise and removed a single picture of the man in black who had wreaked havoc among her family. "You've already confiscated all the security video disc records of the two places that were attacked. You have pictures of the man who did this." She dropped the picture on top of the ones the police inspector had shown her, as if she were upping the ante in the game that they were playing.

The picture was the best among the footage that had been shot by the video cameras. Even with the digital nature of the records and the effort that had gone into cleaning up the image, the man's face was revealed well. It was as if the man had known where the cameras were at all times and was successfully able to dodge the best shots.

De-Ying Wu, the private investigator Saengkeo kept on retainer in Vancouver, had been present at the time of the man in black's attack on Eric Barnes. Wu had been assigned to keep surveillance on Barnes because Saengkeo hadn't trusted the man. The man in black had saved Wu's life, which hadn't fit in with the destruction that he had unleashed upon the Moon Shadow's business holdings.

Simons regarded the picture on the table but made no move to touch it. "Evidently we didn't confiscate all of the security recordings. You know that holding evidence back is a crime in this country."

"I didn't hold evidence back," Saengkeo said. "If you match that frame against the records your detectives and constables were given, you'll find that image came from a duplicate recording."

"You—"

"Those recordings," Saengkeo said, "were given willingly, without the benefit of a court order. My attorneys suggested I keep copies of those recordings. I have. They're in possession of those attorneys now."

"How do I know that those recordings haven't been tampered with?"

Saengkeo stood and picked up the microcassette recorder. She knew that the tape had only another two or three minutes of running time. She'd kept an eye on the time during the whole interview. "We're done here, Inspector Simons. If you need anything further, contact me through my attorneys." She dropped a business card onto the table.

"My superiors could take a dim view of your actions, Miss Zhao."

"Your superiors," Saengkeo said, "have already turned a blind eye toward the real crime that happened last night, it seems. A dim view doesn't worry me."

"Eric Barnes was a known associate of the Zhao family," Simons stated.

Saengkeo waited.

"Would it surprise you to know that a large amount of drugs and cash were found in a business he owned?"

"No," Saengkeo said. "It's amazing to me that you had to wait until the event of his death to find them."

Simons became quiet.

"Everyone knew that Eric Barnes trafficked in drugs," Saengkeo went on. "If you want to know about that part of his business, check with the American television and movie studios that are based in this city or frequently travel here." She paused. "Or maybe leaning on Hollywood studios isn't as politically correct as putting pressure on struggling Asian immigrants."

Simons's face darkened. "Miss Zhao, I hardly think that's fair—"

"For once," Saengkeo said, "we find something we agree on."

An unhappy look skidded across the police inspector's face.

Saengkeo glanced at the picture of the man in black. "Find that man, Inspector Simons. Find him and you'll find the answers to many of the questions you're asking me. As for this conversation, I'm done here. If you need any further contact, call my attorneys."

"I trust you're going to be looking for this man, as well, Miss Zhao."

"Yes."

"And if you find him?"

Saengkeo paused at the door. "We'll turn him over to you."

"This department doesn't condone vigilante activity."

Locking eyes with the man, Saengkeo said, "And I don't condone the murder of people who have put their faith and trust in me." She clicked off the recorder and stepped through the interview room door.

"Her name is Deborah Ames Carter. She's a CIA agent."

Mack Bolan sat with Jack Grimaldi in the living room of the houseboat on Burrard Inlet that Barbara Price had established as their temporary base of operations. A plane engine buzzed by overhead. In addition to offering slips for several fishing boats, pleasure craft and houseboats, Burrard Inlet also offered a marine runway and docking used by seaplanes for the tourist business, corporations and private companies.

The houseboat had a full sensor array in place to monitor activity around the location, both above and beneath the water. Kurtzman also had a team providing additional visual surveillance from a satellite link. The expense of human resources monitoring the houseboat was costly in terms of time, but the Executioner's mission in Vancouver against the Moon Shadows rated the additional security.

"She's a current CIA agent?" Bolan asked. In New York City not even a week ago, a two-man team of ex-CIA agents had killed the Russian *mafiya* man they'd taken prisoner and gotten information from. The two men had also tried to kill Bolan and Grimaldi.

"Yes," Price confirmed.

A notebook computer sat on the small coffee table bolted to the houseboat living-room floor. Suction-cup mounts on the bottom of the computer kept the device locked to the tabletop. The internet computer connection was encrypted, feeding through the local phone service that plugged into the houseboat. Even if a hacker chose to intercept the signal, he or she wouldn't be able to decrypt the transmission without risking serious hard-drive damage. A speakerphone using a secondary phone line, also heavily encrypted, put them in touch with Stony Man Farm.

The notebook computer's screen showed a quartet of pictures of the woman bartender from the Nautilus Club. Beside the typical front and profile shots, there were two more shots of the woman in riot gear during a firefight and aboard a plane in full paratrooper outfitting.

"Her interest at the Nautilus Club couldn't have been Jack," Bolan pointed out.

"No," Price agreed. "She was there on assignment."

"Watching Barnes," Bolan said.

"Yes. She'd been in place for the past seven weeks."

"The missiles went missing from *Kursk* about then."

"True, but there's been nothing to tie the missiles to Eric Barnes."

"But Eric Barnes was tied to Saengkeo Zhao," Bolan said. "And Barnes handled a lot of legal and illegal shipping business for the Moon Shadows."

"You think they might have planned on moving the third nuke across the Pacific Ocean and holing it up in Canada?" Grimaldi asked.

Bolan considered the possibility. "Depends on whether the terrorists' target was the United States or Israel. We haven't even been able to ascertain that. Or have we?"

"No," Price responded. "Our intel coming out of the Middle East is scattered and sketchy. You can get the same story six different ways over there now, or you can find one incident that breeds six different false rumors. We're tracking them down now, but at the moment we're getting closer to finding out who the weapons brokers were in Russia."

"And when you find out?" Bolan asked.

"You'll be the first to know. The Man doesn't want to ruffle any more feathers in Russia than he has to. CIA won't be sent over there to check out maybe-information, and they'll want to move on whoever is named as the broker when that person moves out of country."

"That may not happen for a while," Grimaldi said. "The Russian *mafiya* hasn't made delivery on the last two nukes, and the terrorists haven't gotten the goods. There are some pissed-off people out there waiting for whoever brokered the deal."

"Agreed," Price said, "but we're working on correlating information we've been able to ferret out at this end. When that much money is moved, it leaves a trail. Finding out who the players were in New York and in the Indian Ocean has helped us out a lot."

"What about the other two men with Carter?" Bolan asked.

"Both were CIA agents," Price answered.

New images flashed up on the computer monitor. Two men in front and profile shots lined up from left to right.

"Agents Hoskins and Trudeau," Price said. "Both career men."

"Assigned to Vancouver, as well?" Bolan asked.

"For the past seven weeks," Price said. "Evidently they were working backup on Carter's bartending job. They operated a telemarketing agency within the same building as the Nautilus Club."

"That gave them plenty of reasons to work through the building's phone system," Grimaldi said. "And plenty of opportunity to tap phone lines and security camera feeds."

"Interestingly enough," Price said, "Vancouver police investigating the attack last night have uncovered surveillance equipment in Eric Barnes's security network. However, they haven't been able to make the tie to the telemarketing business."

Bolan stood and walked to the galley. He poured himself a fresh cup of coffee, then held the pot up to Grimaldi.

The pilot nodded and raised his cup.

"So why watch Barnes?" Bolan poured coffee into Grimaldi's cup, then returned the pot to the coffeemaker.

"When you had custody of Pei-Ling Bao," Price said, "we found out that the CIA was trying to put a triad family member deeper into the Chinese government to act as a deep throat."

Bolan remembered the information Price had revealed to him after the raid against the Soaring Dragons down in Arizona. That was the first mention that had been made of such an operation, and that was why the CIA wanted no outside intervention that might expose what they were doing. Rance Stoddard was the section chief in charge of the operation. "Someone in Saengkeo Zhao's group?"

"Why not Saengkeo Zhao herself?"

Crossing the room, Bolan gave the suggestion consideration. He peered through the starboard port hole. The afforded view was small, only revealing a small section of the harbor area. Nearly a hundred yards away, a small cargo boat off-loaded cases of beer and boxes of food to a big-bellied man in an apron. A bar sat a short distance up the rise behind the man.

"What would Saengkeo Zhao have to gain?" Bolan asked. "According to the intel you've turned up, the Moon Shadows are one of the most aggressive triads around when it comes to staking their territory or protecting their interests."

"Yes."

"How can they protect those interests by working with the CIA?"

"I told you that the Moon Shadows have been heavily investing in legitimate businesses since the seventies."

"Yeah. But that can be said of all long-term crime families or organizations in the same time period. They've made fortunes, and the only way to hang on to them in the face of increasingly effective law-enforcement efforts is to diversify and go legit."

The trend wasn't new.

"We've been tracking Moon Shadow business activity since you turned them up. They've been doing more toward going legitimate than nearly any other crime family or organization you can name. Saengkeo Zhao's father and her brother were both selling off part of the illegal businesses."

"What do you mean?"

"Territories. Concessions."

"Are you sure they weren't being coerced into giving them up?" Bolan wrapped his mind around the information, trying to figure the angles.

"Yes. There's a triad leader, Wai-Lim Yang—"

"The leader of the Black Swans." Bolan had briefed himself on all the files pertinent to the Moon Shadows.

"The day before she met you in the Indian Ocean," Price said, "Saengkeo Zhao had a conflict with Yang."

The computer monitor flickered, then video footage rolled across the LCD screen. A large boat burned in a harbor.

"This is *Goldfish*," Price informed. "The flagship of the Black Swan's miniature navy of flower boats servicing the tourist trade and high rollers of Hong Kong."

"Flower boats?" Grimaldi said. "Prostitution?"

"Yes. Yang and the Black Swans have a strong interest in that trade. Drugs and extortion feed off that business."

"Saengkeo destroyed the boat," Bolan said. He remembered seeing a few news clips while he'd been in Singapore.

"She led a team onto that boat," Price said. "They evacuated the clients and the women without any of them getting harmed, then took the Black Swan crew apart. Later, when she was having a face-to-face meeting with Yang, she had the boat sailed into the harbor. As Yang watched, she had the boat blown up."

The image on the computer screen showed the boat blowing up against the Hong Kong skyline. Flaming debris shot through the air like comets.

"That'll send a message," Grimaldi said. A cold grin tugged at the corners of his mouth. "I gotta admit, Sarge, I respect the hell out of this woman. She's got nerves and the savvy to back it up."

"Yeah," Bolan said, and it bothered him that part of him felt the same way about Saengkeo Zhao.

"Saengkeo Zhao," Price went on, "was tentatively identified as the woman that was involved in a brief firefight on Hong Kong Island at the same time *Goldfish* blew up. A team of unidentified men and one woman who might be Americans or Europeans backed her. They were more than that."

Bolan waited.

"They were CIA agents," Price said.

"Who?" Bolan asked.

"Special Agent Rance Stoddard," the mission controller said. "I pulled his jacket. He's also the agent responsible for moving a triad member into the Chinese government's good graces. Aaron managed to track the Internet link on the computer you and Jack retrieved after the Nautilus Club. Aaron also managed to track a piggyback video feed back from the Carnation Building. The trail ended at an office on the twenty-seventh floor in the Bank of China Tower in Hong Kong. Guess who has offices there."

"Stoddard," Bolan replied.

"Actually," Price said, "the correct answer is the CIA. Under a shell holding company. But I'm betting Stoddard is the one the Agency has in place there."

"How much do you know about him?"

"I'll be sending an e-mail packet over." Price paused. "Stoddard has been a good agent, but he plays fast and loose with the rules. He gets the job done—no matter how dirty he has to get to do it."

"Does Stoddard have a connection to the missing nuclear devices?" Bolan asked.

"None that I've been able to turn up. Doesn't mean it's not there, though."

"Saengkeo Zhao may be working with the CIA to protect her legitimate businesses," Grimaldi said.

"Yes," Price agreed.

"Then why go for the nuclear weapon in the Indian Ocean?" Bolan asked.

"I don't know," Price admitted.

"The CIA has an interest in recovering the weapons," Bolan said.

"Yes. Special Agent Anthony Tripp is heading up the investigation regarding the nuclear devices."

"Where's he?"

"Based in Prague. Apparently, the head brass at the Agency believes the weapons are going to make their way through the Czech Republic before making their way into the Middle East."

"What do you think?"

"Prague is a good bottleneck," Price answered. "The city is bohemian, a lot of East and West business is done there, and everybody goes there these days."

"But if the weapons slip through," Grimaldi pointed out, "it's going to be late in the game to try to stop them."

"The CIA thinks they can break the chain there," Price replied.

"Maybe they can," Bolan said. "But we're going to try to stop it before then. What do you think Stoddard would do if he knew Saengkeo Zhao was after the weapons?"

"I don't know," Price admitted. "However, an even better question might be, how could Stoddard not know that the Moon Shadows were involved with the nuclear weapons?"

"What's the Zhao woman's motivation for pursuing the weapons?" Grimaldi asked.

"The cash," Bolan answered. "She stands to make millions of dollars even if she only decides to sell the weapons to the United States."

Grimaldi scratched his chin. "How did Saengkeo Zhao know about the weapons? That the one would be on *Charity's Smile*?"

"If the chance comes up," Bolan said, "we'll ask her."

Price was gone from the connection for a moment, then a new image flickered to life on the LCD screen. "We just picked up a live news broadcast you will be interested in."

Bolan studied the broadcast television image. Flames twisted outside of a modest supermarket. A young, blond television anchor stood in front of the scene, and the tagline showed that the footage was being shot in Vancouver.

"—and authorities are wondering if the attacks last night at Sports Fan Bar & Grill and the Carnation Building are connected," the anchor said. "As you'll recall, those businesses were attacked by a person or persons as yet unknown. Now, with this market burning behind me, the police and local residents are wondering if that night of horror is really behind them."

"What happened?" Bolan asked.

"A local Asian street gang called the Scarlet Waters attacked the supermarket," Price said. "The Moon Shadows own the supermarket."

On the screen, EMTs in pale blue scrubs moved through a crowd of injured people. Uniformed Vancouver police accompanied the rescue workers. Several windows in the supermarket had been shot out.

"Miss Saengkeo Zhao is the CEO of Zhao Family Investments," the anchor went on. "Unfortunately, no one appears able to contact Miss Zhao. As you may recall, Miss Zhao is already wanted for questioning by the Vancouver Police Department regarding attacks on other businesses that were attacked last night."

The camera zoomed in on the flames spiraling against the blue sky. The tall buildings of downtown stood out behind the supermarket.

"Who do the Scarlet Waters belong to?" Bolan asked. Nearly every street gang was sponsored by a major triad or was working toward such sponsorship.

"The Golden Peacocks," Price replied.

"I'll need a dossier on them." Bolan watched the newscast.

"The other triads see Saengkeo Zhao as weak," Price said. "This could just be the start of a serious turf war up there."

"I know," Bolan said. On the screen, one of the EMTs pulled a bloody sheet over the prone body of an adult male. The supermarket wasn't a turf war; it had been a massacre. "Where is Saengkeo Zhao?"

Price took a moment to answer. "She's left the Cambie Street police station. We've got a vehicle lock on her that shows she's en route to the supermarket site."

Bolan wondered at that. With all the notoriety she was receiving in the media and from the police, Saengkeo Zhao's presence at the war zone didn't make sense. Being there was going to guarantee greater exposure to the media and to the police.

"I've got to go," Bolan said.

"She's taking a chance going there, Striker," Price said.

"I know."

"And you will be, too, if you go."

"I've got to," Bolan said. He put down his coffee cup and picked up his jacket. "I'll be in touch soon."

Price broke the connection without comment. A moment later, the Internet feed to the notebook computer ended. The screen blanked, then switched back on to the screensaver.

Without being asked, Grimaldi stood and slipped into a flight jacket. He pulled his ball cap low over his face. "Want company?"

Bolan nodded. "I could use another point of view on this situation, Jack."

"Don't know how much good I'll be on that," Grimaldi said. "I'm beginning to feel confused about Saengkeo Zhao myself. We're getting two different images of the woman—triad boss and humanitarian."

"And possible CIA deep throat," Bolan said.

"Lots of combinations, lots of possibilities."

"She's walking a tightrope, Jack." Bolan went up the gangway and stepped out onto the deck. Bright afternoon sunlight took some of the chill out of the wind cooled by the water. Ahead of the downtown area, over where English Bay was, a smudge of smoke stained the clear blue sky.

"It's her choice."

"Maybe."

"No matter what, she's still the head of a very serious crime family."

"I know." Bolan stepped from the houseboat to the dock. The Mercury sedan that the Stony Man team had also provided sat in the parking area along the waterfront. "If she had the remaining nuclear weapon from *Kursk,* why be here now? And if she doesn't, why isn't she out there hunting it?"

Grimaldi held his silence only for a moment. "Because she's waiting. On someone. On something."

Bolan nodded. "At this point, maybe it's in our best interests to find out what she's waiting on."

3

"You shouldn't get out here, Miss Zhao. It's too dangerous."

Seated in the back of the Lexus sedan, Saengkeo Zhao looked at Johnny Kwan. He regarded her quietly from behind the sunglasses. The lenses reflected the street scene ringing them, captured the plume of smoke that rose from the still burning building.

"What would you have me do?" she asked. "Sit here?" They had just come from a meeting with De-Ying Wu, the private investigator Saengkeo employed to keep watch over several facets of Moon Shadow business in Vancouver. During the night, Wu had been rescued and questioned by the man in black who had been aboard *Charity's Smile* only three days earlier, and who had attacked illegal Moon Shadow enterprises in the city last night.

"Yes." Kwan's answer was instant.

Saengkeo switched her gaze from Kwan to the milling crowd that surrounded the Blue Lotus Supermarket. While the supermarket hadn't been a thriving business on a profit-and-loss statement, it had been an important fixture in the neighborhood. Men and women in the community had gathered there to discuss common and personal problems. Sometimes they had solved the problems among themselves, and sometimes a spokesman had been chosen to represent them to the Zhao family heads. Chinatown in Vancouver centered around Pender and Main Streets, just east of the downtown area. The neighborhood was the second-largest community of Chinese in North America, after San Francisco, California.

Police cars with flashing lights blocked off the intersection and controlled the flow of traffic. Firemen manned hoses from big trucks, flooding the small building with streams of water that unleashed clouds of steam from the ruin of the structure. A news helicopter circled overhead. Evidently nothing else more media worthy had happened in Vancouver.

Or else, Saengkeo thought, someone saw the potential for a much bigger story to come. The thought filled her with unease.

"I'm not going to sit here," Saengkeo said.

"Even if getting out of this car means your death?" Kwan asked.

"We've been attacked. If I were to cower from the people that did this, I might as well be dead. I can do no good for my family."

"Do you think you can do more by dying?"

"No one is going to kill me here," Saengkeo said.

"You don't know that."

Saengkeo looked at Kwan. "Would you kill me here? In the middle of all this?"

Kwan returned her gaze full measure. "If I wanted you dead, I would have someone do it that was willing to trade years of his life for a good deal of money. Such men exist, you know. And there are those that are sworn enemies of your family."

"No one wants me dead, Johnny." Saengkeo gave him a small smile. "They know you would be there to avenge me. No amount of money or hatred is worth a person's own death."

Kwan wasn't amused, but they both knew what she said was true.

"The people who did this don't want me dead. They want me to live so that I can learn to be afraid of them." Saengkeo stared out at the dozens of Chinese families that ringed the streets around the burning building. "They want me humbled. They want the Moon Shadows broken in spirit."

"You are the last of the Zhao line, Miss Zhao," Johnny Kwan said. "After you, there is no heir to take your place."

Saengkeo knew that was true. Her brother hadn't married because he had always figured there was time later, and no woman could quite hold Syn-Tek's heart. Her father had two sisters, both of whom lived out and away from the family. Her uncle had been killed in a boating accident when he and her father were young men. The sisters had stepped away from the family at her father's insistence. The children they had would never know the Moon Shadow triad, nor would they be accepted as leaders. Once family members were placed outside the triad's activities, they were kept out.

"Perhaps that is the way it is supposed to be," Saengkeo said quietly. "My great-grandfather always told my father that Chi-Kan Zhao, our ancestor who first turned to the pirate ways, brought great shame to our family. Jik-Chang Zhao worked with the Green Gang Society and Chiang Kai-shek, and he was an opium user."

"I know," Johnny Kwan said.

Of course he knew, Saengkeo thought. Kwan had been raised in her house with the rest of the Zhao children. But she couldn't stop herself from repeating the story. She thought perhaps she was afraid of stepping out onto the street in the plain view of the police and whoever had fired the supermarket. She wanted to remember why she had to risk so much.

"Jik-Chang was responsible for the death of his brother," Saengkeo said. "On that day, my great-grandfather vowed to repent his ways. He quit opium, which few people in those days were able to do, and he started putting the Moon Shadows on the path of honesty and righteous living. So that his brother did not die in vain." She looked at the people lining the street. A few of them had already seen her, already recognized her. She couldn't simply have the driver pull away. "I can do no less. Whoever killed my brother planned for a day like this to come, as well. To walk away from the task my brother died for would be dishonorable. Those people need to know that I know their pain and their loss."

"There is another time you could do this."

Saengkeo opened the door. "But now is the right time." She stepped out onto the street and into the full face of the wind. Despite the warmth of the afternoon, the wind still carried a chill.

Johnny Kwan emerged from the Lexus on the other side.

Saengkeo wore no weapons. She reached into her pocket and took out a rubber band, quickly pulling her hair back.

An elderly woman started wailing. Her anguished screams cut through the noise of the fire engines and the loud hailers the police used and the constant *whup-whup-whup* of the helicopter rotors overhead. The old woman fell onto her knees in the street near one of the paramedic groups. Two young men moved to help her, kneeling beside her. The paramedics stepped back from an elderly man they had been working to resuscitate.

Even from the distance and through the crowd, Saengkeo saw the charred flesh that covered most of the old man's frail body. She steeled herself for the tumultuous emotions she was about to encounter, then started forward.

"Who did this?" Saengkeo asked Kwan, who walked at her side.

"The Scarlet Waters," Kwan answered.

Saengkeo didn't bother to ask if Kwan was certain. If he weren't certain, he wouldn't have answered. "They are affiliated with the Golden Peacocks."

"Yes. The Scarlet Waters wish to have the Golden Peacocks as their patrons."

They both knew the Golden Peacocks were linked to United Bamboo. Than-Hua Du ran the Golden Peacocks in Vancouver. Over the years that the Zhao family had been conducting business in British Columbia, Du had been waiting impatiently in the wings for some sign of weakness on the part of the Moon Shadows, or a blessing from the United Bamboo triad to make an attempt to add to his empire.

"I want whoever did this found," Saengkeo said.

"Of course," Kwan agreed. "I already have men who are seeking those people. According to witnesses, one of the killers was wounded."

Saengkeo knew she didn't have to spell out what Kwan was supposed to do when he found those responsible.

The people reacted to her at once. Saengkeo and Syn-Tek had made efforts to be among the people they had relocated to Vancouver even as they'd made sure they were known to the people left behind so far in Hong Kong.

At first, the bystanders pulled away. Perhaps some were in awe of the triad leader's presence among them. Maybe some even feared that she might find them somehow accountable for the destruction of the supermarket. With the evidence of something so terrible taking place in the midst of them, on the heels of the attacks that had taken place in the night, paranoia ran rampant through the people who lived in the neighborhood.

Saengkeo didn't respond. She felt saddened, but she kept her attention on the old woman kneeling and wailing at the side of the dead man. The EMTs tried to keep the woman back from the body, as did the two young men.

Without a word, Saengkeo joined the woman beside the dead man and knelt. The stomach-churning stench of cooked flesh was thick in her nostrils. Gently but firmly, she took hold of the old woman's wrists.

"Grandmother," Saengkeo called softly in Mandarin, trying to meet the old woman's gaze. She used the familiar address as one would to any elder when respect was offered. "Grandmother, I need you to come away with me. There is nothing more that you can do here."

The old woman wailed, "He is my husband! He is my husband!" She rocked back and forth disconsolately.

"There is nothing more you can do for him," Saengkeo said. "Come from here. He would not want this for you."

The old woman's eyes opened slightly as she focused on Saengkeo. Tears slid down the withered cheeks. Her eyes resembled shattered emeralds. "Miss Zhao!"

"Please, Grandmother," Saengkeo whispered. "Please let me take you from this." Her heart nearly broke as she looked at the old woman. For a moment, she remembered the funeral home where she had first seen Syn-Tek after his body had been recovered. As least she could remember her brother like that, not like the horror that the old man had become.

"They killed him," the old woman said hoarsely.

"I know," Saengkeo said. "Whoever did this, Grandmother, those people will not get away with it. I swear to you on my family's name."

Slowly, the old woman rose on trembling legs. When she stood, she wrapped her arms around Saengkeo.

Overcome by echoes of her own grief over Syn-Tek's loss, Saengkeo felt burning tears slip from her eyes. The errant wind cooled them on her cheeks. She held the old woman tightly, feeling the clutch of bones beneath the bird-thin flesh.

"Your father sent us over here, Miss Zhao," the old woman whispered in a frail voice. "Mr. Zhao asked us to come here to help build the neighborhood, to be leaders in your father's stead, to carry out the wishes of what he wanted done."

"I know," Saengkeo said. She knew the family. She had only been a little girl at the time herself, but she could remember going to the airport in Hong Kong with old Ea-Han to watch the families debark. "My father was very proud of the work that you did here among this part of his family, Grandmother."

The woman peered around Saengkeo's shoulder as the EMTs loaded the corpse onto a stretcher and covered it with a body bag.

"My poor husband," the old woman whispered.

"He will never be forgotten," Saengkeo promised in a thick voice. "My father and my brother are with your ancestors in the celestial heavens. They have already welcomed him." She turned and led the woman away. "Let me take you home, Grandmother."

MACK BOLAN STOOD on the outside of the crowd gathered around the supermarket. Jack Grimaldi was at his side.

The crowd remained thick as the fire engines continued hosing the building. Sunlight glinted from the helicopter's Plexiglas cockpit as the aircraft continued to cycle overhead. Sawhorses and police tape marked off the crime scene. Most of the neighborhood was Asian, and most of those were Chinese. But several other nationalities were represented there, as well. Bolan was comfortable that he and Grimaldi wouldn't stand out.

He watched as Saengkeo Zhao went to the old woman and talked with her. The way that Saengkeo spent time talking to the old woman, then quietly and easily took charge of her impressed Bolan.

At first, he had thought Saengkeo Zhao had arrived at the scene only to make an impression on the people in the neighborhood who were under the protection of the Moon Shadows. But the way that she obviously cared for the elderly woman was unmistakable.

The image jarred in Bolan's mind, conflicting with the background information he'd read about Saengkeo Zhao and the things he'd seen aboard *Charity's Smile*. Yet, at the same time, the sight of the triad leader fit with what he knew had to be true if her family was so interested in getting her extended family out of the crime business.

"That's no act, Sarge," Grimaldi commented quietly. "She really cares about that old lady, and about what happened here."

"I know," Bolan said. He watched Saengkeo Zhao intently.

"She doesn't quite fit the part of triad princess, does she?" Grimaldi asked. "Or nuclear arms dealer, either."

"No."

Zhao led the woman to the waiting Lexus and helped the woman inside.

"She's taking a big risk showing up here like this," Grimaldi said. "You put a guy up on one of the buildings around here with a good sniper scope, and she's out of the picture."

Bolan nodded.

"Maybe she hasn't thought of that."

"She's thought of it," Bolan told him. "The way she sees it, she doesn't have a choice."

Johnny Kwan stayed at Saengkeo Zhao's side. He moved restlessly, like a panther on the prowl. He kept his head up and his eyes moving, and Bolan didn't doubt that the man would put himself between Saengkeo Zhao and a bullet in a heartbeat if he saw it coming.

Before the triad leader could get into the Lexus, an unmarked sedan rolled to a stop beside her. A blond man got out on the driver's side. The wind caught his jacket just long enough to clear the holstered side arm at his hip for a fraction of an instant.

Kwan stepped forward immediately, placing himself between Saengkeo Zhao and the guy in the blue suit. Kwan kept his hands spread out away from his body. Every time the man in the blue suit moved to get around Kwan and get to Saengkeo, Kwan took a small step and made the path impossible.

Three more men got out of the unmarked car and came around to confront Kwan. They drew their weapons and pointed them at Kwan. The crowd around the Lexus suddenly broke and ran for cover.

Bolan reached into his jacket pocket and took out a cell phone and a wireless telephone-ready Palm Pilot. The cell phone was chipped to handle two separate lines, and the Palm Pilot, also specially chipped by Kurtzman and the tech crew at Stony Man Farm, automatically accessed the phone line and the Internet when the device was switched on. He pressed an earbud into his left ear and used the speed-dial function.

Barbara Price answered on the first ring.

"You're watching?" Bolan asked.

"You've got a three-ring circus going on there," Price acknowledged.

"Who's the guy in the blue suit?"

"Vancouver Police Department Inspector Paul Simons. He interviewed Saengkeo Zhao earlier."

Bolan knew they didn't have to worry about the cell phone being tapped or hacked into. The connections, phone and Internet were heavily encrypted. "Where does he play in all this?"

"Simons handled the Asian community for a lot of years," Price answered. "He has a history with her father. It wasn't a friendly history."

The Palm Pilot juiced the LCD screen with a quick sheen of gray, then reintegrated into a picture of Inspector Paul Simons of the Vancouver Police Department. Two other pictures followed.

"I've updated the intel packet you're working from," Price advised. "You'll have a more complete history of Simons if you need it."

"What's his involvement?" Bolan asked.

"I think he's only interested from the law-enforcement side."

Bolan watched the police inspector pushing himself nose to nose with Kwan. "But you don't know," Bolan said.

"No," Price agreed. "We've already got CIA agents looking for you and Jack. I can't establish perimeters on any of this yet."

Simons took another step forward. Kwan placed a hand on the inspector's chest, hitting the man so deftly with a nerve punch that Bolan barely saw the movement. Simons stumbled back immediately, grabbing at his chest and at his throat. Bolan was impressed; he hadn't even seen the throat blow.

The reaction of the three detectives was immediate. Two of them closed in, prepared to use their pistols as clubs. The third man yelled at Kwan to get facedown on the ground.

"They're going to kill him," Grimaldi said.

"NO!" SAENGKEO ZHAO'S VOICE rang above the confusion of the men's voices surrounding her. She couldn't believe that Simons had confronted her at the scene of the attack.

"Get your fucking hands up!" the police inspector with the pistol pointed at Johnny Kwan's head shouted. "Get your fucking hands up or I'll blow your fucking head off!"

Kwan remained as smooth as silk, stepping slightly to one side and using another of the plainclothes inspectors' bodies to block the other man's line of sight. Saengkeo recognized the implacable, relaxed set to Kwan's face. He wouldn't stop unless they killed him or incapacitated him.

"Surrender to them," Saengkeo ordered in English, hoping that her command would at least stay the police inspector's trigger finger for a moment.

Like a marionette, Kwan suddenly stood straight and tall. He kept his arms low, hands lifted slightly so his palms faced the ground.

"I surrender," Kwan stated in a cold voice.

"Don't!" Paul Simons groaned. "Don't kill him! Don't...kill the son of a bitch!" He staggered back among his men. One hand still gripped the underside of his jaw. "Arrest him!"

The two police inspectors quickly took charge of Kwan while the other man with the pistol held steady on Kwan's head. Spinning the man, the two inspectors slammed Kwan across the back of the Lexus.

"Inspector Simons," Saengkeo said, "hold your men back. There is no reason to hurt him."

"Lady," Simons growled, "that bastard just assaulted a police officer."

"That man," Saengkeo stated archly, "was performing his duty as my bodyguard."

Simons shook his head and massaged his jaw.

Silver flashed as one of the men whipped a pair of handcuffs into view. He snapped one cuff around Kwan's right wrist, raising his arm painfully behind his back. Kwan never uttered a sound. The other man kicked Kwan's feet apart, nearly knocking him to the ground.

Glancing around, Saengkeo locked eyes with a nearby reporter. "Do you want an exclusive interview with me?" she asked.

The female reporter immediately answered, "Yes." She was young and pretty, and her eyes lit up at the unexpected possibility.

Saengkeo and Syn-Tek had made it a point to stay out of the media's view as much as possible. Their father had done the same thing.

"Record this," Saengkeo said, pointing at the police inspectors controlling Kwan. "I'll give you an interview later today if you can get this on tape."

The reporter waved to her cameraman. The man hustled over and settled into place with the camcorder over his shoulder.

Simons turned on the reporter at once. "Get that damn camera out of here," he croaked, obviously still in pain.

The redheaded reporter looked at the police inspector innocently. "And miss this opportunity to see our metropolitan police force in action, Inspector Simons?" the woman asked. She shook her head. "I don't think so."

"I'll have that camera confiscated," Simons blustered.

"Could you speak up, Inspector Simons?" The reporter extended the wireless microphone she carried. "We're broadcasting live. I don't know if the mike picked up your threat clearly."

Inarticulate rage showed on Simons's face. He turned back to Saengkeo. "Your friend is going to be arrested for assaulting a police officer in the performance of his duty."

Saengkeo ignored Simons, turning her attention to the reporter. "What is your name?"

"Cameron Murray," the reporter replied.

"Take pictures of Mr. Kwan," Saengkeo instructed. "Show that he has no bruises on his face or hands."

The cameraman leaned in closer, shooting the footage with quick, practiced ease. The two officers who had placed Kwan in cuffs straightened him, holding him by an elbow each and keeping him between them.

"Get him into the car," Simons ordered.

"Inspector Simons," Cameron Murray said, "can you tell us why this man is being arrested?"

"Get the camera out of my face," Simons ordered.

"The public has a right to know, Inspector," Murray insisted. "Miss Zhao says this man is her bodyguard."

"That doesn't give him the right to interfere with me."

"What were you doing here?" the reporter continued.

Simons waved toward the destroyed building. "Lady, there was an explosion earlier."

"Yes," Murray said. "From what I've been able to piece together, Miss Zhao was in voluntary police custody only minutes before the Blue Lotus Supermarket was blown up. Is Miss Zhao a suspect in the explosion?"

"I'm not giving an interview here," Simons said.

"Did you have a reason for accosting Miss Zhao?" Murray asked. "Did you identify yourself to Mr. Kwan? Because I don't think you did. I can review—and *will* review—the footage we shot of this incident. I'll be interested in seeing if you identified yourself to him. Miss Zhao is a known figure, a businessperson and investor in the Asian community here. I'm certain a lot more people than just myself will be interested in knowing if you and your men are arresting a man guilty only of performing his duty."

"There was no need for the bodyguard to interfere," Simons said.

Murray waved toward the smoking wreck of the supermarket. "Not even after the complete destruction of a business and building owned by Miss Zhao's family?" She paused. "If you ask me, that seems to be the perfect time for a bodyguard. And the perfect time for a bodyguard to be as protective as he can be."

Simons looked at Saengkeo. "I'll want to talk to you again."

"From this point on," she replied, "you're only going to be talking to my attorneys."

"You're making a big mistake," Simons said.

"I don't think so," Saengkeo said coolly. "The only mistake I made today was agreeing to accompany you to the police station. I won't make that mistake again."

Simons shook his head. He turned to the two men holding Kwan and took a step forward. "Get him in the—"

Without warning, the police inspector's head shattered like a pumpkin smashed with a sledgehammer.

Hong Kong

"Son of a bitch!" Rance Stoddard spat out a mouthful of coffee as he watched the police inspector's head go to pieces on the live broadcast he was currently receiving from Vancouver, British Columbia.

David Kelso yanked his head up from the other camera feeds he was currently monitoring. "What?"

Leaning forward, Stoddard watched the action taking place on the monitor. Even as Simons dropped dead, his head nearly obliterated by the heavy round that had ripped into him, Kwan tore himself free of the two inspectors holding him.

Stark cold fear filled Stoddard as he watched ropes of blood from Simons's falling corpse spray across Saengkeo Zhao and other bystanders. The CIA agent didn't doubt that the Moon Shadow triad leader would be next.

Kwan reached Saengkeo first, his hands bound behind him with the police handcuffs. He threw himself across Saengkeo, knocking her down. Then he jerked, going down in an eye blink, and Stoddard knew Kwan had been hit by sniper fire, as well.

"Sniper," Kelso observed with sudden intensity.

"No shit," Stoddard said. His mind was already racing, figuring out the angles that would give the unknown sniper the necessary field of fire. Anger burned within him. Things had constantly skidded out of control since Saengkeo Zhao had traveled to Los Angeles the day before. "Do we have any links to other camera feeds?"

The view on the screen whipped around, suddenly focusing on the street. From the odd angle, the scene was greatly reduced, but Stoddard was able to see several people lying on the ground around the camera operator.

"No," Kelso responded. "We're only tapped into the one feed. I can try to access others."

"We don't own anybody there?"

"No."

Stoddard cursed and reached for the phone.

Vancouver, British Columbia

HUNKERED DOWN, Mack Bolan raked the surrounding buildings, searching for the sniper. He didn't think the first bullet had been meant for Simons; the police inspector had only gotten in the way of a rushed shot.

"Do you see the shooter?" Bolan asked Grimaldi.

"No." The pilot lay flat on the ground.

Most of the people had cleared out of the intersection, racing for cover behind nearby buildings. The police and the firemen took up positions behind their vehicles.

"Striker," Price called over the earbud.

"Go," Bolan replied.

"We have the shooter."

"Where?"

"North of your present position."

Bolan looked to the east. A large section of the downtown metro area lay in that direction. "No help," he replied.

"We're putting the shooter's location through the Palm Pilot."

Glancing at the device, Bolan watched as the feed changed from the downloaded information on Paul Simons to a satellite's view. The feed was thermographic, rendering the screen dark around the red, yellow and orange figure of a person scrambling through the barely revealed corridor of a building.

"Got the sniper," Bolan said. "Can I make him?"

"Not from where you are," Price said. "We're going to try to maintain contact and find out who he belongs to."

Bolan knew the chances were slim. Vancouver was huge and densely populated. Reading one heat signature out of thousands was going to prove impossible without some real luck.

"We're sifting through video feeds from the various news sources," Price went on. "Also through security cameras in the area. Maybe we'll find something."

Slowly, as they understood there would be no more shots, the crowd around the crime scene gathered its wits and courage. They stood and they walked away, but a few of them clustered around the area where Simons, Kwan and Saengkeo Zhao had gone down.

Bolan got to his feet and made his way over to the downed policeman. He knew nothing could be done for Simons, but he didn't know if Kwan or the woman had survived. He was certain that the round had been a heavy caliber with enough penetrating power to get through a man's body.

EMTs rushed to Simons but gave up immediately. The man's head and face were ruined. Instead, the emergency medical crew turned its attention to Kwan and Saengkeo Zhao.

Kwan had gone down atop Saengkeo. His hands remained bound behind his back, and he wasn't moving when Bolan saw him. Saengkeo gently rolled him from her. She looked dazed and hollowed out. Blood trickled from a cut on her cheek. Kneeling, hands shaking, she laid her fingers on the side of Kwan's neck.

"He's alive," she told the EMTs as they came forward to take over. "He's alive. I mean for him to stay that way."

One of the nearby Chinese men dressed in a dark suit reached down and helped pull Saengkeo to her feet. She looked at the police inspectors standing around Simons's body. "Get the cuffs off him. Now!"

None of the inspectors moved.

"Dammit!" one of the EMTs shouted. "I've got to treat this man! Get those cuffs off him so I can do my job! He's unconscious from the impact of the bullet! He's wearing a Kevlar vest, but his heart may have stopped from the shock of the blunt trauma!"

Reluctantly, one of the inspectors stepped forward with a handcuff key. He opened the cuffs and took them off.

Hair mussed, cheek bleeding, Saengkeo Zhao stood her ground defiantly. If another bullet had come her way, she'd have taken it head-on.

Bolan respected the woman's courage, but he also knew her position trapped her into her reaction. If she'd acted frightened, she would have lost a lot of the power she needed to keep her family together and her enemies at bay.

"Striker," Price called over the earbud.

"Go," he replied.

"We picked up something else interesting. Take a look at the Palm Pilot. We accessed the security cam from the bank ATM across the street and the convenience store farther down the block."

Bolan looked at the image and found he was staring at a young blond woman. The Palm Pilot showed her in the crowd. Behind wraparound blue-tinted sunglasses, her expression was one of icy interest. Bolan looked for her in the crowd but couldn't see her from his position.

"Her name is Jacy Corbin," Price said. "She's a CIA agent who is currently assigned to Rance Stoddard in Hong Kong."

"Then what is she doing here now?"

"I don't know."

"Where is she?"

"I don't know. We video-recorded the crowd and ran the footage through a photo-ID program. Aaron had fed in the faces of everyone we've been able to connect with this thing."

"Was she the shooter?" Bolan asked.

"I don't know," Price replied.

Bolan stared at Saengkeo Zhao. For a moment he felt as if he were gazing at an island, an entity adrift in a sea of chaos. She looked...alone—and vulnerable. Compassion touched the soldier. He respected the woman for how she met death and defeat, but she was the enemy.

Uniformed police officers spread through the crowd, taking command of the new scene of violence and pushing everyone back.

Bolan knew the time had come to go. In a few more minutes even more police would arrive. He got Grimaldi's attention and led the way through the crowd.

"She's going to be covered over in law enforcement and rival triads," Grimaldi said. "So what's our next move?"

Bolan thought about how fragile and alone Saengkeo Zhao looked. He also reflected on the compassion the triad leader had shown the elderly woman who had lost her husband.

"I'm going to have a face-to-face with her," Bolan said.

"Not exactly the brightest move I would recommend," Grimaldi stated.

"It has to be done."

"Maybe you didn't hear me when I said the triads and the police are going to be watching her," the pilot suggested.

"I heard you," Bolan said. "I didn't say doing that was going to be easy. The first thing I'm going to do is create some breathing room."

NIGHT HAD DESCENDED over Vancouver before Saengkeo Zhao reached the hotel where she was staying under an assumed name while in the city. She'd spent the time prior to her arrival at the hospital, making certain Johnny Kwan and the other people who had been grievously wounded in the explosion that had claimed the Blue Lotus Supermarket were taken care of. Other phone calls had been made to secure funeral homes for the dead after they were released by the law-enforcement agencies.

Kwan's own injuries had resulted only from the blunt trauma of the rifle bullet striking his Kevlar vest. The attending physician had wanted to keep him overnight for observation. Kwan had refused, and he had suffered stoically, refusing painkillers for the cracked ribs he'd received.

Tired and frustrated, myriad faces racing through her mind, Saengkeo entered the hotel's opulent grand lobby. Her eyes narrowed against the bright lights of the chandeliers hanging from the high ceiling.

Three night clerks in dark suits manned the desks. All of them stared at her. A large television occupying a corner of the lobby replayed footage of the supermarket scene that Saengkeo had grown weary of while at the hospital.

Saengkeo turned her steps to the elevators on the left. Her cell phone rang in her purse. Knowing no one would call her on that line unless it was an emergency, she took the phone out and said hello.

Rance Stoddard's voice came across the phone connection as clearly as if he'd been standing next to her. "You need to get out of there."

Saengkeo stopped next to the elevators. Kwan and a half-dozen men took up positions around her, a wall of flesh and blood that would die to defend her. She didn't feel any more secure. The whole city felt unsafe.

"I can't," Saengkeo said.

"Can't or won't?" Stoddard asked. The frustration was evident in his voice.

"This call is a mistake," Saengkeo pointed out. "For all you know, the Vancouver Police Department could be monitoring my cell phone."

"It wouldn't matter," Stoddard said. "The Vancouver police and I both want the same thing—you out of that city and on your way back here."

"That may not be possible."

"Make it possible."

Saengkeo struggled to contain her temper. She kept seeing the faces of the dead in her mind. "The police—"

"The police can't hold you. That's what you have that law firm on retainer for. Let them handle the police."

"I need to talk to the people here."

"What are you going to tell them? That it's not your fault some of them got killed today?"

Saengkeo kept silent. Only the fact that Stoddard might be able to help her find her brother's killers and could help her get more immigration visas for her family out of Hong Kong kept her on the phone.

"Those people today did get killed because of you," Stoddard went on mercilessly. "Don't lie to them, and don't lie to yourself."

"Damn you," Saengkeo said.

"I'm trying to help."

Saengkeo surveyed the lobby. It was a few minutes before 9:00 p.m. Couples and small groups drifted in and out of the lobby, coming from or going to dinner or an evening out. They all looked remarkably normal and carefree. For just a split second, Saengkeo hated them for that.

"You're not helping," she told Stoddard.

"I'm trying." His tone softened and he waited a moment before continuing. "As long as you remain in that city, you're going to be a target. The man in black is looking for you, too."

Saengkeo took a shot in the dark, hoping to get more information. She'd known since her first meeting with the CIA agent that he never told everything he knew. "He could have been behind all of this."

"The Scarlet Waters took out the supermarket," Stoddard said. "You and I both know that. And the Vancouver Police Department knows that. One of the Scarlet Waters gang members killed Simons."

"What makes you think that?"

"The bullet that was recovered from Simons's head matched a bullet taken from another assassination two months ago. The

Scarlet Waters had also marked that victim for death. Some of their members had military training in the Chinese army, and spent time as mercs and assassins in Southeast Asia."

Saengkeo considered that. If Stoddard was telling the truth, the knowledge proved that the CIA section chief was capable of getting into the Vancouver Police Department's records, as well.

"I can't leave this situation right now," Saengkeo said.

Kwan glanced at her. His complexion was more pale than usual, but his sunglasses masked whatever emotion might have been revealed in his eyes. But she knew that he would agree with Stoddard in wanting her out of Vancouver.

"You'll have to," Stoddard stated. "I've got a lead on the third package."

Saengkeo felt torn. "I've got to stay here. There are people here who need to be reassured."

Stoddard's voice hardened. "You don't have a choice. You and your brother and your father have circumvented your own organization. You don't know as much about your enemies as you used to. The people that once spied so easily for you now look to other masters. Without me, you're going to be blind and deaf as to what is going on with the other families. I now know more about them than you."

For the first time, Saengkeo realized how far out of the triad organization her family had come. Her father had expected to be able to make the transition during his lifetime. He hadn't planned on his death interrupting the flow of change carrying their family out of the crime cartel.

Without Syn-Tek, who maintained more business among the other triads than she did, Saengkeo grew more and more aware of how far behind she was. With his contacts, Syn-Tek might well have known that the Scarlet Waters were going to attack before they did. Syn-Tek would have cut a deal with them if possible, or he would have loosed Kwan and his shadows of death among them as a warning.

She had done nothing except get caught by surprise. She had arrived at the Blue Lotus Supermarket in time to watch people she was responsible for die or be spread out already dead on the street.

"They'll be coming for you, Saengkeo," Stoddard said.

Saengkeo knew it was true. Johnny Kwan had said the same thing on the way back from the hospital.

"Maybe," she admitted.

"Don't be a fool, dammit. You need me."

"And you need me," Saengkeo said. She breathed into the long, hollow silence that followed.

Stoddard pulled no punches. "I can get you the person who killed your brother."

Saengkeo listened to the words roll like thunder through her mind. She knew he was tempting her, baiting her at what he thought was her weakest point.

"I can't talk now," she told him. "There are things I must attend to." She broke the connection and felt immediately as though a giant weight had been lifted from her shoulders. But she knew the relief was only an illusion. The problems she had still existed, and Stoddard would call again.

"He is right," Kwan stated.

"I'm not leaving," Saengkeo said stubbornly.

"Faugh!" Kwan's face creased in anger. He took a step away from her and turned his back.

"If you want me to go so badly," Saengkeo said, "then I will. On one condition."

Kwan turned back and looked at her. Suspicion tightened his eyebrows.

"If I leave," Saengkeo said, "you go with me. At the same moment."

"You know I cannot."

"Why?"

"Because your father raised me to protect this family's interests."

"My father," Saengkeo said, "raised me to do the same thing."

"I can serve your interests here," Kwan said. "In the interests of the Zhao family."

"But you are not the leader of the Moon Shadow triad. Whoever attacks my family is going to pay a dear price. The Scarlet Waters and perhaps the Gold Peacocks are going to know this before I leave this city."

"I could—"

"You could," Saengkeo agreed. "But *we* will."

Kwan met her gaze for a moment, then nodded. "As you wish, Miss Zhao."

Saengkeo softened her voice. "That is what I wish, Johnny. But most of all, I wish that those people had not been killed today."

Kwan pressed the elevator button. The digital readout started dropping numbers, showing the cage's descent.

Saengkeo's phone rang again. She started to ignore the phone, thinking that Stoddard had immediately called back. Then she noted the number in the Caller ID screen showed the call was originating in the Vancouver area code. Stoddard's call had come from Hong Kong, though she doubted the whole number was traceable.

Thoughts of the man in black filled Saengkeo's mind. She pressed the Send button and said hello in English.

"Saengkeo?" a woman's voice asked.

"Yes."

"This is the woman who saved your ass the other night. I want to meet with you."

"Why?"

"To maybe set the record straight on a few things."

"I don't know if that will be a good idea."

"Trust me. It's a good idea."

"I don't think you can convince me of that," Saengkeo said.

"Stoddard is lying to you about some things. He's the reason that Syn-Tek sold Pei-Ling Bao to the Soaring Dragons. She knows that. Did she tell you why your brother sold her to the Soaring Dragons?"

"She said it was because she had seen Stoddard with him," Saengkeo said.

"She lied."

"Why?"

"Do you want to know the truth?"

As soon as she was asked the question, Saengkeo asked herself if she trusted the woman to tell her the truth. The immediate answer was no.

"Perhaps," Saengkeo answered.

"The offer's on the table now," Jacy Corbin said. "It's not going to stay there forever."

"Why would you tell me this?"

"Because he's lying to me about some things, too. I want to compare notes and see if we can fill in any of the blank spots together."

"Where are you?"

"In the hotel bar. At a back table. You'll know me when you see me. Leave Kwan and the others at a distance or I'm going to vanish like a smoke ring in a hurricane."

The phone connection broke with a sharp click.

"STRIKER, THE BALL is in play."

Standing in the darkened stairwell of the Manchester Building deep in the heart of Vancouver's Chinatown, Mack Bolan tapped his headset. "Affirmative, Stony Base. The ball is in play."

The soldier wore loose denim coveralls with the patch of a nonexistent electrical company printed on the back. The ball cap he wore bore the same patch on the front. He wore a tool belt around his hips. The Beretta 93-R was snugged in shoulder leather under his left arm.

Reaching down, he took up the massive tool kit he'd been using for the past hour while working on the junction boxes. Only five people had traipsed through the apartment building's stairwell in that hour instead of using one of the four elevators. He and Grimaldi had worked on the electrical connections for the seventh floor earlier, setting up the power relays that Price and Kurtzman could operate through a digital link from Stony Man Farm.

Bolan stepped through the stairwell door and walked down the hallway. Three people stood in front of the bank of elevators ahead of him.

"Striker," Price called over the headset.

"Yeah."

"We took the security cameras off-line when the hallway was empty. The security people on-duty are staring at empty hallways for the next few minutes."

"Okay." Bolan walked to the elevators and stood waiting.

A young guy in a suit jacket and sweater looked at him, then at the toolbox. "Don't tell me something's wrong with the elevators. Man, I hate when that happens."

"It's just a maintenance call," Bolan said, not making eye contact.

"Elevator three," Price said.

"Just stay off elevator three," Bolan said to the three people standing in the hallway.

"Elevator one is on its way," Price said. "I'm holding elevator three for just a moment to give you time to clear the hallway."

Bolan stepped forward as elevator one came down from the tenth floor. "You'll probably want to take this cage down."

The elevator doors opened and Bolan held them while the three people got on.

"Cage three is on the way," Price said.

The doors on the first elevator closed.

"Kill the lights," Bolan said. Before his voice trailed away, all the lights in the hallway went out, filling the area with darkness.

None of the backup security lights came on, their photosensitive relays overridden by Kurtzman's control over the systems. He took a pair of sunglasses from his ball cap and slid them on. The darkness retreated as the world became limned in greens. The sunglasses lenses were specially treated and powered to provide light amplification.

"The elevator is one floor below you," Price said. "On your go."

Bolan reached inside the coveralls and unleathered the 93-R. He slipped a flash-bang grenade from his tool belt. The grenade was one of the new munitions developed by Sandia National Laboratories. As big as a soda can, the flash-bang grenade was filled with aluminum-powder dust that was forced through sixteen quarter-inch diameter holes and into the air by the ignition of a fuel-air explosive. The aluminum powder ignited and burned almost immediately as it mixed with air. The soldier pulled the pin and held the plunger.

"Go," Bolan said.

"We're opening the door," Price responded. "The cage will be suspended between floors. Yun-Fat Lua and his people are on edge."

Bolan lifted the 93-R, aiming the pistol at the center of the cage. The doors came open, revealing two men standing with their weapons braced over their forearms.

The Executioner fired immediately. Yun-Fat Lua was the leader of Vancouver's Golden Peacocks triad. In addition to the drugs and illegal immigrants he ran, as well as the extortion and protection rackets he operated, he also pandered to the American Hollywood people shooting in Vancouver.

Lua also produced a few Chinese action-adventure pictures about Shanghai gangsters in the 1920s that were basically hardcore porn with an attempt at plotting and an excuse for the accompanying violence and bloodshed. At the moment, a young American starlet named Krystal Sands had captured Lua's attention and was trading lust for a step up in her career. The intel Price and Kurtzman had access to was nothing short of amazing or prodigious. The sniper they had locked on to through the satellite earlier had led them to the Golden Peacocks leader. They had stayed with him all day, and had confirmed his rendezvous with Krystal Sands by tapping his phone lines.

The 93-R's 9 mm rounds slammed into the throat of the man on the left and tracked up two hard-hitting steps to his face. Tracking right, Bolan squeezed another trio of bullets that shattered the second gunman's forehead and punched his head backward.

Lua, grossly fat and dressed in an expensive Italian suit, cowered in a corner of the elevator cage. He yelled for his men.

Bolan heaved the grenade into the stalled elevator cage even as the first two men fell back over Lua and three other bodyguards. The soldier stepped away from the open doors as bullets crashed through. Even though the Manchester Building was heavily soundproofed to provide for a well-moneyed clientele, Bolan knew the sound of the shots could be heard and would trigger alarms.

The flash-bang went off with a thunderous roar. From his position beside the open doors, Bolan watched the cloud of aluminum powder jet out into the open air. A heartbeat later, the dust ignited into a rooster tail of flame and heat and sonic concussion that completely disoriented the four surviving men in the elevator cage. Fierce light ignited the dark hallway for five long seconds.

Curses and yells came from the elevator.

"Stop shooting, you fools!" Lua screamed fearfully.

"The eighth floor is clear," Price informed him.

Bolan stepped back around the corner, remaining somewhat shielded by the open elevator doors. "Elevator up," he said.

Immediately, the elevator rose, getting trapped between the seventh and the eighth floors. The men reacted at once, trying desperately to see well enough to use their weapons.

Moving forward, the sunglasses lenses still reacting somewhat to the sudden flash of light that had expired, Bolan gazed into the elevator cage and spotted Lua huddled against the back wall. The Executioner reached into the cage with his free hand and seized Lua's suit coat. Then Bolan yanked, sliding Lua across the slick wooden floor of the elevator cage.

Lua yelled in fear. "Someone has me! Someone has me!" He slid over the edge of the elevator cage and fell at Bolan's feet.

"Elevator up," Bolan said calmly.

"Done," Price replied.

Screwing the 93-R's barrel under Lua's triple chins, Bolan ordered, "Get to your feet."

"No English," Lua squalled, holding his hands over his head.

"You speak English," Bolan growled. "Get up or I'm going to leave you lying here."

With a grunt and considerable effort, Lua got nearly four hundred pounds of sweaty flesh up from the floor, helped along by the Beretta's front sight cutting into his throat. Bolan grabbed the back collar of the man's jacket and got him moving toward the stairwell.

"What do you want?" Lua asked.

"Keep your hands up," Bolan instructed. "The minute I stop seeing them, I put a bullet into your throat."

"Who are you?"

"Someone who didn't like what happened at the Blue Lotus Supermarket today." Bolan kicked the stairwell door open and hauled his prisoner through.

"I can pay you," Lua offered. "Whatever the Zhao woman is offering you, I can double. No—I can triple that."

"The Zhao woman didn't send me." Bolan pushed Lua up against the stairwell railing. The soldier took two pairs of handcuffs from his tool belt and used them to cuff Lua to the railing. He knew he had only a couple of minutes before Lua's men found them.

"Then who?" Lua demanded. He blinked owlishly, striving to get his vision back.

"This is plastic explosive." Bolan took a heavy chain wrapped with C-4 from his tool belt and draped it around Lua's shoulder. He shoved a digital timer into the plastic explosive. He took a detonator from his shirt pocket and pressed buttons. "If I set this off, you're over."

Lua stared at the detonator. The fear that filled his eyes told Bolan that the triad warlord could see well enough to make out the detonator and knew from experience what it was.

"Getting to you was that easy," the Executioner said in a graveyard voice. "This is the only warning you get."

"Warning? Warning about what?"

"Stay away from the Moon Shadows," Bolan said. "Stay away from Saengkeo Zhao. Next time I won't even get close enough for you to see me."

"What is the Zhao woman to you?" Lua demanded.

Bolan held up the remote control and flicked the switch. The detonator armed with a treble cricket chirp. "Any more questions?"

"No." Sweat trickled down Lua's brow and cheeks. His thick, blubbery jowls quivered in fear.

"Then we understand each other."

"Yes," Lua agreed.

Without another word, Bolan turned and went down the stairwell. The night was young. Getting to Saengkeo Zhao was going to be even harder. But he had a plan.

"Are you armed?"

Peering through the darkness of the hotel bar at the young blond woman she remembered from the night before, Saengkeo Zhao said, "What do you think?"

Jacy Corbin sat, as she'd claimed during the phone conversation, at one of the booths in the back of the hotel bar. The emergency exit door was only three short strides away.

The bar was called Hammett's. Colorized black-and-white posters from old gangster movies decorated the walls. Someone had added neon tubing, layering pale limes, bright turquoise and soft reds in with the dark motif. Dark wood paneling and chairs and tables upholstered in oxblood set off the fluttering tea candles in brown glass bottles. The bar was an avant-garde mixture of elegance and seediness.

"I think you're probably carrying at least one weapon," Corbin said. She nodded toward the table. "That's why I'm holding a .44 Magnum Smith & Wesson aimed right at your stomach. If you look at me funny, or if Johnny Kwan or one of his boys comes through that back door, I'm going to blow a hole in you I can walk through."

Even after everything she had been through the past few days, Saengkeo thought she would at least be a little afraid. She wasn't. Her nerves felt steady.

"Are you drunk?" Saengkeo asked.

Jacy appeared to consider the question. "I wouldn't say I'm drunk, but I've had a few drinks. I've been waiting on you for a while."

"I'm sorry you were inconvenienced."

Corbin's expression turned sour. "Okay, so we both get extra points in the bitchiness department."

Studying the woman in the darkness of the hotel bar, Saengkeo knew she had something seriously bothering her. "Maybe I could sit down."

Corbin turned over a palm to the booth across from her. "Please. Sorry. My manners aren't quite what my mother expected them to be."

Saengkeo sat. She left both hands in plain sight on the tabletop.

"What are you drinking?" Corbin asked.

Glancing at the glass containing an icy skeleton and a pink-and-white umbrella, Saengkeo said, "I'll have whatever you're having."

"Earl," Corbin called. When the young bartender glanced up at her, she ordered two more Mai Tais. While he prepared the drinks, the CIA agent used her free hand to shake out a cigarette. The pack was American. Placing the cigarette between her lips, she bent forward to get a light from the fluttering flame in the brown glass container. She exhaled a slow mouthful of smoke, then inhaled the curling gray wisps back in through her nostrils.

Saengkeo waited. She knew Kwan and his men were in the lobby and wouldn't take the passage of time well.

Earl brought over the drinks. Corbin paid and tipped immediately.

"Thank you," Saengkeo said.

"Are you always so polite?" Irritation sounded in the woman's words.

"No."

True humor showed in the CIA agent's smile. "Neither am I." She gazed with open interest at Saengkeo. "What is it that Rance Stoddard finds so damn attractive about you?"

Saengkeo sipped her drink. The alcohol was disguised by the fruit taste. "I don't think that he's attracted to me."

"That's because you haven't seen how protective he is of you."

Saengkeo said nothing.

"Trust me when I say that he's got more interest in you than he should."

For a chill moment, Saengkeo guessed that the CIA agent wasn't as drunk as she appeared to be. The professional way she'd handled the attack in Los Angeles the night before weighed against the act she was putting on now.

"How much interest do you think he should have in me?" Saengkeo asked.

"Not this much." Corbin's eyes narrowed against a stream of smoke as she took another hit off her cigarette. "Not unless he was sleeping with you."

"That's not the case." Saengkeo eyed the other woman. "How long have you been sleeping with him?"

Corbin grinned, showing clean white teeth. "Months. But don't worry. I'm not the jealous type. Unless you get in my way." She shrugged and took a sip of her drink. "I'm sleeping with Rance Stoddard because it's an easy way to get close to the heart of the mission we're on."

"And what mission would that be?"

"Getting a triad leader sympathetic to the American cause involved with the Chinese government. I was more comfortable when Stoddard was showing this much interest in your brother."

Saengkeo focused on the woman. "Do you know who killed my brother?"

"No. I wish I did. That would give me a bargaining chip with you, wouldn't it?"

Saengkeo said nothing.

"But," Corbin replied, "I get the impression that you would know when I was lying. At least, about that. I'm a good liar."

"Does Stoddard know who murdered my brother?"

Corbin looked puzzled. "I don't know."

"Would you tell me if you knew?"

Shaking her head, Corbin said, "I don't know. Maybe. If it helped me out. I sleep with Stoddard because I like sex and he's a healthy guy and ambitious in bed. Sleeping with him also gives me a chance to further my career."

"With your agency?"

"Yes. If Stoddard is successful in getting a deep throat into the Chinese government—that would be you—then he's up for promotion. The other guys I work with? None of them are hungry for promotion. They've been there ten and fifteen years longer than me. They're putting in time until they pull the pin and sit out the rest of their days on some Caribbean beach and hope no one they pissed off ever recognizes them."

"What do you want from me?" Saengkeo asked.

Corbin was silent for a moment. "I want the same thing you're giving Stoddard."

"I'm not giving him anything."

The CIA agent leaned back in the booth. She kept her right hand concealed below the table. "I don't buy that."

"Why?"

"Because you drop off our radar screens from time to time, but Stoddard always seems to know where you are."

"Stoddard always knows where I am," Saengkeo said. "Eventually."

"I've tried to keep up with you, but Stoddard shuts me out sometimes. That makes me antsy. It makes me wonder what the two of you have going on. At first, I thought it was an affair, but you're not his type."

Despite the tension and the other issues bearing on the confrontation, Saengkeo felt her ego sting a little. "And you are his type?"

Jacy grinned, and the effort lessened the years between her twenty-something age and her teen years. "I...blow...Stoddard's...mind. I know. He doesn't quite know how to handle me." She paused. "When I first came over here, like I said, I thought Stoddard's interest in you was purely sexual. I just wanted to take a look at the competition."

"I'm not competition."

"Not in that area, you're not," Corbin agreed. "I don't mean that in a bad way. I bet you're hot enough when you're inspired to be. I can just tell that when it comes to sex you wouldn't give Stoddard the time of day. But there's something about you. Something you're not telling me, or something you don't know yourself yet." She smiled wistfully. "And wouldn't that be a kick in the ass if it's something you don't know and I figure it out before you do?"

"Not if it got my brother killed." Saengkeo put ice in her words. "You said Pei-Ling Bao lied about the reason Syn-Tek sold her to the Soaring Dragons."

"Yeah. She did. Think about it. Would it be a big deal if she saw Syn-Tek with Stoddard?"

"She knew he was CIA."

"Big deal. A lot of people know Stoddard is CIA. At least, the triad people do. Trading information about the Russians, the Middle Eastern countries and terrorists is one of Stoddard's primary functions. The only danger to the triads is someone like you."

Saengkeo looked back at the woman.

"Yeah, you. You're so caught up in your own personal agenda that you're willing to betray and risk getting caught by the Chinese government. None of the other triads are willing to do that. They're tied too tightly to the Chinese government these days." Corbin shrugged. "Or you're willing to bullshit Stoddard with promises about helping us get information about the Chinese government until he makes you put up or shut up."

Instinct slithered cold tendrils through Saengkeo as she listened to the other woman. So far they had talked about everything but the nuclear weapons that had gone missing from the Russian submarine *Kursk*. Thinking about it now, she realized that would have been one of the first things that Jacy Corbin would have talked about.

That could only mean that Jacy herself didn't know about those weapons. And yet, how could that be? Thinking back on the conversations she'd had with Stoddard about the nuclear weapons, she realized then that no one else from the CIA team had been around.

"If Stoddard wasn't the reason Syn-Tek had the Howling Dogs kidnap Pei-Ling and sell her to the Soaring Dragons," Saengkeo said, "what was the reason?"

"Simple. She saw someone else."

"Who?"

"A man named Sebastian Cain."

Saengkeo recognized the name. Sebastian Cain was an American millionaire who was lobbying for oil rights in the Middle East. The current difficulties in Afghanistan and the erupting crop of new problems in Israel and Iraq had shifted the balance of power in that part of the world. Cain had also heavily lobbied for American involvement in the Taiwan issue, to see that a democratic form of government existed there rather than the reemerging Communist rule of China.

"Cain was in Hong Kong?" Saengkeo asked.

"Yeah. I saw him myself. Stoddard doesn't know, though."

"What was Cain doing there?"

"I don't know. It's kind of hard for me to find out."

Saengkeo regarded the woman. "You want me to find out."

"You're the one with the friend who hops from bed to bed. Maybe she learned something."

Saengkeo shelved the instant biting remark that came to mind regarding Jacy Corbin's own sexual practices.

"Where is your little friend?" Corbin asked. "I didn't see her check into the hotel with the rest of your entourage. Did you leave her back in L.A.?"

"No," Saengkeo said. "I sent her back to Hong Kong. She's probably still on the flight."

The flip attitude dissolved from Jacy's face. "That wasn't a good idea. At least she's still in the air. See if Kwan or one of his guys can put a shackle on her when she arrives in Hong Kong."

"She's with guards now."

Jacy shook her head. "If they're not good, she'll slip them the first chance she gets. Whatever Pei-Ling Bao knows, it must have been enough to get her nearly killed. And it was enough to get her to lie to you."

"Pei-Ling has always tried to lie to me about different things. She hasn't always been successful."

"But you didn't know about Cain."

"No," Saengkeo agreed. "I didn't know about Cain."

"Check it out and let me know," Corbin suggested.

"That may be the last thing I want to do."

Corbin shrugged. "I wouldn't be surprised if you find you need a friend." She slid out of the booth, crushed out her cigarette, stood and slipped a silver pistol out of sight behind her handbag. "I don't know what kind of game Rance Stoddard is playing, but it's not going to cost me my career. And one thing I can tell you right now—you can't trust him. He's looking out for his own interests. Whatever the hell those are."

"What about you?" Saengkeo asked. "Are you going to let me know what you find out?"

"Maybe." The woman smiled. "Maybe I'll need a friend one day soon. Until then, you take care." She turned and walked through the emergency exit. The alarm went off at once, bleating stridently, but the CIA agent passed through and disappeared into the alley outside without an apparent care in the world.

Earl, the bartender, came over and shut off the alarm. He closed the door and turned to Saengkeo. "You know," he said, "your friend is a real jerk."

That, Saengkeo thought, was an understatement. She sat at the booth for another moment trying to collect her thoughts. The effort didn't really help. Everything seethed inside her head like dying snakes. Finally, she gave up trying to make sense of it and walked back to the lobby. She had phone calls to make, then she had to get some sleep before she collapsed.

CLOUDS OBSCURED the moon over Vancouver, but neon advertising and street lamps ripped away the lower layer of the night. Mack Bolan fell through the sky, suspended beneath a rectangular black sport parachute. He was dressed in the blacksuit to blend with the darkness, and camou cosmetics robbed his features of highlights. A durable, high-impact resistant black case hung from a strap between his feet.

He wore slimline ANVIS AN/AVS 6 generation 3 high-resolution aviator's night-vision goggles clipped to his helmet. The light-amplification system built into the goggles stripped away most of the night, leaving an undercurrent of green illumination running through the lower levels of the metropolis like a river of light.

The parachute's passage through the night air was almost silent. Grimaldi had dropped him west of the city and he'd drifted in, riding the breeze. In a town where Hollywood came to play and work, Bolan thought even if someone saw him they might not think anything of it. If his arrival was called in to the police station, there was a good chance that investigating officers would insist on someone making calls to the studios first before action was taken.

A summer replacement police television show was already filming in Gastown. Two streets three city blocks long had been shut down by police officers. A science-fiction anthology series was currently filming out in the Burrard Inlet harbor area. Despite the late hour, Vancouver was humming with activity.

Bolan wasn't surprised that he could parachute onto the roof of the hotel where Saengkeo Zhao was staying, but he was surprised that Vancouver didn't have more security problems.

"Striker," Barbara Price called over the headset, "do you copy?"

"Striker copies five by five, Stony Base," Bolan replied. "Mustang, do you copy?"

"Affirmative, Striker," Grimaldi replied. "Mustang copies. Have settled back into the water. Will be mobile in ten, fifteen minutes from your go."

"Understood, Mustang." Bolan pulled on the parachute's elevator lines and adjusted his descent. Grimaldi had put together the information he'd needed to make the drop, plotting from the meteorology reports Price had given him.

After putting Bolan into the air, Grimaldi had called back to the tower in Burrard Inlet and reported engine trouble. Once he was back on the ground, he would travel by vehicle toward the hotel and await contact from the Executioner about possible exfiltration depending on mission success or a scrub.

With expert skill, Bolan landed on top of the towering hotel. The building was roughly oval, giving a good view of the mountains and the shoreline.

Bolan worked quickly to collapse the parachute. Then he shrugged out of the smaller sport parachute he'd worn across his chest and the durable plastic case that had dangled between his legs. Once the parachute was collapsed, he used a pneumatic cordless nail gun to shoot nails through the parachute and into the rooftop to hold the parachute in place. When he was satisfied the blowing folds of the parachute wouldn't draw any undue attention any time soon, he dropped the nailgun on top of the parachute.

He slipped a micro block-and-tackle rig from the equipment bag at his waist. He attached the rig to the HVAC closest to the side of the building where he planned his descent.

"Striker, this is Mustang."

"Go, Mustang," Bolan replied. He tested the tension on the block-and-tackle rig, then made a quick adjustment.

"I'm en route."

"Affirmative." Bolan shifted line through the block and tackle, then made his way to the edge of the building. Bracing his feet against the edge, he peered down. A brief moment of vertigo assailed him because of the night-vision goggles, but it passed. He leaned back on the rope that he held, gradually letting the block and tackle take his weight.

Saengkeo Zhao had taken rooms on the top floor, occupying one side of the hotel.

Cradled in the mountaineering seat harness, Bolan lowered himself down the side of the building. "Stony Base," he said. Street noises came up from below, sounding even more distant than they were, but echoing clearly to his ears because of all the humidity in the air.

"Go, Striker."

"Confirm lock on subject."

"Confirm. We still have subject. Subject is in the target rooms."

The Kernmantle climbing rope slid through Bolan's gloved fingers as he made the descent. He stopped beside the small balcony that afforded a breathtaking view of the harbor and the cruise-ship terminals.

"Balcony," Bolan said, resting lightly on the balls of his feet. The pale light issuing from the room pawed at the darkness gathered on the balcony. Elegant patio furniture and a few potted plants occupied the balcony.

"Balcony is clear," Price said.

Bolan took a glass cutter from the small kit at his chest. He walked along the building's side and reached the balcony, then pulled himself up and over. Standing on the balcony, he slid out of the seat harness and tied the rope to the railing with a sailor's fast-release reef knot.

The Beretta 93-R rode in shoulder leather under his right arm, and the .44 Magnum Desert Eagle rode his right hip. He carried a 12-gauge Jackhammer shotgun with a 10-round capacity cylindrical magazine in a bullpup configuration behind the trigger and handgrip on a Whip-it sling over his right shoulder.

If everything went right on the op, he was overdressed. But after seeing Saengkeo, he'd wanted a face-to-face.

"What's the sitrep on the room, Stony Base?" Bolan affixed a suction cup to the glass, inscribed a quick arc with the glass cutter, making a small circle, then yanked out the piece of glass. Then he reached inside the room and unlocked the door. With the piece of glass out of the door, he heard the television on inside. From the constant news reports, he figured the woman was tuned to a local station or to CNN.

"Subject is clear of the egress point, Striker," Price reported. "Subject is in the back rooms."

"Alone?"

"Affirmative."

Bolan slid the balcony door open and peered through the heavy drapes.

The door opened onto a large living area. On the other side of the suite was a kitchen with a breakfast nook and a bar that overlooked the living area. A pair of matched couches occupied the center of the floor, flanking a pair of matching easy chairs.

Paintings of Vancouver sights hung on the walls. The carpet was plush, thick and white.

No one was in the room.

Recalling the room's layout from the intel packet Price had sent to him, Bolan knew the master bedroom was to the left. The door was only partially open.

He glanced at the bar and saw a single drink on the counter. Evidently Saengkeo Zhao was alone and not expecting company.

The Executioner drew the Beretta 93-R and used his free hand to push the drapes aside as he stepped into the room. He shoved the silenced pistol out before him and let the Beretta lead him into the room. Crossing the room, he took a chair from the breakfast nook and jammed it up under the door. He made sure the door was locked, as well. Then he turned his attention to the bedroom door.

Darkness filled the bedroom, but light came from a source to the right. The television continued to drone on, talking about a bomb that had gone off in Israel and a demonstration along the West Bank that had gotten bloody. Afghanistan and Iraq remained hot topics.

The Executioner paused at the bedroom door. He wanted Saengkeo Zhao alive if he could manage it; he didn't plan to harm her. "Stony Base."

"You're clear, Striker. Subject remains in the small room off to the right. There's a bathroom there."

"Affirmative." Bolan stole through the door as silently as a wraith. The sound of running water reached his ears in the large bedroom.

A circular bed occupied the center of the room. An entertainment system filled the wall to Bolan's left. A freestanding wardrobe stood in the corner next to the bedroom door.

"The bathroom has two rooms, Striker," Price said. "There's a vanity first, followed by the shower area. The heat from the shower is throwing off the thermographic view, but she's in the shower."

Bolan went forward, moving quickly and soundlessly through the door with the Beretta resting in both hands. The strong smell of herbal soap filled the soldier's nostrils. His black-clad image in the mirror drew his attention for just a moment, then he focused on the naked woman on the other side of the steamed-over glass of the shower vestibule. She faced away from him, showing him her nude back, curved haunches and slim legs. Scented candles burned on the vanity.

Saengkeo stood relaxed under the water, as if enjoying the slow heat of the needle spray. She was lush and more rounded than her file pictures had suggested, and her complexion was a dusky olive that had reddened somewhat under the shower. The curved hint of her left breast peeked from under one arm.

For a moment, Bolan hesitated. The shower made things complicated. If violence broke out, the glass walls could rapidly become jagged shards that would cut them both to pieces. Knowing he was already working on borrowed time, that the Moon Shadow leader kept a full schedule, the Executioner moved forward.

The woman was naked, alone and vulnerable. She would listen to reason. He wouldn't give her a choice.

Bolan stepped toward the shower door, moving so that his body didn't fall between the vestibule and the light from the vanity area. His shadow never touched the glass wall.

Even as he touched the door, she turned to face him. Water from the shower cascaded over her shoulders and raced down her full breasts, over her flat stomach and hips and through the small, intimate triangle at the juncture of her thighs.

If the woman's beauty hadn't taken away the Executioner's breath, the pistol clasped in both her hands would have. She aimed through the steamed glass directly at his head. Her eyes were as cold and hard as steel, as black and dark as the heart of a frozen sea.

Saengkeo stared through the steam-covered shower glass at the man dressed in black on the other side. Even after the pictures and video footage she'd seen of the man, and the detailed description she'd been given by private investigator De-Ying Wu, Saengkeo was unprepared for the raw and feral presence the man exuded. She held her matte-black Walther Model P-990 QPQ in both hands, framing the sights on the man's eyes.

Even though the security cameras inside the Sports Fan Bar & Grill and the Carnation Building had captured images of the man, none of them had gotten revealing pictures of his face. Black greasepaint disguised his features now, but the volcanic blue eyes pierced her. He was wary, but he wasn't afraid.

The shower hissed around her, and clouds of steam scudded against the glass walls, creating a cottony world trapped inside the glass. Droplets gathered on the glass, then grew too heavy and skidded down, leaving winding wet paths behind.

The man in black had been quiet, and the fact that he hadn't tripped any of the security Johnny Kwan's teams had put into the hotel room spoke volumes about his skill. Only his reflection in the high-gloss finish of the shower tiles had given away his approach.

Saengkeo's breath felt tight in her lungs, dry against the back of her throat. Her finger rested on the Walther's trigger a half-pound pull away from firing. Even if the glass deflected the bullet somewhat, she felt certain that the round would strike the man in the face. If the shot didn't kill him outright, she knew he'd be grievously wounded.

But she would be dead.

She mastered her breathing and took control of her voice. "Well?" she asked. She spoke in English because the survivors of the attacks he had orchestrated said that he spoke that language.

The man's face remained impassive. The silenced Beretta cupped in his hands never wavered.

For a moment, Saengkeo considered trying to move, to drop below his line of sight and fire. But she knew that she would throw off her own aim and probably miss him or hit him in the chest. The Kevlar would deflect the bullet.

"You came here to talk," Saengkeo said.

A faint grin touched the big man's lips.

"Otherwise you would have shot me from the door," Saengkeo said.

"Or tossed in an antipersonnel grenade," the big man agreed.

A chill ghosted through Saengkeo. She had believed herself safe behind Johnny Kwan's devices and the men he had placed around her.

"I've seen your work," Saengkeo said. "In the tapes from the Sports Fan Bar & Grill and from the Carnation Building. I also saw you up close and personal on the decks of *Charity's Smile*. You get around."

"And I seem to find you everywhere I go."

Saengkeo waited for him to continue speaking, then realized he wasn't going to. "You're not much for conversation."

"No."

"But you're here to talk now."

"Yes."

Shampoo slid from Saengkeo's hair and caught in the corner of her eye. Pain gnawed at her like a biting fly. She ignored the pain, pushing it away and feeling her eyelid jerk just the same. "I've got shampoo in my eye," she said. "I'm going to release the pistol with one hand and wipe my eye."

"All right."

Carefully, keeping the pistol pointed at the man's face the whole time, Saengkeo wiped the shampoo from her eye. Then she replaced her hand on the Walther. The man's gaze never wavered from her eyes despite the fact that she was naked in front of him.

"Talk," Saengkeo said, "or I'm going to open fire."

"Why?"

"Because I'm going to start thinking you're stalling and you've got a friend planting a bomb in one of the outer rooms designed to take out this whole floor of the hotel."

"That's not happening."

"Drop your weapon," Saengkeo said. "Maybe I'll believe you."

He smiled. "That's not happening, either."

"I will shoot," she told him. "You should believe that's happening."

"I do."

"Then talk."

"I have some questions that I want answered," the man said.

"So do I. Perhaps we can trade."

"You're not in a position to trade."

"I think that I am." Saengkeo breathed out normally, willing her hands to remain steady. "If I shoot, and I will, my men will come and alarms will be set off in this building. I'm betting that, after today, the Vancouver Police Department also has this suite under observation."

"They do."

"Then we both can lose."

The man in black nodded. "Where is the third nuclear warhead?"

Saengkeo answered without hesitation. "I don't know."

"How did you know about the one aboard *Charity's Smile*?"

"No," Saengkeo objected. "You asked a question. Now I get to ask a question."

The man regarded her. "All right."

"Did you murder my brother?"

"No."

Silently, Saengkeo cursed her lack of forethought. She should have asked him if he knew who had murdered Syn-Tek. If the answer would have been no, he was either lying or he hadn't killed Syn-Tek. The question had been too small. She had to do better.

"How did you know about the nuclear weapon aboard *Charity's Smile*?" the man in black asked.

"I was told."

"That's half an answer."

"I can't tell you any more."

"You mean you won't."

"Give me a reason."

"What reason?" the man in black asked.

"Whom are you working for?"

"Myself."

"I don't believe you."

"Then we have a problem."

The Walther started to feel heavier at the end of Saengkeo's arms. She got the impression the man in black could have held his weapon forever. "How do we trust each other?"

"We haven't fired," he said. "I guess we already are."

"Do you know who killed my brother?"

"No. He was tied up in this business with the nuclear weapons, wasn't he?"

Saengkeo considered her answer. She guessed that the man already knew that or he wouldn't have asked. Even if he was only speculating, Syn-Tek's death happened too closely to the other events involving the nuclear weapons not to be somehow related.

"Yes," she answered.

"Was he killed because of them?"

"I don't know."

The volcanic blue eyes remained as steady as gun sights. "But you think so?"

She paused only for a moment. "Yes. He was working to recover the first nuclear weapon."

"From the Russian ship *Jadviga*?"

Saengkeo was surprised. "You're very well informed."

"Yes. There were three nukes aboard that ship."

"My brother found only one."

"He told you this?"

"No. He was dead before I saw him again."

Something in those blue eyes softened. "I'm sorry for your loss. I've lost family."

Saengkeo heard the ghost of pain in his voice even though he spoke in the same graveyard tone. He was telling the truth about his losses. For a moment she felt a connection between them, then she walled the feeling away as she remembered the carnage that had been revealed in the tapes from the Sports Fan Bar & Grill and the Carnation Building. Several body bags had been used to bring out members of the on-site security teams. "You killed several of my family."

He nodded. "Yeah, but they weren't innocents. They were killers long before I got there. They knew the risks involved in the businesses you had them in." He fixed her with his gaze. "You knew those risks when you assigned them there. And if I hadn't killed them, they wouldn't have hesitated to kill me."

"No." Saengkeo kept his face in her sights.

"What did your brother do with the nuclear weapon?"

"He threw it over the side of the boat. I was told the United States Navy recovered that one just like they recovered the one you sent down with *Charity's Smile*."

"Was your brother working for the same person you're working for?"

Saengkeo met his gaze and returned it full measure. She saw her own image in the steamed glass of the shower cubicle, aware of her own nakedness. Self-consciousness worried at her, but her instinct for survival was stronger.

"You're ahead of me in questions," she pointed out.

"Ask."

"Are you working for a triad?"

"No."

"Then why did you target my family?"

"I was tracking down the nuclear weapons."

"How?"

"Through the Russian *mafiya*."

"I have no dealings with them."

The man in black nodded. "They set up the buys for the nuclear weapons."

"How did you find out about me?"

"There was a woman I found."

"Pei-Ling Bao."

"Yes."

"How did you find out about her?"

"From the Russians."

"How did they know?"

"I don't know."

"Did Pei-Ling tell you about me?" Saengkeo asked.

"No. I identified her as a Moon Shadow from the tattoo she wears."

"And that led you to me?"

"That led me to the Moon Shadows. I was told that *Jadviga* was attacked by Chinese pirates."

Saengkeo couldn't help thinking about Chi-Kan Zhao, her ancestor who had first turned to piracy. "No."

"Your brother attacked the ship and took the weapons."

"One weapon," Saengkeo corrected.

The man in black gave a small nod. "Someone told your brother about the weapons *Jadviga* carried."

"Yes."

"Who?"

"I'm not going to tell you that."

"Because you're protecting someone?"

"I'm protecting my family." Saengkeo paused. "When I think about the way you chose to sink *Charity's Smile,* I can't help but wonder if we are protecting the same person."

The man in black appeared to give that consideration. "Do you," he asked after a moment, "know a man named Rance Stoddard?"

"I DON'T KNOW ABOUT YOU, Stoddard, but I think that's a big fucking security problem that I'm looking at."

Seated at the conference table in the large office, Rance Stoddard glared at the images on the flat-screen plasma monitor that emerged from the recessed area of the ceiling. He recognized Saengkeo immediately as she stood in the steaming shower.

"It's a controllable situation," Stoddard insisted. But it was also a totally unexpected one. If anything, the CIA section chief had been figuring on trying to keep Saengkeo Zhao alive against the man who now confronted her. There were still no guarantees that he wouldn't shoot her down where she stood in the shower. Acidic tension boiled in his stomach. *He hasn't shot her yet* became a mantra that ran through his mind over and over again.

"Who the hell is this son of a bitch?" the man at the other end of the scrambled phone connection and computer link demanded.

"I don't know," Stoddard admitted. He sat in front of an open laptop that he'd been working with. The room was located in one of the high rises along the Kowloon mainland overlooking Hong Kong. Tight security guaranteed that he remained alone and unobserved. No one, including the agency he worked for, knew the safe room existed.

"This is the same guy that put in the appearance on *Charity's Smile.*"

"Possibly." Stoddard stared at the image on the notebook screen that matched the one on the flat-screen plasma hanging from the ceiling.

"Possibly?" The snort of derision over the speakerphone blasted into the larger room.

"My best guess is that this is the man," Stoddard said. "Or at least the leader of the men who have been active in the operation we've undertaken."

"You don't even know if we're up against one man or an organization? Or even why he has involved himself?"

"No."

"And you mean to tell me that even with the resources of the American Central Intelligence Agency that you can't identify this man?"

Stoddard glanced at the inset window regarding the latest query he'd sent off to the CIA only hours ago.

"Results negative. Keep searching? New search parameters?"

"No." Stoddard had pulled the pictures that Saengkeo Zhao and the Moon Shadows had uploaded from the security camera's digital files from the places in Vancouver the man had attacked the night before.

"This is bullshit, Stoddard. Do you expect me to go back to my investors and tell them that you can't even identify the man that we're up against?"

Anger flared through Stoddard. He turned to the small digital camera that sat on the conference table, then tapped one of the notebook computer's keys. A window opened up on the notebook's monitor and revealed the man at the other end of the connection.

Michael Taylor was an internationally known lawyer. As an attorney specializing in Pacific Rim business and operating out of Seattle, Washington, Taylor had been regularly featured in law reviews, *People* magazine and on MSNBC interviews regarding the Middle East. He had brokered several oil deals for U.S. investors.

Trim and fit at thirty-seven years old, Taylor wore business suits like a second skin. His short-cropped blond hair, horn-rimmed glasses and round face made him look almost twenty years younger. He stood in an opulent den outfitted in black metal and glass. A floor-to-ceiling window overlooked Puget Sound and the wharf area. The reflection of the Space Needle in the distance stood out against the glass. The wall to Taylor's right held shelves filled with law books, which were unnecessary given the attorney's digital references, but they impressed the select few that he invited to his aerie.

The wall on Taylor's left held a huge home entertainment system that sublet itself as a communications station. The software that ran the communications relays tied into geosynchronous satellites was top-of-the-line, better than most currently used by the CIA. The consortium that Michael Taylor represented had a number of resources.

Taylor had a drink in one hand and stared out the windows.

"The problem isn't that I can't identify the man," Stoddard said calmly. "I only haven't identified him yet. This man is obviously well connected."

Taylor glanced at the screens, unaware that he was being observed himself. He stared at the image of Stoddard on the screen that showed the conference room interior. The camera in the conference room sat inset in the wall across from Stoddard and didn't reveal what was on the notebook computer screen.

"So you say," Taylor replied. "That statement could also cover any number of errors on your part."

"I haven't made errors," Stoddard stated.

"Pei-Ling Bao is still alive."

"Pei-Ling Bao," Stoddard said, "only became a problem because of one of the people you represent."

Taylor swirled his drink. "Pointing out the mistakes made by others is a cheap defense."

"Sebastian Cain didn't make a mistake. The man fucked up

my security layers when he decided to put in an unexpected appearance in Hong Kong. Choosing to have a prostitute accompany him to the meeting with me was an even bigger mistake."

"He couldn't have known Pei-Ling Bao was part of the Moon Shadow organization," Taylor said.

"Counselor," Stoddard stated, leaning forward, "Pei-Ling Bao isn't a member of the Moon Shadows, but she has affiliations with the triad. If you had reviewed the dossier I had sent you regarding this operation, you would have known that then and you would have known it now."

"Cain has used Pei-Ling Bao's services before when he was in Hong Kong."

"And that," Stoddard pointed out, "was something that I should have been made aware of."

"You don't need to know all of our business."

"I do when it crosses over into my territory." Stoddard glanced at the plasma flat screen, amazed that Saengkeo Zhao and the man in black hadn't shot each other yet. "That mistake won't be made again."

"Cain is the chief investor in this operation," Taylor said. "I'd step cautiously there, if I were you."

"You're not me, Counselor," Stoddard said. "And you're not running this end of the operation. When we first agreed to this, I told you I needed total and complete control over the handling of these matters."

"Cain hasn't interfered with your operation. His visit there was unfortunate and—"

"Bullshit!" Stoddard leaned back in the ergonomic chair and watched Taylor on the notebook screen. "Cain's presence here necessitated action on my part that left us open to attacks by this unknown man or the organization he represents. He traced her to Arizona, then made the connection to the Moon Shadows."

"How did he track her to the woman?"

Stoddard had put the story together by reviewing the man's moves through New York. Saengkeo didn't know the man confronting her now had been there, as well. "Your Russian *mafiya* constituents. I told you they were unreliable. This man picked up the trail in New York City."

Taylor's tone never wavered, never became agitated with the accusation. "Unfortunately, we had to deal with those men. No one else seemed to have nuclear warheads for sale." He sipped his drink. "You would have served our interests better by eliminating the threat posed by Pei-Ling Bao."

Resting his elbows on the chair arms and steepling his fingers, Stoddard drew in a breath and let it out. "Before I was properly able to address that situation, Syn-Tek Zhao intervened and sold her to one of the other triads. I hadn't thought we would see her again."

"Syn-Tek Zhao was another mistake you made," Taylor accused.

"Pei-Ling Bao told Syn-Tek who Sebastian Cain was. Knowing that Cain has been fomenting unrest between Taiwan and China, Syn-Tek started looking more deeply into the assignment I gave him. He figured out that he wasn't stealing nuclear warheads for the United States." In the end, Stoddard had been given no choice but to kill Syn-Tek and clean up the situation as best as he'd been able. That had meant dealing with Saengkeo Zhao instead, and that had proved difficult.

"Where is Pei-Ling Bao now?"

Stoddard opened another window on the notebook computer. A clock image generated. "On a flight out of Los Angeles. She'll be back in Hong Kong in less than eight hours."

"She talked with the Zhao woman."

"Yes."

"Was there any mention of Sebastian Cain?"

"No."

"What makes you so certain?"

Stoddard smiled coldly and looked at the location where the camera was inset into the wall across the room. "Because Pei-Ling Bao called me from LAX before she left. She's blackmailing me, threatening to expose my connection to Cain to Saengkeo Zhao."

"I suggest you make arrangements to rectify that situation," Taylor said.

"I've made arrangements," Stoddard said, "to rectify a number of situations." He tapped another series of keystrokes. A brief second later, the screen that Taylor was watching changed from a view of Stoddard to a view of Taylor within his own den.

To his credit, Taylor took in the new view without much reaction. He took a sip of his drink to cover what little there was. As an attorney, Taylor was stone cold in the courtroom; all emotion was manufactured as needed, from outrage to a call for empathy.

"You've been busy," Taylor observed.

"Yes," Stoddard answered. "After Cain's obsessive need to put in an appearance here to throw his weight around, I thought know-ing where all the players are at any given time might be helpful."

"You can track us?"

Stoddard enjoyed the experience of having the upper hand in the relationship with Taylor for the first time. "Only within rea-son, of course. I have learned your usual haunts. Here. Your law office in Seattle, as well as those in Tokyo and Hong Kong. The apartments you keep with your three mistresses. But if you vary too much from your normal routine, I'll know. And I'll take steps to get you back into that routine."

"You've done the same for the other investors?"

Leaning forward, tapping the computer keys again so that Taylor would once more see his face, Stoddard said, "All five of them. Including Sebastian Cain." He watched Taylor step toward the camera angle he had revealed. Even if the lawyer removed the small camera, there were three others in place in that room. And Stoddard now knew how to make arrangements for others.

"You know who they are?"

"Yes," Stoddard answered. He punched in another series of keystrokes. In quick succession, recorded live-cam shots of Cain, three other men and the only woman of Taylor's group flashed across the screen. Cain was shown with a petite Chinese prosti-tute that he'd thought was underage but that Stoddard had veri-fied was twenty-four. One of the men was sexually involved with another man. The woman was involved with a man and a woman in a tangle of limbs. The other two men had no real vices outside of greed and a willingness to circumvent the law.

Taylor smiled, but there was no humor in the expression. "Perhaps I know why you haven't been able to ascertain the identity of the man now talking to Saengkeo Zhao. You've been too busy spying on your employers."

"These cameras have been in place for weeks," Stoddard said. "Long before this man put in his first appearance in New York a few days ago."

"The investors are not going to be happy with your efforts," Taylor warned.

Stoddard tapped the keyboard and the last of the live-cam shots faded from Taylor's screen. "They don't have to know."

"I have to tell them."

"Do that," Stoddard said evenly, "and they're going to be unhappy with you, too. You were supposed to protect their interests. Even from me."

Taylor saluted Stoddard with his glass. "True." He returned to the mini-wet bar in the corner of the room and made himself a fresh drink. "So you think you can blackmail me into compliance?"

"I think you'd be a fool to expose yourself to the dissatisfaction of our employers before there's a need."

"Still, a preemptive strike would be better than waiting for you to drop the other shoe."

"The shoe won't drop," Stoddard pointed out, "as long as I feel you and I can work together. We have a common interest, you know. Both of us want the money we've been promised. We'll both do what we have to in order to earn it."

Taylor remained quiet for a moment. "Perhaps." He sipped his drink. "So what do you want, Stoddard? Blackmail never comes without a price."

"Nothing more than we've already agreed to, Counselor."

"I don't believe it."

"You will." Stoddard smiled into the camera. "I'm a greedy man, but I also know the cost of a greed that grows out of control. For the fee I'm netting out of this job, I can live more than comfortably for the rest of my life under another identity. I intend to do that."

"You still sought out the identities of the investors."

"I don't like secrets. Also, I like knowing my interests are protected."

"And if you find yourself out of money at some later date?"

"Then I'll find a means to get whatever I need then," Stoddard said, "without resorting to blackmailing you and your client list. By the time that happens, the things I know about what your employers hired us to do won't be much in the overall scheme of things."

Taylor sipped his drink. "You're an opportunist. You acknowledge that there is a time limit on the damage you can do with what you know. Likewise, you know that there is a time constraint on how long the knowledge you have is worth anything. For blackmail purposes."

Stoddard took a breath, knowing the situation he now faced with Taylor was as dangerous and volatile as the one confronting Saengkeo Zhao. Probably more so. At least the woman triad leader would know immediately when her situation went south on her.

"I wasn't expecting this situation to arise when it did," Stoddard said. "If I find myself needing or wanting money at a later date, something will come up. There's always work for a man with my talents who doesn't mind getting his hands dirty."

Taylor sipped his drink in silence. "We'll see. But you do realize that you have encumbered yourself with increased risk that I hadn't allowed when I had kept the identities of Mr. Cain's fellow investors from you?"

"Risk, certainly," Stoddard agreed. "But increased risk always carries increased worth."

"Worth?"

"My presence is worth more to you now than it was. Time is running out on the events you and Cain have engineered. You can't find someone to replace me in the time that you have left to pull this off."

"What do you believe you have gained by coming to me with this?"

"An interest on your part, Counselor," Stoddard announced. "Should something go wrong before we've finished with this thing, I don't believe you'll be so quick to wash your hands of me and let me take the fall. I think that our relationship won't be so one-sided in the future. You can see that protecting my interests with regards to our employers will be in your interests, as well. In other words, Counselor, if you and your people decide to throw me to the wolves, I'll take you with me."

"Sebastian Cain isn't a man that you can arbitrarily change games on. If I were to tell him of your impropriety given the parameters of our agreement, I believe he would have you...*relieved* of your participation."

"Probably," Stoddard admitted. "But the fact remains that I am the only man he has at this point that can do for him the things I've hired on to do." The CIA section chief raised his shoulders and dropped them. "Unless Cain and his co-investors would like to wait until another nuclear warhead falls into their laps. Provided, of course, that they can find another patsy to take the fall as I have."

"And that's not blackmail?"

"That's job security, Counselor."

"For the moment," Taylor agreed. "The instant you veer from this agreement we've made today, I won't hesitate to drop an avalanche on you."

"I'll keep that in mind." Stoddard didn't feel threatened. Taylor was forced by his nature to at least try to recoup his own self-worth. "Are you a betting man, Counselor?"

"All lawyers are. Why? Do you want to make a wager?"

"I already have," Stoddard replied. "I'm betting Cain and his constituents in this investment need a man of my talents more than they need a lawyer right now. But I'm also betting that you're intelligent enough to realize that and set aside whatever ego damage I've done today."

Taylor smiled coldly. "It remains to be seen if you've increased your net worth, Agent Stoddard, or conscripted your own death sentence." He turned his attention to the screen where the man in black and Saengkeo Zhao faced each other across drawn pistols. "I can guarantee you, however, if the woman dies your worth will go down considerably."

"He won't kill her."

"What makes you think that?"

"Because if he was going to, he would have done it already."

"You think you know him so well?" Wry amusement lifted Taylor's eyebrow. "Yet you don't even know who he is or why he's involving himself."

"I've seen this man operate. He doesn't hesitate."

"Then maybe you should be more concerned about the conversation they're having."

"I am concerned." The steady rush of water emanating from the shower interfered with the audio pickup. Stoddard wondered if the man in black had deliberately confronted Saengkeo Zhao there. "I also have a security team in place in the hotel. I put them into motion the minute I spotted the security breach. We'll know more in a few minutes. Either way, that son of a bitch isn't leaving that hotel room alive."

Bolan stared through his grayed reflection on the streaked glass of the shower cubicle. Steam glided across the naked woman on the other side of the glass. Water cascaded down her hips and over her breasts, but the pistol muzzle never wavered.

"Do *you* know someone named Rance Stoddard?" Saengkeo countered over the rushing hiss of the shower.

"We've never met," the Executioner replied, "but he's involved with this thing on a number of fronts. Including yours."

"What thing?" Saengkeo kept her hands locked around the Walther, her left hand casually supporting the right.

"The missing nuclear weapons from *Kursk*," Bolan said. "With you. Stoddard never seems far. I was told that Stoddard is CIA, and that one of his current operations is to help place a triad deep throat in the Chinese government."

Saengkeo never batted an eye. "Such a proposition would be very dangerous."

"Yeah," Bolan agreed. "If the other triad leaders found out one of their own was in bed with the American CIA, or if the Chinese government found out they were being spied on by someone they gave their trust to, that person's life expectancy would be measured in negative numbers."

"Anyone that agreed to something like that would have to be very foolish."

"Or," Bolan said, "desperate." He studied her, seeing the fear in her eyes but knowing that she—like he—was in complete control of that emotion. Fear was a survival skill. A warrior who didn't learn to fear was a dead man walking. A man who learned to give in to his fear was no warrior. The only safe harbor was control.

"Why are you telling me this?" she asked.

"Because I think you're working with Stoddard. I've reviewed the visas granted to your business and your family interests. You and your brother have made a major push to get out of Hong Kong over the past few years. De-Ying Wu confirmed that last night."

"Profits lie outside of China," Saengkeo replied evenly. "Everyone knows the biggest markets are in the Western world, primarily in the United States. The Chinese government takes all the profits from in-country."

"Your family and your businesses are getting more visas than most. You're getting help from inside the American government."

"So now you would try to blackmail me by accusing me of being that person?"

"I didn't come here to blackmail you."

"Really?" A doubtful look filled Saengkeo's beautiful face. "Didn't you think you could blackmail me by telling me this, then threatening to expose me if I don't give you the information you want?"

"No."

"Then why are you here?"

"I want the nuclear weapons secured and my country out of harm's way."

"I don't have those weapons."

"What does Stoddard have to do with your interest in the weapons?"

"Nothing."

The headset crackled in Bolan's ear. "She could be lying about not knowing Stoddard," Barbara Price said. "Aaron tapped into the hotel's digital security system and uploaded the files for the time period that Saengkeo Zhao has been checked in. Forty-seven minutes before you invaded her penthouse, the bar security cameras recorded her talking to another woman. I just IDed that woman from Stoddard's file. Her name is Jacy Corbin. She's a CIA agent working under Stoddard's supervision in Hong Kong."

Bolan thought about that. He gazed at Saengkeo over the Beretta's sights. Over the years, through all the danger and the missions he'd undertaken with all the people he'd come in contact with, he'd learned to trust his instincts.

"Do you know Jacy Corbin?" he asked.

The woman's eyes flickered. "I'm through answering questions."

"She met you here," Bolan stated, "less than an hour ago."

"We're through talking," Saengkeo replied coldly. "And I'm through with my shower. If you don't leave in ten seconds, I'm going to pull this trigger. I won't live in fear of you, and I won't tolerate your insistence on controlling me any longer."

Trusting his instincts, knowing the woman meant every word that she said, Bolan slowly lowered his weapon but didn't put it away. He watched her, feeling his heart thud against his rib cage, feeling the adrenaline spike in his blood. The uncertainty over whether he had made a judgment mistake rattled inside his skull. He kept his arms away from his sides, telling himself if she attempted to fire that he could still hope to survive the shot, possibly even escape it completely. The glass would help deflect the .40-caliber round.

"I want the nuclear weapons," he said.

Her eyes narrowed and he knew she kept track of his pistol through her peripheral vision, but her gaze never left his. "Why?"

"I want them off the playing field. I don't want another terrorist attack launched against the United States."

"You're American?"

"Yes."

"CIA?"

"No."

"NSA?"

Bolan smiled a little. "Unaffiliated. Private enterprise. Just like you."

"Why did you come here?"

"Because your family has been in harm's way since the nuclear weapons disappeared from *Jadviga*."

"Weapon," she corrected.

"Your brother is dead," Bolan said. "Probably because of that weapon. I know that Pei-Ling Bao ties back to you and your family. And then there's the meeting we had on *Charity's Smile*."

"Where the second nuclear weapon was lost."

"And recovered by the U.S. Navy. Do you want those weapons in the hands of terrorists?"

She answered without hesitation. "No."

Bolan gazed at her. "I believe you."

She arched a brow at him. "And, in turn, I should believe you?"

"Believe me, yes. Trust me?" Bolan shook his head. "I wouldn't expect you to trust me. I don't trust you."

"Yet there you stand while I have a pistol pointed at you."

"You haven't fired yet," Bolan said. "And even if you fired, maybe I'm fast enough to anticipate the bullet and get out of the way. Maybe the glass will deflect the round."

Suddenly, with a liquid ease that mirrored the water sluicing down from the showerhead, Saengkeo Zhao relaxed her arms and let her pistol drop down to her side. "You must still leave."

"I want to talk about Stoddard. He's playing a key part in this."

"No," she replied. "No talk about Stoddard."

"He sent you to *Charity's Smile*, didn't he?"

Saengkeo made no comment.

"How did Stoddard know the weapon was going to be there?"

"How did you?" Saengkeo asked.

Bolan ignored the question. "Does Stoddard know where the third weapon is?"

"I don't know."

"What did Jacy Corbin want?"

"Ask her."

Bolan stared into the woman's eyes, recalling images of how she had appeared aboard *Charity's Smile* and earlier in the day at the bombing of the Blue Lotus Supermarket when she had led the old woman away from her dead husband. She was a deadly warrior and she was a compassionate woman. Both sides of the same coin.

Her eyes, her body language, held defiance. She stood naked before him with a pistol in her fist and she wasn't about to back down.

"Striker," Barbara Price called over the headset.

Bolan lifted his hand slowly to the earpiece so Saengkeo would know he was talking to someone else. "Go." The hissing sound from the shower interfered with the audio pickup.

"The thermal imagers just picked up two groups of men en route to the top floor."

"Law enforcement?" Bolan backed out of the bathroom, keeping his eyes on Saengkeo Zhao.

"No. We've been monitoring the police department's movements. They've got units on the street below and plainclothes officers in the foyer, but this isn't coming from them."

"What is it?" Saengkeo asked.

Before Bolan could reply, the ratcheting growls of suppressed auto fire ripped loose outside in the hallway. The room's walls further muffled the noise, but there was no mistaking the noise. Screams and curses in English and Chinese followed, punctuated by cries of warning and pain.

"You're under attack," Bolan told Saengkeo, then shifted his attention back to the headset. "Base, have you IDed the groups?"

"Negative, Striker. We're trying to access the hotel's security video system, but that it appears to be shut down. Someone interrupted the feed."

"You brought these people here." Saengkeo swung open the shower cubicle and stepped out. She pulled on a pair of loose black silk pajamas with crimson dragons embroidered on the legs, then pulled on a matching top. Reaching under a towel on the vanity, she took out another Walther that matched the first.

Bolan ignored the accusation and strode toward the living room. He leathered the Beretta and lifted the Jackhammer

12-gauge shotgun on the Whip-it sling. The crunching growls of the silenced weapons in the hallway grew louder, interspersed now with unsuppressed gunfire.

A cell phone lying on the bed rang. Saengkeo picked up the handset. She spoke in Chinese too rapidly for Bolan to hear over the thunder of the weapons. After a brief exchange, she pocketed the cell phone.

"They're not police," she told Bolan. Her eyes gleamed with suspicion. "And they're not members of a rival triad."

Bolan took up a position beside the door. "They're not with me." His mind raced, going over the options he had.

"Then they're after you," Saengkeo said.

"We need to get out of here."

"They're not after me."

"They're cutting their way through your people to get here," Bolan pointed out. "Whether they're after me or after you, you're not going to be safe in here."

"I can't leave those men."

"You've got to move, Striker," Price said. "The Moon Shadows are caving in front of them."

"Your men are out there dying for you," Bolan growled. "If you stay, more of them will die. Get free. Use the phone to call Kwan and tell him to pull those men out of here."

Indecision flickered across the beautiful face for just a heartbeat, then grim resolve smoothed the emotion. "How?"

"The balcony." The thunder of gunshots ripped into the suite of rooms, making normal conversation impossible. A handful of bullets crashed through the door and the wall, letting in shafts of light from the hallway. Plaster dust from the thin wallboard swirled through the light.

Saengkeo nodded.

"Let's go." Bolan stepped into the living room. Saengkeo followed him immediately. The Executioner stayed between the woman and the door leading out into the hallway, offering her the added protection of the Kevlar he wore.

They were two long strides from the patio windows and sliding when the front door blew open. The doorknob and lock blew across the room and embedded in the wall, letting the warrior know the men had brought at least one shaped charge with them. The door swung into the room, buckling on the hinges and revealing the hellzone that had dawned outside the entrance.

Bolan brought the Jackhammer to his shoulder and fired into the center of the first man through the door. The double-aught buckshot slammed into the man and staggered him backward. Tatters of the gunman's dark sweater revealed the navy Kevlar vest beneath. He also wore a riot helmet and face shield.

A second man elbowed the first man out of the way, spinning expertly into place with an MP-5 SD-3 clenched in both hands. The submachine pistol jerked in his hands and spit out a stream of 9 mm rounds that chopped into the room. The bullets tore holes in the carpet, raked splinters from the coffee table and punched through the sofa. A stray round crashed through a lamp on a side table and dropped the ceramic base in jagged shards to the floor.

Targeting the new gunner, Bolan squeezed through two quick rounds, placing the first at the man's knees and riding the shotgun's recoil up to the guy's chest. The initial blast of buckshot cut the man's feet from under him and spilled him forward. Instead of impacting against the Kevlar on his chest and knocking him backward, the shotgun pellets shattered his face in a violent crimson spray that dropped him in his tracks.

Saengkeo slid the patio door open as the gunfire hammering the room increased and exploded through the walls. Fist-sized sections of the wall opened up, letting in the hallway light.

Bolan pulled a flash-bang grenade from his vest, popped the pin and tossed the explosive toward the wall beside the open door. He fired two more shotgun rounds through the wall as Saengkeo slipped out onto the balcony. Then he turned and followed her, catching her and pressing her against the wall beside the balcony door.

"Close your eyes," he said, and closed his own. "Open your mouth." He opened his own mouth, hoping that the effort could equalize the sudden pressure of the coming explosion so he wouldn't suffer temporary partial deafness.

The flash-bang detonated before the Executioner could draw his next breath. Despite the fact that he had closed his eyes, the bright lights painted his eyelids. The explosive blast robbed him of his hearing, but the pressure equalized in an instant and his hearing returned.

"Move," Bolan said.

Saengkeo gazed out over the balcony's edge. Cars filled the streets below, passing through pools of neon lights from the bars and clubs that remained open. "Where?"

"To the balcony below," Bolan answered. "I'll help you." He offered his left hand.

She looked at him but made no move to clamber over the side.

"Striker," Price called over the headset, "they're regrouping."

"Trust me," Bolan said. "Or you can stay and hope that those men are really after me and not you."

Resolutely, Saengkeo pulled the drawstring from her pajama bottoms, threaded the string through the trigger guards, and looped them around her neck. Lithely, she hopped over the wrought-iron railing that topped the balcony walls. She shoved her left hand out.

Bolan took her hand and leaned over the balcony as she crawled down. More bullets ripped into the room behind them. When Saengkeo ran out of balcony that she could safely descend by herself, she looked up at Bolan.

"I've got you," the Executioner said. "Trust me."

Without a word, Saengkeo released her hold, surrendering her fate to him. Her eyes held his.

Bolan felt her weight settle at the end of his arm. He'd hunted her for days. On board *Charity's Smile,* if things had gone differently, he might have killed her if it hadn't been for the bulletproof vest she'd been wearing. Or she might have killed him, because she and her team had tried.

Now...all he had to do to claim her life and rob the Moon Shadow triad of their leader was just let go. The irony of the situation wasn't lost on him.

Her free hand seized the butt of one of the pistols hanging from the drawstring around her neck. Defiance marked her features. If he let go, she would shoot him. Maybe she would even shoot him the instant she had her feet on the lower balcony.

They recognized each other as enemies, and in that moment Bolan realized how open he'd left himself to an attack by her. If he had judged her wrong, he could be dead in seconds. The trust had gone both ways, and he had made that judgment in an eye blink.

Arm trembling from the strain, Bolan guided Saengkeo Zhao toward the lower balcony. He had to bend at the waist as far as he could to get her close enough to reach the railing with a foot.

"Striker!" Price called. "Behind you!"

Half turning, Bolan spotted a shadow stepping into the hotel room. Saengkeo dropped six inches as he spun and tried to bring up the Jackhammer.

Then a double-tap of concussive force ignited liquid fire against the right side of the Executioner's chest. The Kevlar armor stopped the bullets from penetrating, but the blunt trauma bruised the flesh beneath and nearly threw him over the wrought-iron railing. The contusions he'd received aboard *Charity's Smile* still hadn't faded. The impact knocked the breath from his lungs and threw him off balance. He almost released his grip on Saengkeo, felt his hold on her slip a fraction of an inch before he could secure his grip again.

Below, Saengkeo swung dangerously out from the building. The change in the weight distribution and the awkward angle pulled at Bolan's shoulder socket until he thought the joint was going to come apart. More bullets struck sparks from the wrought-iron railing. The impacts rang in the warrior's ears and vibrated against his side.

Grimly, knowing his life was measured between seconds, the Executioner lifted the 12-gauge shotgun and aimed at the center of the gunner. The double-ought load caught the man and spun him backward.

Glancing below again, Bolan saw that Saengkeo had reached the lower balcony with the toes of both her feet. However, she couldn't reach a handhold that would allow her to scramble to safety. The rail was out of reach and she was too short to reach the balcony above to steady herself.

"Hold on," she called. "I'm going to swing out, then you have to let go."

"Let's do it," Bolan growled.

The woman kicked against the balcony railing. The additional strain on Bolan's arm and back burned fiercely. She arced out over the street far below, reached the apex of her swing just as Bolan's arm started to grow numb, and swung back toward the balcony below.

"Let go!" she yelled.

Certain that she was going to make her destination, and facing the fact that he couldn't hold her much longer in the present situation, Bolan let go. He stayed bent over the railing and watched as Saengkeo slid out of sight across the balcony floor below. Patio furniture crashed, and a glass-topped table overturned against the wrought-iron railing and smashed to a thousand glittering pieces.

"Get going, Striker," Price called over the headset. "She made it. She's up and moving."

Fire coursed through Bolan's flesh under the Kevlar armor. His left arm still felt pulled from the socket. Moving by instinct and with the adrenaline spiking his system, the Executioner pulled up the Jackhammer as two more men invaded the hotel room. Holding the trigger, he cycled through the remainder of the combat shotgun's magazine. When the action blew back dry, he released the weapon to hang from the sling. Ripping a smoke grenade from his combat harness, he popped the pin and heaved the grenade into the room.

"Grenade!" a man yelled inside the room.

The gunners crowded for the door and the hole blown in the wall.

Bolan ran toward the nylon rope still hanging from the mini-block-and-tackle rig hanging from the building's roof. Gripping the rope, he vaulted up onto the wrought-iron railing and pulled himself up.

The grenade went off in the hotel room, and a moment later, acrid black smoke belched from the room out over the balcony.

"It's just smoke!" a man yelled.

Bolan's combat boots thudded against the side of the building and found traction. He went up the rope quickly, then threw an arm over the roof's edge. "Base," he said.

"Go, Striker. You have Base."

"Where is she?"

"She broke into the room below," Price replied. "She's making her way down the fire escape."

That was dangerous, Bolan knew. The groups of attackers would probably take the same route to the ground. "What about the police?"

"On their way. She's pulled her people back."

"Are the newcomers pursuing them?"

"No. They seem focused on you."

Bullets chipped splinters from the stone only inches from Bolan's face as he hauled himself up. His left shoulder trembled from the strain, and for a moment he thought it might not hold him.

"Up there!" a man shouted from below. "Bastard's headed for the roof!"

More rounds ricocheted from the building's wall and whined through the air close enough for Bolan to hear them even over the car noises in the street below. He flipped over the roof's edge.

As he pushed up from the rough surface, the Executioner saw the rope grow taut. He pulled the Cold Steel Tanto blade from his combat harness and drew the razor-sharp edge across the Kernmantle line. The rope, although strong enough to resist sharp rock and frozen ice, parted instantly. The rope's end whipped out of sight, followed a moment later by a man's scream.

"The group is going back through the hallway," Price said. "There's a roof access at the other end of the hall."

Bolan sheathed the knife and ran toward the area where he'd left the parachute. He grabbed the case he'd brought with him and snapped the latches open. "Mustang."

"Here, Sarge," Grimaldi radioed back.

"I need you in front of the building."

"Affirmative. I'm on my way."

Working with tense efficiency, Bolan drew the collapsible hang glider from the case and popped out the struts. The dark gray nylon material drew taut as the locks snapped into place.

"It's confirmed, Striker," Price said. "The men are after you. They're making their way through the roof access."

"What about the woman?" Bolan asked as he lifted the hang glider and eased into the harness.

"She's made it back to her security team. They're headed for the ground floor."

Metal grated behind Bolan. In the next second, a pistol blasted and bullets struck something metallic.

The Executioner judged the wind, hefted the hang glider and sprinted across the hotel's roof to the front of the building. Landing on either side of the building or behind the structure would have been much harder than trying to land on the four-lane street in front of the hotel.

Full-throated autofire erupted behind Bolan, bullets ripping through the HVAC units and throwing swarms of sparks in all directions.

Without hesitation, Bolan kept sprinting, driving himself over the roof until the edge fell away and gravity reached up to claim him. He dropped, hurtling down the side of the building.

8

Bolan watched the side of the hotel hurtle by him. He moved so fast that the lights of the passing floors whipped into and out of view like a strobe light. Automatically, he counted them. The stream of traffic in the street in front of the hotel looked like ants. Wind pushed at his face and raked talons through his hair.

He held the control bar in both hands but didn't push it forward. The updraft wasn't enough to push him back up again, but the hang glider would take longer to decelerate. During that time, he'd be a target for the rooftop gunners.

With less than twelve stories to go before his plunge ended up with him smeared across the street, the Executioner pushed the control bar forward. The nylon moved grudgingly, refusing to grab hold of the air easily because the wind kept it shoved in position, streamlining the air.

Bolan's left shoulder screamed in protest at the continued abuse. A hot shower and a few hours of rest would probably put the shoulder back to rights, but that wasn't happening now.

Two floors later, less than a second, the hang glider gave in to the warrior's strength and determination. The plummeting descent stopped with a suddenness that threatened to suck Bolan's stomach through his shoe soles. Caught by the air but still maintaining the speed he'd built up, the warrior rose a short distance and shot forward like an arrow released from a bow.

Before Bolan had time to take a breath, the hang glider knifed through the air and across the street, heading for the tall office building across from the hotel. He pulled on the control bar and shifted his weight, managing to pull up the hang glider just short of impact. He got close enough to run up the building a couple steps, then the glider twisted over, slinging him through the air and shooting him forward again. Traffic passed dizzyingly beneath him.

Bolan arched his body and fought the glider, bringing the unit under his control. A line of bullets scarred the building wall beside him, tracking after him and crashing through a line of windows. Once the glider righted, he slid east along the four-lane.

"Mustang," Bolan called over the headset.

"I've got you, Sarge," Grimaldi called. "Do you see the light?"

Bolan raked his gaze along the traffic. Despite the neon signs around the street and the pools of vehicle headlights, the soldier spotted the mini-Maglite the pilot brandished from the driver's seat of a sport-utility Jeep. The hardtop had been removed, leaving the seat area open.

"I see you, Mustang," Bolan replied. "Get moving." He pulled on the control bar, shedding height and streaking along the street.

Grimaldi jumped into the flow of traffic, igniting a barrage of horns from infuriated and startled drivers. The pilot ignored the irate responses and kept moving.

Bolan shifted, trying to ease the strain on his shoulder. The joint ached fiercely and his fingers felt numb, the feeling growing with each second.

"Striker, you've got company coming from the hotel. They're approaching from your six, gaining ground rapidly."

Glancing back, Bolan spotted five men racing along the sidewalk. They bulled through an open-air café that spilled out from a bar in the lower floor of the building adjacent to the hotel. The men left patrons and tables overturned in their wake. Other passersby along the sidewalk saw what was happening and quickly stepped from the path the men took.

Farther behind the men, Bolan recognized Saengkeo Zhao sprinting from the hotel with her security team in tow. A black limousine, sliding forward with a heaviness that assured body armor had been added, jumped the curb in front of the hotel and pulled to a stop. A man inside the luxury car opened the back door and Saengkeo darted inside.

Bullets from the running men below cut through the air near Bolan, leaving no doubt that he was the primary target of the attack. A round glanced off his back, turned by the Kevlar. The blunt force knocked the breath from him and caused him to jerk the control bar as he swooped toward Grimaldi and the Jeep. Three more rounds holed the nylon material covering the glider.

Another struck the aluminum frame with a metallic spang that hurt the soldier's ears. The frame bent where the bullet had struck. Partially out of control, Bolan dropped toward the street.

"Mustang," Bolan said, "I'm short."

"I see you," Grimaldi replied. "Hang on."

Struggling to maintain control, feeling the pain from his strained shoulder knifing into him, spreading along his side, Bolan dropped toward the street. Several motorists had frozen in the lanes as they stared up. Pedestrians stood at attention, some of them pointing in the soldier's direction.

Grimaldi brought the Jeep around in a tight U-turn, locking bumpers momentarily with a taxi, then tearing free and shooting forward again. They'd chosen the Jeep for the exfiltration vehicle because of the open top and the short wheelbase, as well as the power. With tight-turning capability and four wheel drive, the Jeep presented power and mobility. Unfortunately, the Jeep also came with a distinctive look and would have to be quickly dumped before the Vancouver police tracked the vehicle down.

"Striker," Price said, "the police department has ordered a chopper into the air. If you don't clear that area shortly, they're going to be able to track you."

"Understood," Bolan said. He whipped along the street, dropping to within ten or twelve feet. Yanking the quick-release straps, he abandoned the glider and dropped. Freed from the extra weight but now out of control, the glider rose briefly, drawing a barrage of gunfire that tore and twisted the frame and the stretched nylon. The glider smashed into a display window, crashing through and setting off a burglar alarm that screamed stridently.

Bolan dropped to the street, going down immediately in a paratrooper roll to lose his momentum. He continued to roll, coming up on his feet but still wasn't able to stop before slamming into a minivan marked with the logo of a pizza chain.

Grimaldi threaded through the traffic, leaving the street and speeding along the sidewalk.

Bullets stuttered into the minivan and shattered the lighted pizza advertisement atop the vehicle. The driver yelped and cursed and took cover. Other bullets punched holes in the windshield.

Shoving himself into motion, Bolan ran through the stalled traffic. Panicked faces flashed through his vision as drivers and passengers of the vehicles trapped in the cars in the street ducked down. For a moment, the soldier felt bad about that. He tried to keep most people from the path of violence that he followed while on a mission, but that wasn't always possible.

The stakes in the present operation had warranted the risk. But if he had known the response was going to be coming from an outside third party and that the response would be as aggressive and punitive, he would have planned on confronting Saengkeo Zhao another way. Still, the attack had conferred a lot of knowledge that he hoped to be able to use.

A police siren split the night.

"Striker," Price warned, "you've got a car coming up ahead on your left."

Bolan spotted the heavy sedan muscling through the traffic. The driver had abandoned all hope of negotiating the traffic without collision and rammed through the stalled cars. Metal ripped with agonizing screeches that reverberated between the canyon of tall buildings.

A passenger leaned from the open window and pulled an assault rifle to shoulder. Muzzle-flashes lit up his hard-planed features.

The Executioner drew the Desert Eagle from his hip, came to a brief stop in a modified Weaver stance, left hand cupping his right, and sighted on the man. When the tritium dots lined up on the center of the man's chest, Bolan squeezed the trigger.

The .44 boattail hollowpoint crashed through the gunner's sternum and through his heart. His corpse dropped from the sedan and sprawled across the street.

Moving again, Bolan ran toward the car because Grimaldi and the Jeep were in that direction. The driver tried to cut off the Executioner, swerving sharply. Bolan leaped as he closed on the sedan's side, throwing his feet forward and over the vehicle's hood. He skidded across the front of the car, but the sedan's forward momentum buffeted him up onto the windshield.

From the corner of his eye, Bolan spotted one of the two men in the back seat of the car lifting a machine pistol and thrusting the weapon forward. Muzzle-flashes blossomed at the end of the machine pistol's wicked snout. Bullets chopped through the windshield, blowing glass out, then ripped through the sedan's roof as the warrior rolled up over the vehicle.

Dropping to his feet on the other side of the sedan, Bolan landed with his knees bent, crouching, sliding and shifting and centering himself behind the Desert Eagle. The man in the back of the sedan tried to bring his weapon to bear. Bolan knew the man wouldn't care that innocents were in line behind his target.

The Executioner stroked the Desert Eagle's trigger, rode out the recoil, then fired again. Both bullets struck the gunner and knocked him into the other man in the sedan's back seat. In the next moment, the sedan collided with a large garbage truck mired in the traffic.

The driver reached for the column gearshift. Dropping his sights over the back of the driver's head, the Executioner squeezed the trigger again. The man's head went to pieces inside the sedan and his body slumped across the steering wheel.

Wheeling, Bolan sprinted for the Jeep. Grimaldi screeched to a halt, allowing the Executioner to haul himself into the passenger seat.

"Well, I'd say we've about worn out our welcome here," the pilot stated dryly. He shoved the gearshift into reverse and glanced back over his shoulder.

Bolan thumbed shells into the Jackhammer from the pockets of his combat harness. "Yeah."

Just as Grimaldi let out on the clutch, a black limousine skidded to a halt behind the Jeep. Purple light from the nearby tavern coated the driver's-side windows.

Bolan leaned back over the seat with the Jackhammer in his hands. He aimed at the rear passenger window, expecting the threat to come from there. He guessed that the glass would be bulletproof, but the people inside couldn't shoot through it, either.

Johnny Kwan sat near the door. His face was implacable on the other side of the dark glass. A pistol showed nakedly in his fist. The back window started to roll down smoothly.

Seated on the other side of the man, Saengkeo Zhao put her hand on Kwan's pistol. Bolan read her lips through the glass: "No."

With obvious reluctance, Kwan lowered his weapon. The glass slid back up. Saengkeo turned her attention to the driver and spoke again. An instant later, the limousine surged forward, picking a treacherous path through the paralyzed traffic. Metal scraped against other cars, but the heavy luxury vehicles never surrendered forward momentum.

"New convert to the fan club?" Grimaldi asked dryly.

"No," Bolan answered, lowering the shotgun. "A truce. For the moment."

Grimaldi let out the clutch and got the Jeep into motion.

"YOU SHOULD HAVE LET me kill him."

Saengkeo gazed at Johnny Kwan. His face was still and quiet, seemingly as malleable as stone. She curbed her immediate response to point out that Kwan's attempt could have resulted in both their deaths. The man in black was deadly, and she had seen the man in action up close and personal twice.

Still, she knew that Kwan's ego was bruised. The unanticipated attack in the hotel had caught his security team flat-footed. Recovering from the injuries he'd received earlier in the day at the Blue Lotus Supermarket had left him thickheaded. Even though he'd refused painkillers, his thinking wasn't back to one hundred percent.

"I don't think killing him is the answer," she stated.

"He tried to kill you aboard the Russian freighter," Kwan said.

"And he could have killed me tonight," Saengkeo said, "but he chose not to."

"The next time he meets you, he may change his mind again."

The limousine driver broke clear of the snarled traffic and streaked through the city. A police car with whirling lights and a shrill siren passed by them.

Saengkeo glanced through the luxury car's back glass but couldn't see the Jeep the man in black had used to escape. She didn't even know if he'd gotten clear of the traffic.

"The next time we meet won't be by his choosing," Saengkeo said.

"What do you mean?"

"We're going back to Hong Kong. Our strength lies there. No one can get close to us there—unless we choose to let them."

Kwan visibly relaxed. "I'm glad you've made this decision, Miss Zhao."

"I feel badly about leaving our family and our business in disarray," Saengkeo said. "Many will feel as though we have abandoned them."

"If you stayed, the Vancouver Police Department would hound you. And you would continue to be a target for the rival triads based in this city. There is blood in the water, Miss Zhao, and many may feel that a great deal of it is yours."

"A lot of it is." Saengkeo thought of Syn-Tek and wondered how her brother would have handled the present situation.

"You're not weak," Kwan stated.

"If Syn-Tek were here—"

"Miss Zhao," Kwan interrupted smoothly, "this situation has come from the same one that got Syn-Tek killed. In fact, things have gotten worse since you have involved yourself directly. You have dealt with our enemies and shored up the Moon Shadow's position among the triads. Syn-Tek could have done no better."

"Thank you."

Kwan nodded. "What did that man in black want?"

"To know where the third nuclear weapon is."

"What did you tell him?"

"That I did not know."

"Did he believe you?"

"Yes. Then, when he knew those men were coming, he stayed to protect me." Saengkeo remembered how she had felt dangling at the end of the big man's arm. The situation had been, oddly, the most dangerous and most secure place she had ever been in. Even when he had been shot from a man inside the room, she had known he wouldn't drop her. He hadn't allowed himself, and she had seen the determination in those volcanic blue eyes.

"How did he know those men were coming?" Kwan asked.

"He talked to someone over the headset he wore."

"The man in the Jeep?"

Saengkeo thought for a moment, then shook her head. "No. I got the impression that the person he talked to while he was with me was female."

"He didn't call her by name?"

"He called her Base."

Kwan stared out at the city. Reflections flashed across his black eyes. "I saw him on the street. I saw how he wore his gear and the kind of gear that he carried with him. He came from the top of the building. That's where he left the hang glider. This man is a soldier, Miss Zhao."

"I think so, too."

"But what brought him into conflict with us?"

"The Russian *mafiya*." In terse detail, Saengkeo relayed the story as the man in black had told her.

"He did not find out about the Moon Shadows until he rescued Pei-Ling Bao?"

Thinking that Kwan intended to talk about Pei-Ling's failings again and not wanting to hear them, Saengkeo said, "Pei-Ling didn't tell the man in black about the Moon Shadows. He saw and identified the tattoo she carries."

To his credit, Kwan didn't suggest how such a sighting could have come about. "That was the first he knew of the Moon Shadow's involvement?"

"That's what he told me."

Kwan gazed at her. "Then there's no way he could be Syn-Tek's killer."

"He told me he was not."

"You believed him?"

"Yes."

Shifting in his seat, Kwan leaned forward. Pain flickered across his face and his breath hissed through his lips as his bruised ribs caused him to sit up straight to adjust them, but his features smoothed out in the next moment. "So he came to Vancouver to draw you to him?"

"He didn't say that."

"De-Ying Wu's report suggested that." Kwan had been at the debriefing. "If he did come here to draw you out, which I believe he did, then you must be the only lead he has to work with."

"I don't think so. There are the men who attacked me tonight. And he knows about Stoddard."

"How?"

"He didn't say."

Kwan cursed softly, something he rarely did in Saengkeo's presence. "Now this man has two targets. It will be interesting to see which he chooses."

"He didn't want me dead." Saengkeo remembered again how she had dangled from the big man's hand. She didn't think she would ever forget that.

"Does Stoddard know where the third weapon is?"

"I don't know." Saengkeo patiently endured Kwan's questions. They were the same ones she had been asking herself, but it was helpful to know that she and Kwan, whom she considered to be clever and adroit, were thinking in the same direction. "He knows about the deal my family struck with the United States government through Stoddard."

Kwan regarded her, his gaze flat and black. "That is dangerous."

"It also means this man is well informed about his government's dealings."

"He is American?"

"He told me he was."

"Do you believe him?"

Saengkeo remembered how the man in black had stated that he wouldn't allow another terrorist attack on the United States, and his simple declaration that he was American. "If you had heard him, you would know he could be nothing else." There had been a fierceness about the statement that had run as deep and as true as her own feelings about her family and her commitments to those people.

"Why did this man bring up Stoddard?"

Pressing the button on the arm console, Saengkeo opened the intercom to the driver. "Take us to the airport. Have our plane readied."

"Yes, Miss Zhao."

Saengkeo closed the intercom. "He told me that I couldn't trust Stoddard."

"In that," Kwan said, "we agree." He took a breath. "It will be interesting to find out what the Vancouver Police Department finds out about the men that attacked the hotel room."

"Who do you think they were?"

"Americans." Kwan reached inside his jacket. "I took a wallet from one of the dead men." He flipped the wallet open, revealing a United States driver's license with a picture of a smiling, innocuous man in his late twenties or early thirties. His home address was listed as Cleveland, Ohio. "I also think that these identifications are going to prove dead ends for us, as well as the Vancouver Police Department." He put the wallet back inside his jacket, moving gingerly. "What concerns me most is how quickly those men knew the man in black was inside your rooms."

Saengkeo nodded. "I've been thinking about that. There's only one way."

"Your room was rigged with cameras and audio pickups. Only one person could have done that so efficiently and known you were going to be at that hotel tonight."

"Stoddard." Saengkeo had reached the same conclusion. "That was the same message Jacy Corbin gave me when I met her tonight."

"Why would she tell you that?"

"Because she's sleeping with him and he's keeping secrets from her," Saengkeo said. "Also, I get the impression that she wants to get ahead in her chosen career. If she has to, she'll step over Stoddard to do that."

"She doesn't trust him, either."

"No. Jacy Corbin is of the opinion that Stoddard is more interested in me than the present operation warrants. Also, during the time we were together, she made no mention of the nuclear weapons."

"You don't think she knows about them?"

"No. I think Stoddard is hiding the existence of the weapons from her."

"The American agencies keep intelligence from each other sometimes."

"Jacy Corbin works closely with Stoddard from what I've seen," Saengkeo said. "If she has had questions about his behavior and decisions, she's not had them dealt with."

"Hong Kong," Kwan said, "may not be as safe as we think. Stoddard is well-versed in your activities there."

"I don't intend to let him have the chance to act," Saengkeo said.

"What are you going to do?"

"Jacy Corbin told me she believes that Syn-Tek made a deal with the Howling Dogs to kidnap Pei-Ling Bao because she saw a man with Stoddard."

"What man?"

"Sebastian Cain." Saengkeo saw the recognition dawn in Kwan's eyes.

Cain was an international industrialist who specialized in munitions, pharmaceuticals and cutting-edge technology. Some of the Moon Shadow's holdings included labor-management agencies that provided workers at factories the industrialist owned in Hong Kong and Taiwan. Cain was also a major proponent of Taiwan's continued separation from the Chinese mainland. He maintained lobby groups in Washington, D.C., that pushed for American involvement in the Chinese-Taiwan question.

"Where is Pei-Ling Bao?" Saengkeo asked.

Kwan glanced at his watch. "Four hours out from Hong Kong."

"Reroute the jet," Saengkeo said. "Have the pilot put in to Shanghai. Arrange our flight so that we put in to Shanghai as well, but I want the plan to read that we are going to Hong Kong. We'll change course later." She thought the destination was fitting. That was where her family's future had begun to change, when her great-grandfather Jik-Chang Zhao had sworn the oath to his dying brother.

"Stoddard may still have contacts in Shanghai," Kwan pointed out.

"Even so," Saengkeo agreed, "there will be fewer there than in Hong Kong."

"We have fewer people there, as well."

"We won't be there long," Saengkeo said. "Just long enough to get the truth from Pei-Ling."

"Do you think," Kwan asked evenly, "such a thing is possible?"

Saengkeo quieted her anger and her immediate impulse to protect Pei-Ling as she had been doing since they were both girls. Even old Ea-Han, who had been Saengkeo's chief mentor when she'd been growing up, hadn't spared as much time for Pei-Ling as he had the other children. Pei-Ling lived with a high sense of drama that fueled the lies she wove with skill and the fantasies that lifted her life even in her eyes.

"You can always get the truth from Pei-Ling when you already know the answers to the questions you ask," Saengkeo replied.

The limousine's phone buzzed for attention.

Kwan answered the phone, listened briefly, then covered the mouthpiece with a hand, and said, "It's Stoddard."

Heart speeding a little from the anger and sense of betrayal that filled her, Saengkeo took the phone from Johnny Kwan. "Saengkeo," she said.

"Are you all right?" Stoddard asked. He sounded properly agitated and concerned.

"Yes," she answered. She stared through the limousine's front windshield as the driver negotiated the heavy traffic.

"News of the attack on the hotel just broke on MSNBC and FOX," Stoddard said.

"That was fast," Saengkeo replied noncommittally.

"You haven't exactly been maintaining a low profile while you've been visiting Vancouver." Stoddard sounded irritated. "CNN is still running the video footage of the police detective getting shot down in front of the Blue Lotus Supermarket. Fox has put together a special regarding Chinese triads, with the Moon Shadows in the starring role. I have to tell you, this is going to make selling you and your group to my people harder to do."

"This isn't my fault," Saengkeo argued. "Nor is it the fault of my family. Your business has spilled over onto our business. The man from *Charity's Smile* is here."

Stoddard hesitated. "Are you certain?"

"I saw him." Saengkeo made her voice hard. "It was the same man."

"What did he want?"

"He's the one who has attacked the Moon Shadow's businesses in Vancouver."

"Why?"

"He wants the third nuclear weapon."

After a brief pause, Stoddard said, "What did you tell him?"

"That I didn't know where it was."

"Did he believe you?"

"I think so. There was no time to be certain because we were attacked at that time."

"How long did you talk to him?"

He knew, Saengkeo thought. He was watching. The cold certainty filled her, trickling down her spine. "For a little while," she admitted. "I don't know how long. We both had weapons."

"Why didn't you shoot him?"

"He would have shot me."

"Why didn't he?"

"Because I would have shot him."

"He was afraid of you?"

"I believe so. He didn't shoot." Saengkeo waited to see if Stoddard was going to say anything else. Then she said. "You need to investigate the men who attacked the hotel."

"Why?"

"Because Kwan and I believe they were American."

"Working for the man in black?"

The description was another giveaway that Stoddard had watched the scene unfold. Saengkeo hadn't told the CIA section chief how the man in black had been dressed. "No. They tried to kill him, as well."

"Maybe one of the triads hired outside help," Stoddard suggested.

Saengkeo didn't point out that the possibility was slim. The

Golden Peacocks had performed the action against the Blue Lotus Supermarket on their own. The triads generally handled their own battles because the action generated respect and showed the other triads the cost of any action that might be directed against them.

"I want you to find out what you can," Saengkeo said.

After a brief pause, Stoddard said, "I will. What are you going to do?"

"I'm coming back to Hong Kong," Saengkeo answered. "I can't stay in Vancouver. I'll be covered over in law-enforcement agencies."

"Good. I think I'll have the location of the third nuclear weapon by the time you arrive here." He paused. "Have you seen Jacy Corbin lately?"

The question caught Saengkeo off guard. Even during the short amount of time she required to get over her surprise, she knew she couldn't lie about that. "Yes."

"Have you talked to her?"

"Twice. Once in L.A. and once here."

"About what?"

"You," Saengkeo answered.

"Why would she discuss me?"

"I think she's jealous. From the impression I got, she believes the two of us are involved." Saengkeo decided to give him that. The answer would flatter Stoddard's male ego and give Jacy Corbin plenty of room to maneuver in an argument Saengkeo felt certain would ensue. Also, the woman would have an emotional outlet that would allow her to step away from a full-blown interrogation if she needed or wanted it.

"She's a better agent than that."

Saengkeo put an edge on her reply and added frost. "Then I suggest you ask her why she was here demanding to know if I was sleeping with you."

Stoddard laughed. "That's ridiculous."

"Under less stressful circumstances," Saengkeo said, "I might take exception to that assessment."

The CIA man sobered at once. "That's not what I meant. This has nothing to do with you."

"Are you sleeping with her?" Saengkeo pressed the question, knowing no matter what Stoddard's thoughts were that the man would be uncomfortable with the direction the conversation was going. Spy or not, he was a man, and most men had problems with discussions about sex or relationships.

"That's none of your business."

"It is," Saengkeo countered, "when it interferes with my business."

"That was a mistake," Stoddard said.

"I don't want to be the one to pay for a mistake that you made."

Stoddard hesitated for a brief instant, then pressed on. "What did Jacy discuss with you?"

"Only the question of whether I was having a relationship with you."

"Didn't that seem extreme to you?"

"My brother had the Howling Dogs capture Pei-Ling Bao and sell her into slavery because she had seen you," Saengkeo said. "I thought that was extreme."

"That's what Pei-Ling told you?"

"Yes."

"Do you believe her?"

Saengkeo hesitated only long enough to indicate indecision. By seeding that fact instead of mentioning Sebastian Cain, she hoped to gain some time. If Stoddard thought he knew what she knew, he wouldn't guess at what she was beginning to suspect. Even with Pei-Ling's plane making an unscheduled stop in Shanghai, Stoddard might have access to agents or mercenaries that would find her before Saengkeo reached her.

"Pei-Ling," Saengkeo said, "has a history of lying about things. She could have lied about that. But she was taken by the Howling Dogs."

"Maybe Syn-Tek didn't have anything to do with Pei-Ling's disappearance. Why would he do such a thing?"

"I don't know."

"That could have been another lie. Something she fabricated to gain your sympathy. From what I had observed, Pei-Ling and your brother didn't get along well."

"I intend to talk to Pei-Ling again when we get back to Hong Kong. I'll find out the truth soon enough."

"I'll see you here," Stoddard replied. He paused a moment, then asked his next question as if it were only an afterthought. "Did Jacy Corbin give you a number to reach her?"

"No."

"Did she say when she would be in touch again?"

"No."

"Or where she was going to be?"

"She didn't say." Saengkeo stared at the skyline. The taller buildings gave way as they neared the airport, forming the semi-circle of architecture that fronted the harbor area. A bubble of hazy golden light glowed like a dawning sun over the landing strips and the tower. Anxiety twisted fishhooks inside her stomach.

The fact that she had been staying in the hotel and that the rooms that were destroyed had been hers had to be a fact of record by now. After the police inspector's death that morning, she had no doubt that the Vancouver Police Department would try to keep her plane grounded till they questioned her. But that would take a court order. If her luck held, she would be gone before that could be granted and served.

"I need to confess something to you," Stoddard said. "I had your rooms at the hotel wired for video and audio."

"You've been spying on me?" Saengkeo tried to put ire and disbelief in her voice, hoping it would cover any false notes of the surprise she tried to convey. She felt confused by the CIA agent's admission. If she had chosen to confront Stoddard, she had expected the man to admit to the electronic eavesdropping, but she hadn't guessed that he would be the one to bring the matter into the open.

"I did it for your protection," Stoddard replied. "And to protect the investment I've made in backing your family to my government."

"I would never have allowed—"

Stoddard cut her off. "I know. And that's why I did what I did. You have to remember, Miss Zhao, I need to present a preponderance of evidence on your behalf to convince my agency to go to bat for your family and secure those visas outside of Hong Kong. I have to be able to tell those people that I am working with what you've been doing at any given moment. The Moon Shadows are known international criminals. It's going to take a lot of concentrated effort to convince the people I need to get on our side that we're playing according to the rules we agreed upon. Keeping you under constant surveillance when I could was one way to accomplish that."

Saengkeo remembered Jacy Corbin had mentioned that Stod-

dard had always known where she was. Even when the rest of
the team lost sight of her. The woman hadn't mentioned when
those times had been, or how she and the rest of the team had
been left out of the loop.

But had the female agent been telling the truth about Stoddard? Or herself?

Jacy Corbin had found Saengkeo twice: in L.A. only seconds
into a blistering attack that had left several people dead, and then
again in Vancouver to warn Saengkeo not to trust Stoddard only
minutes before another attack that was triggered by the arrival
of the man in black.

Maybe triggered by the arrival of the man in black, Saengkeo
amended silently. She also realized in that moment that Stoddard
hadn't asked her about the two times Jacy Corbin had visited her.
Had he known? Or did he think those times didn't matter in light
of everything else going on?

"Why are you telling me this now?" Saengkeo asked.

"Because Jacy's knowledge of those video and audio taps may
explain the attack on the hotel room," Stoddard said. "Jacy
Corbin knew about the surveillance taps. She might have hacked
into those feeds for her own use. I've got my team checking on
that now."

"Why would she do that? And who would she be working
with?"

"I'm going to ask her," Stoddard promised, "as soon as I find
her."

"You don't know where she is?"

"No. Jacy Corbin went missing at about the same time you
left Hong Kong."

"You should have told me."

"Perhaps," Stoddard agreed.

"We're going to talk when I get back to Hong Kong,"
Saengkeo said.

"Of course. I think we should."

With the tone of contriteness in Stoddard's voice, Saengkeo
decided to see if the CIA section chief really meant it or if he was
only faking. "In the meantime, I want you to see what you can
turn up regarding the identities of the men who attacked the hotel."

Stoddard was quiet for a time.

For a moment, Saengkeo thought he was going to refuse, then
she heard Stoddard sigh tiredly.

"According to the news reports, the attackers carried the bodies of the dead and the wounded from the building. They had vanished by the time the police arrived."

"Do what you can to network with the local police. There should be fingerprints, shell casings or other forensic evidence. I'll have my people investigate, as well." Without saying goodbye, Saengkeo broke the connection and cradled the handset.

Kwan looked at her with interest.

"Stoddard says that Jacy Corbin might have instigated the attack," she said.

"What do you think?" Kwan asked.

Saengkeo considered the problem. Her mind felt as if it were filled to bursting with bread dough that was still rising and had no place to go. The pressure increased slowly inside her head, threatening to overwhelm her. So many things had happened over the past ten days after Syn-Tek's murder. During the past three days, though, everything had started happening even faster. The attack on *Charity's Smile* seemed like months ago, and at the same time it felt as if only minutes had passed.

Fatigue gnawed at her concentration, splintering her attention across several fronts. She never slept well on planes, and she'd spent considerable time on them these past few days.

"I think there are so many lies involved in this now," Saengkeo said in a measured voice, "that we may never fully sort them out." She gazed at Johnny Kwan. "But we are going to try. Starting in Shanghai."

BOLAN WOKE IN DARKNESS in an unfamiliar bed. The sway of the ocean danced under him and the stink of fish and sea salt filled his nostrils and momentarily tightened his breath in his lungs. He gazed up at the low ceiling over the bunk built into the boat's side.

Barbara Price had arranged transportation out of Vancouver. That transportation had been a fishing trawler setting out at night for an early-morning run. The captain was a retired naval intelligence man who had put in time with the special forces. Captain Murdock had also spent time on Stony Man Farm as one of the special blacksuits that maintained the hidden base's security. When she'd asked a favor, Murdock had agreed without hesitation.

The trawler had slipped from the harbor unobtrusively while the Vancouver police thronged at the airport and alerted the border guards farther south. An oceangoing escape route allowed for a low profile, and there was nothing immediately pressing. The vessel also provided a warm bed and relative security where Bolan and Grimaldi could rest for a few hours.

The soldier threw his feet out of the bed and sat up with a little reluctance. A quick glance at his watch showed him that he'd slept five and a half hours. The downtime hadn't been enough, but it was all he could spare. The previous night's events would heighten the chase for the final nuclear weapon and push the stakes closer to the edge. His eyes still felt grainy, and he hadn't quite rested enough to get the edge on the lethargy that knotted his muscles.

Gingerly, he worked his left arm and was surprised to find that only a little stiffness remained from the strain the limb had undergone only a short time earlier. He grabbed the duffel Captain Murdock had kept waiting for him and took black khakis, a black long-sleeved pullover and a black woolen sweater from inside. A side pocket contained a black watch cap. He was thankful Price had thought enough to order the extra layers. Out on the ocean away from Vancouver, the temperature was cool, especially so early in the morning.

Bolan took the Desert Eagle from the combat harness that he'd kept in the bed with him, then slipped the harness into the duffel. The fishing boat didn't come with any amenities like a shower, which the soldier would have relished for cleanliness and because hot water would have sluiced the chill and fatigue from his body.

He dressed quickly then took out a pair of waterproof work boots that cinched tightly around his calves. He shoved the Desert Eagle into a left-handed paddle holster, then tucked the holster into the waistband of the khakis at the small of his back. A down-filled jacket covered the weapon and provided pockets for extra pistol magazines.

After snugging the watch cap down over his head and the tips of his ears, Bolan bundled the duffel back up and slung it over his shoulder. The joint shrilled a little, but the pain quickly passed.

He passed through the narrow hallway belowdecks and made his way to the hold. Fishermen were already busy laying out the nets that would be used shortly before daybreak to catch their quarry.

The six sailors were a motley mix of old and young, interested and disinterested, all of them busy preparing the nets for the morning's cast. They talked in low voices that fell silent at Bolan's approach.

"Cap'n Murdock's topside," one gaunt old man told Bolan.

"Thanks," Bolan said, then directed himself to the companionway that led up to the main deck. Gazing through the open hold, the soldier spotted a lightening in the eastern sky that had turned the night from sable to a violet infused with a pink-tinted glow.

The wind whipped in from the south, southwest when Bolan ascended the companionway to the deck. His face tightened against the blowing cold. Looking back to the east, he saw that the mainland was out of sight. Long, slow waves curled past the boat, cresting white foam. The canvas sails and rigging popped overhead, clinging to both masts. The fishing boat was also equipped with diesel engines, which had powered the craft out of Vancouver the previous night.

Captain Murdock stood at the stern starboard railing. He was in his early fifties, tanned and fit, weathered by the elements and the sea. Iron-gray hair showed around the edges of the hooded sweatshirt he wore beneath a thick pea coat. Rubber waders with built-in boots encased his feet and lower body. He smoked a pipe and regarded the sea with a jaundiced eye.

"Morning, Mr. Belasko," Murdock said.

"Captain," Bolan replied, going to join the man. Michael Belasko was a frequent pseudonym the Executioner used while out in the field. He'd used the name for years and responded to it easily.

"Sleep well?" Murdock took his pipe from his mouth and knocked the bowl empty against the boat's railing.

"Well enough for what there was of it." Bolan stood at the man's side. The cold wind chased his hands into the pockets of the down-filled jacket.

Murdock turned and focused his hazel eyes on Bolan. "There's a message waiting for you. From the woman that arranged your little excursion aboard ship."

Bolan didn't say anything. Murdock had been a professional soldier and knew that everything in the intelligence field functioned on a need-to-know basis.

"Part of the equipment that was left for you includes a notebook computer," Murdock said. "You can set up in my quarters."

"I'd appreciate that."

MURDOCK'S QUARTERS were cramped and spare, a cubbyhole carved out of space in the stern. Personal effects, consisting of family and career pictures and medals from his military career, decorated the walls. A lean assortment of sailing novels and re-source materials, DVDs and audiobooks occupied the built-in shelves. The small desk held a desktop computer and a box containing a partially constructed model of a clipper ship put together with handmade parts.

Taking the box containing the ship's model from the desk, Murdock grinned. "Guilty pleasure," the man admitted. "*Scarlet Queen* is a working boat, but she's also my home most of the time. Between the fishing and the pension I get from the military, we stay afloat. I'm making this one for one of my grandsons. Have a seat."

Bolan sat at the desk.

Murdock put the box on the bed. Then he reached up to the cabin's ceiling, pushed at the fitted wood, and revealed a hidden compartment. "*Scarlet Queen*'s an old boat, Mr. Belasko. Hand-built by my grandfather and my father when he was a young man. She's got a number of hiding places aboard her. Unless a man knows them, or strips her down to her bones, he'll never find them all." The captain reached into the hidden space and took out a metal briefcase.

Bolan took the briefcase and placed it on the desk. He rolled the combination numbers with a thumb, then lifted the lid to reveal a slimline notebook computer and two satellite phones.

"I'll be up on the deck if you need anything," Murdock said.

Bolan nodded.

Murdock paused in the doorway. An apologetic look framed his features. "The crew's apt to be curious after last night. Sailors and fishermen are always looking for tales to tell. I trust those men with my life and my boat every day, so I can't offer you anything more than that."

"That's good enough," Bolan said.

"They'll still have questions." Murdock grinned. "I told them you and your friend were old military acquaintances of mine, and that we couldn't talk about anything we used to do together or we'd have to kill them. They're young and curious, but they're good men."

"Thanks. I see you have a television. Any chance of receiving a Vancouver news channel?"

"I've got a satellite dish. There might be some interference, but you should be able to get a signal most of the time. Help yourself." Murdock saw himself out, closing the door behind.

Turning his attention to the notebook computer, Bolan powered up the machine. He plugged one of the satellite phones in to the notebook computer, then picked up the other and dialed one of the cutout numbers he had for Stony Man Farm. He crossed the cabin to the television as he listened to the clicks and whistles over the phone line. He punched the television's power button, and the screen juiced with an electronic pop that settled into a hum.

Barbara Price answered on the second ring.

"It's me." Bolan rolled through the channel guide using the remote control that had been left attached to the television set with Velcro. The CNN, Fox, MSNBC and Headline News networks all centered on the continuing tensions in the Middle East. There was no mention of the attack on the hotel in Vancouver, British Columbia, but an early morning local news network out of the city was scheduled to begin in twelve minutes.

"How are you?" Price asked.

"Sore. Tired as hell," Bolan said. He resumed his seat in front of the notebook computer, leaving the television turned so he could monitor it. "Tell me you've got something."

"We do," Price affirmed. "More than we expected. Leo's been busy in New York."

Leo was Leo Turrin, a semiretired undercover cop who was— on the surface—a retired mafia capo. Turrin was also one of Bolan's longest and most trusted friends.

"I thought New York was a dead end." Bolan watched the latest images to roll out of American activities in the Middle East. A montage of shots showed aircraft lifting from the deck of an aircraft carrier out in the Mediterranean Sea and infantry slogging through desert sand dunes with tanks and APCs in the background.

"New York was a dead end," Price agreed, "but you can't count Leo out. Ever. Since he couldn't follow up on the transport because the nuclear weapon never reached American soil, Leo started looking for the broker who handled the money between the Russian *mafiya* and the Green Ghosts."

"The weapon wasn't transported," Bolan said, understanding, "but the money was in place for the swap."

"Right. I hadn't thought of that. Leo was ahead of me on that one, and he never said a word."

"He wouldn't," Bolan said, "until he knew for sure that he had the information. Leo's always played things close to the vest."

"Sometimes," Price said, "I forget how cagey he had to be to live two lives."

"There's not much margin for error." The television switched to stock market forecasts.

"As it turns out, there aren't many people who can carry the kind of weight required on a deal for a nuclear weapon," the mission controller said. "Leo knows most of them. He used De Luca to put pressure on the situation."

Head of one of the Five Families in New York, Don De Luca wielded a tremendous amount of power. He had been the first to find out about the proposed sale of the nuclear weapon recovered from the Russian submarine *Kursk*.

"Leo kept himself out of the picture for the most part," Price went on, "but he got the information De Luca's people got from the money manager."

"What information?"

"The name of the man who handled the money from the Russian end of things. Bring up the computer. I've got a PDF dossier ready for you set up through an FTP protocol." Price read off the password that allowed Bolan entry to the computer's OS.

Once the computer's operating system was up and running, the Executioner opened the FTP program and initiated the file transfer. While he waited for the file to load, he flipped the television over to the Vancouver morning news channel. The lead story was the attack on the hotel.

"Have you followed the story from last night?" Bolan asked.

"Yes. We have more information than the Vancouver Police Department."

"Saengkeo Zhao?"

"She got out of the city before the dragnet closed around her."

"You've confirmed that?" Bolan considered the move, not satisfied with the surface thought that the triad leader would flee because things had turned rocky in Vancouver. He'd seen her the previous night, held her at gunpoint, and she had remained steadfast and calm. Running wasn't her strong suit.

"Yes. Her private jet left Vancouver only minutes after the action at the hotel."

The television camera panned to the hotel, showing police tape that marked off sections of the street and the building's broken windows. The anchor talked, but Bolan hit the Mute button and brought up the Closed-Caption function. He scanned the words.

"Saengkeo wouldn't run from a fight," Bolan said. "She'd run *to* one, though."

"I agree," Price said. Her words carried respect. "She's a hell of a woman, Striker."

An image of Saengkeo Zhao standing naked in the shower filled Bolan's mind. The memory had slid through his sleep time and again. "Did she file a flight plan?"

"To Hong Kong."

The television changed to film footage from the previous night. Evidently a tourist with a camcorder had gotten a chance-in-a-lifetime opportunity to film some of the attack. Bolan watched as he drifted through the night air suspended below the hang glider with gunfire sparking from the hotel's rooftop.

"Is Stoddard still in Hong Kong?" Bolan asked.

"According to his agency chief's files, Stoddard is."

"Something changed," Bolan said.

"Maybe Saengkeo took your advice to heart," Price suggested.

"Or else she got the call about the final nuclear weapon. We know Jacy Corbin visited Saengkeo last night. We don't know what they discussed."

"No," Price agreed.

"Has there been any trace of Jacy Corbin?"

"She's smoke, Striker. I don't know how she got into the country, where she was staying or if she's still there. We got lucky with Saengkeo. Jacy Corbin stepped back into the shadows. Saengkeo Zhao could have chosen to disappear, but she wanted to get out of the country and the quickest way was with her private jet. I had two of Aaron's people hack into Vancouver's airport security and run Jacy Corbin's CIA photo through passenger files containing information on frequent flyers to Vancouver, but we turned up nothing there. She could have been wearing a disguise."

The television showed a brief snippet of the gunplay out on the street, but the cameraman obviously valued discretion as the better part of valor and ducked into a nearby pizzeria. The camera's sweep showed other people down on the floor, arms covering their heads under tables and benches. The scene shifted back to the television anchor.

"Are you tracking the jet?" Bolan asked.

"We've kept a tag on the jet since it left Hong Kong and

while it was in Los Angeles," Price confirmed. "We're following it now."

"Do the police want Saengkeo?"

"There's not a warrant for her arrest," Price replied, "but they do want her for questioning."

"Is she out looking for answers?" Bolan asked, thinking about the woman and how little he actually knew about her. "Or has she been called back to get the third nuclear weapon?"

Price hesitated only a brief instant. "There's no way to judge that yet. We're on top of the situation. That's the best that we can hope for at the moment."

Remembering the way he had held Saengkeo's hand while suspending her above the street several floors below, Bolan knew he'd had the chance to take the triad leader out of the play for good. She was the leader of a crime family, and as such she had blood on her hands. The men the Executioner had killed over the past twenty-four hours in Vancouver were proof of that. Last night, he'd had her. All he would have had to do was open his hand. But he hadn't been able to.

After all their years together as mission controller and combatant, as lovers, Barbara Price knew how the Executioner thought. "You still don't know where Saengkeo Zhao fits in all this. What you did last night by letting her go was the right thing."

Bolan let out a tense breath. "Saengkeo Zhao isn't an innocent."

"No," Price agreed, "and neither are we."

The acknowledgment on the part of the mission controller surprised Bolan. They weren't often given to introspective searching of their chosen careers. "I'm not comfortable with Saengkeo's position in all of this."

"Trying to figure out if she's a good guy or a bad guy?"

In spite of the seriousness of the situation, Bolan smiled. "Yeah."

In a more gentle tone, Price said, "I've looked at her files, Mack. You've looked at her files. Saengkeo has, just as her father and brother before her, been working to get the Moon Shadows out of crime. That choice has weakened her and her family financially, and in the eyes of the other triads, encouraging other triads to seize their business holding, illegal and legal. That's why she was attacked in Hong Kong, and why she had to stand up for herself to the other triads."

"I know."

"If you look at her past right," Price said, "Saengkeo Zhao's mix of guilt and innocence will remind you a lot of someone else you know."

"This isn't about me," Bolan said.

"It is," Price disagreed, "because you're who you are and believe the things that you believe. You go through life your own way. That's why you don't fit comfortably at the Farm and with Farm operations."

Bolan knew that was true.

"I'm not offering recriminations here," Price went on.

"I know."

"But you weren't the example I had in mind," Price said.

"If you look at Saengkeo Zhao's jacket and her history," Barbara Price went on, "she reads, looks and acts a lot like Leo Turrin."

Silently, Bolan considered that. He hadn't made the connection before, but now that Price had pointed it out, the similarities were there.

"Leo was born into the mafia, chose to serve his country in the military and came back to sign on with the OCB."

The memories of those halcyon days rolled back over Bolan. During his first meeting with Leo Turrin, the Executioner had believed Turrin had been responsible for forcing his sister to become a prostitute in order to help pay off the loan their out-of-work father had taken out from Triangle Industries, a front for the mafia. Turrin had been in charge of a number of cathouses. Using Turrin, Bolan had insinuated himself into the organized crime Family to tear it apart from the inside.

And the Executioner had vowed to kill Leo Turrin. In fact, during one of those early encounters, Bolan had very nearly done that, stopped at the last moment by Turrin's wife, Angelina. The second time they had met, with Turrin fully in the Executioner's sights and a hellish war zone taking shape around them, the stocky little Fed had shown Bolan his Organized Crime Bureau identification and revealed the double life that he lived, one that his wife hadn't even known about at the time.

The commonality of being good men trapped by uncontrollable circumstance and a sense of duty had ostracized Bolan and Turrin from the worlds they had known. Bolan's own sense of outrage and grief, as well as the training he'd had in the Special Forces, had pushed him past the point of conventional society. He'd taken up arms against the mafia and had done the job that law-enforcement agencies hadn't been able to, and he had spurned the laws of society, setting himself up as a wanted fugitive dodging warrants scattered across the globe. Turrin had turned away from the easy life that organized crime promised him and gone into the arms of the undercover law-enforcement agencies. Many of those agents that Turrin had labored to help had also despised him. Death had followed them both during those days, as close and as certain as their own shadows.

In the heat of the battle, they'd found each other. Sometimes that friendship had been the only thing that had kept each one going in the loneliest wars men could undertake. Together and separately, then as now, they had worked on a dozen different fronts to stay alive and sometimes to keep the other alive.

Bolan considered what he knew of Saengkeo Zhao. Upon reflection, taking the perspective Barbara Price had given him, the Executioner saw that there was little separating the woman from his friend. Leo Turrin had been able to volunteer for the military, get himself straight and establish contacts in intelligence that would help him change his life forever once he returned to Massachusetts.

Saengkeo Zhao and her family hadn't had those resources. The Chinese government didn't provide the same freedom of choice, and the political corruption ran too deeply. Escape wasn't easily accomplished.

What the woman and her family had done had been nothing short of miraculous.

If, Bolan amended, Saengkeo was innocent. The possibility that the woman wasn't everything her father and brother were still remained. She was, to a large extent, an unknown variable in the whole scheme of things because she had stepped into the family business after her brother had turned up dead. Not enough was known about her even in the files Price and Kurtzman had managed to put together.

But the soldier hadn't let Saengkeo Zhao fall last night. No matter what else he thought or guessed at, that was the bottom line. So had he saved her, or had he set her free to run? He still wasn't certain about that.

Bolan pushed out a breath and wished he'd thought to stop to get a cup of coffee. The incessant chill of the ocean seeped into the fishing boat and bit into his flesh in spite of the clothes and down jacket.

"Okay," Bolan said. "You're tracking her. Keep me close to her."

"Maybe we can do better than that. Have you received the file?"

Bolan glanced at the notebook computer's screen, surprised that he had forgotten about the incoming dossier. "Yeah."

"It's encrypted. I'll give you the keystroke sequence."

After typing in the keystrokes that opened the file, Bolan found himself staring at a man with Slavic features who looked as though he was in his late thirties. The man wore his hair short and dyed platinum blond. Earrings hung from both ears and silver piercings marred his left eyebrow. His brow stood out like a shelf, giving him a Neanderthal appearance.

"Who is he?" Bolan asked.

"Ivar Torvitch," Price replied. "Before the Berlin Wall fell and Russian communism went the way of the great speckled dodo, Torvitch was an up-and-coming manager among the national banks. After the fall, Torvitch headed up a number of the straw banks, straddling the line between legal and illegal business practices. In the end, he got caught with his hand in the till and barely escaped with his life."

"Where is he now?"

"In Moscow."

"He didn't run far."

"Torvitch did for a time," the mission controller said. As she spoke, pictures cycled through the video presentation. All of the pictures showed Torvitch in clubs, on streets, or at open-air cafés in Moscow, Prague, Paris and London. He seemed perfectly at ease.

Bolan noted that two of the men remained constant in the pictures. Two other men were in many of the pictures, though they were never in the same shot. Several of the people Torvitch appeared to be dealing with were evidently repeat customers.

"When Torvitch was first chased out of St. Petersburg in 1994, he disappeared into Europe," Price went on. "He already had a network established in several cities for moving money around—his own, as well as that of the banks he'd worked for. During the bloodletting that crippled the Soviet army, Torvitch helped several high-ranking politicos flee the country with their fortunes more or less intact. He was also caught then helping himself to a greater percentage than had been agreed upon."

"Greedy," Bolan commented.

"Definitely. But Torvitch isn't geared for saving money. He spends cash as fast as he gets it, which makes him a favorite customer of the people he uses, but his lifestyle leaves him constantly searching for the next score."

"I take it he doesn't have trouble getting them."

"No. When Russian business began the fire sale that sold off a lot of their natural resources, military hardware and everything else, Torvitch was there to help broker the deal."

"For a fee."

"For a percentage. Torvitch built himself a rat's nest of accomplices and means to leverage money into and out of the country. Mostly because he isn't afraid to spend money to make money to insure loyalty. Plus, when he makes a deal, he makes it for life. People who have crossed Torvitch have a habit of turning up dead."

"He kills them?"

"Sometimes. Generally, though, the people Torvitch works with only need a finger pointed in the proper direction. The people Torvitch deals with know that."

"Torvitch brokered the deal between the Green Ghosts and the *mafiya?*"

"That's what Leo found out when he started checking around to see who handled money for the *mafiya* in New York. The distribution network is good and it's clever. Torvitch buries his work through dozens of banks, keeping money constantly flowing, splitting and regrouping until it ends up where he wants it to. He's that good, and that's why the politicos in Moscow who should be calling for his head turn a blind eye to his presence there. As long as he remembers his place."

The screen hazed, then re-formed into a bank statement. The screen split, revealing another bank statement. The statement on the left started out in Moscow. The one on the right started out in New York. In quick succession, a number of bank statements of account flickered across the split screen. The statements moved through nearly as many countries as there were documents, then repeated, coursing through different financial establishments.

"Leo also found out how the Green Ghosts handled their finances," Price said. "By comparing the accounts Aaron and his people were able to turn up using the information Leo gave us, we found the accounts that were going to be used for the money transfer between Torvitch and the Green Ghosts."

The screen froze, showing two statements of account. One account was in Taiwan. The other account was in Hong Kong.

"The Hong Kong account belongs to the Green Ghosts," Price said. "While it was open, Torvitch had control of the Taiwan account."

"While it was open?"

"The day De Luca's troops hit the Green Ghosts when you were there, that account was closed. Unfortunately, the money hadn't been transferred into the account from wherever Torvitch was holding it to ransom the nukes back from the Chinese."

"Torvitch was set to buy the weapon back from the Green Ghosts?"

"That's how it looks."

"He wasn't buying it for himself."

"Bingo," Price said. "And the asking price for the nuclear weapon had to have been astronomical, so far out of Torvitch's reach that he'd never have been able to touch it."

"He represented a money man."

"Had to have, Striker."

Bolan reflected on the situation. "One of the nukes was recovered from where *Jadviga* went down. According to Saengkeo Zhao, her brother Syn-Tek threw that one over the side of the ship so it could be recovered by the CIA team he was working with."

"Through Stoddard's people," Price agreed.

"The second weapon was recovered from *Charity's Smile.* The Russians had it. Have we ever confirmed the Green Ghosts had the third weapon in their possession?"

"No."

"So, accepting that *Jadviga* only had one weapon aboard her when Syn-Tek Zhao took her down, when did the weapons get split up?"

"We don't know."

Irritation gnawed at Bolan. The devil was in the details, and they didn't have them all framed properly yet. The movements felt like a three-card monte. The third weapon seemed to be in constant motion, but it was never in any place where it was supposed to be when it was supposed to be there.

The soldier tapped the keyboard's keys and went back to the picture of Torvitch. "Do you know where Torvitch is in Moscow?"

"Yes. I'm putting a travel package together for you and Jack now." Price paused.

"How soon can we move?"

"In a few hours. I'm assembling visas that will allow you into Moscow. Entry is easier these days, but the authorities still examine documents thoroughly. There's another file at the back of this folder."

Bolan tapped keys and brought up the new folder. Thumbnail pictures quickly spread out across the screen. Clicking on one of them revealed that it was a shot from the street battle out in front of the hotel in Vancouver. Cycling through the pictures also showed that someone had gotten pictures of Bolan and his attackers.

"What are these?" Bolan asked.

"A real piece of luck," Price confided. "While Aaron was investigating the hotel for your insertion in Vancouver, he discovered that the area was covered by street cameras that deliver a constant video feed to a Web site supporting tourism in Vancouver. There were also two bank ATMs that provided overlapping fields of view. Before the Vancouver police could seal the video feed or the ATMs, Aaron had already uploaded the data they had. We were able to identify three of the men who attacked you."

"MORNING, SARGE. Captain Murdock told me I could find you down here."

Looking up from the small flat grill in the fishing boat's galley, Bolan spotted Grimaldi standing in the doorway. The pilot was dressed pretty much the same as he was. "Morning, Jack."

The television mounted in the corner of the galley opposite the mess area droned on, cutting out intermittently as the signal was lost and regained. The CNN anchors relayed the latest international news.

"You taking requests for breakfast?" the pilot asked with a grin.

Pointing to two plates heaped with food, Bolan said, "It's a fixed bill of fare. You get out of bed late, you take what you can get or you fix it yourself."

"Ouch." Grimaldi approached the grill and looked at the plates. Both of them held thick pancakes stacked high, hash browns with onions, breakfast chops and a rasher of bacon.

Bolan spooned a soft-boiled egg from a boiling pot of water and laid it over a piece of toasted whole-wheat bread. He fished three more eggs from the pot and dressed three more pieces of toast.

"I was expecting a microwaved breakfast or something out of a box." Grimaldi took the plate Bolan offered. "This is totally unexpected."

"Captain Murdock believes in keeping a fully stocked larder." Bolan took up his own plate and led the way over to the small mess area that contained a small stainless-steel table bolted to the floor. Padded benches sat on three sides of the table, fitting it neatly into a corner of the galley where it was out of the way and afforded the most seating.

"God bless Captain Murdock," Grimaldi said as he seated himself. "I don't think we've had a home-cooked meal since we hooked up for this op."

"We haven't." Bolan retreated to the grill area while Grimaldi held his plate. Bolan brought back two cups of fresh-brewed coffee, passed one to the pilot and took over control of his plate himself. *Scarlet Queen* rode out the relatively calm sea well, but she still rocked from side to side enough to send loose items skidding.

"Anything left for the rest of the crew?" Grimaldi asked.

"They've already eaten. We're late." Bolan managed the coffee with one hand and used his forearm to keep the plate in place. The crew was already above casting nets.

Without another word, both men turned their full attention to the meal. Within minutes of comfortable silence between them, the contents of both plates were demolished.

"A meal like this," Grimaldi said, mopping up egg yolk with a piece of whole-wheat toast, "took some time. We've been friends for a long time, Sarge, but I don't think you were thinking exactly of me. Don't get me wrong, I appreciate the hell out of it, but generally when a man works this hard at something he's usually keeping his hands busy while his mind works."

Bolan peered at the pilot over the coffee cup. "I've been thinking about the woman."

"Saengkeo Zhao?" Grimaldi grabbed the plates and put them in the sink. He returned with the coffeepot and warmed Bolan's cup.

"Yeah."

"What about her?"

Bolan took the notebook computer from the floor beside the table. He opened the device up and turned it on. "Aaron and Barb identified three of the men involved in the blitz on the hotel last night."

Grimaldi sat as the computer screen cleared. The thumbnail photos of three of the attackers spread across the LCD monitor.

Bolan opened each of the files in turn. "All three of these men are ex-CIA."

"Like the two guys you and Leo bumped into in New York," Grimaldi said.

"Yeah."

The pilot rubbed his whisker-stubbled face and stared at the computer with hooded eyes. "The team at the Nautilus Club was a bona fide CIA team."

Bolan nodded.

"CIA and ex-CIA agents," Grimaldi mused. "What's the tie?"

"Rance Stoddard and his team." Bolan sipped his coffee. "Stoddard has worked with or around these ex-agents while they were with the Agency, and Barbara's intel suggests that he and his team have used one of these guys on black-bag operations that had to be conducted off the books and with complete deniability."

"You think Stoddard arranged the attack on the hotel last night," Grimaldi said.

"That's a possibility," Bolan agreed. "But Jacy Corbin's presence there complicates the situation. As one of the people on Stoddard's Hong Kong task force, Jacy Corbin had access to these people, as well."

"How does she factor into this?"

Bolan remembered that he and Grimaldi hadn't discussed the discovery of Jacy Corbin's presence at the hotel the previous night. They'd been too busy fleeing the police cordon and getting to the fishing boat. Quickly he explained who the female CIA agent was and how she fit into the present mission.

"What was Corbin doing in Vancouver last night?" Grimaldi asked when Bolan had finished.

"We don't know. According to the work Aaron and his people have done, Corbin is believed by the CIA to still be in Hong Kong."

"Stoddard is covering for her?"

"It looks that way. But Barb sent the video from the hotel's security system to a lip reader. A complete read of Corbin's conversation wasn't possible, but the expert said that she believed Corbin told Saengkeo that she couldn't trust Stoddard."

"Why?"

"I don't know. If that was mentioned, we didn't get it."

"What about the weapons?"

Bolan shook his head. "There was no mention of them."

"So what are you struggling with?"

Staring at the men's faces on the computer, Bolan answered, "Whether to tell Saengkeo Zhao who these men are."

"Seems like telling her would be the smart move to me," Grimaldi said. "Forewarned is forearmed."

"Unless she's in on it."

Grimaldi scratched his chin. His two-day-old growth rasped under his fingertips. "If you thought she was in on it, you wouldn't tell her."

"And if I thought she wasn't in on the whole operation, I shouldn't tell her because that would tip her hand and let her know more about the little knowledge we have on the organization that's fronting her movements. She might panic and expose us."

"The lady doesn't seem like the panicky type to me," Grimaldi observed. "So what do you think, Sarge? Trust her or don't trust her?"

"She's not an ally, Jack."

"I know. But she's stuck in a bad position. Same as us."

"We don't know that."

Grimaldi nodded. "Don't know, yeah. But you think you know." He paused. "All that firepower those guys used last night? They could have killed her."

"They didn't."

"No. And maybe you stopped them."

"They weren't there after her."

"Probably not.

"A lot of her people got killed in that battle last night," Bolan said. "That's not going to win us any feelings of goodwill."

"And the night before, you shot up a bunch of her hardcases," Grimaldi said dryly. "I'd take away bonus points for that, too."

Bolan knew it was true, but he could still feel the woman's hand in hers, could still feel her strength as she held on. Whether she admitted it to herself or not, she still hung suspended between the life she was reaching for on behalf of her family, and the triad and the Chinese government that would kill her the moment they found out she was working for the CIA.

"The bottom line," Grimaldi said, "is that the lady had you in her sights and didn't drop the hammer. I know you. I know you couldn't have shot her, but we didn't know her."

"Still don't," Bolan said.

"No, but we know more. She's looking for a way out. Judging from everything she's done and the way she acted at the Blue Lotus Supermarket, she's looking for a way to save her family. Maybe you won't be friends, but I think that after last night you two have an understanding. Of sorts. I'd go with that."

"Maybe."

"The downside is that she'll tell whoever is running the CIA that you know ex-CIA agents are in the playing field. Hell, you and I would both figure that little nugget of information is probably blow. Whoever is running those people, whether it's Stoddard or Jacy Corbin, we've got to believe he or she is taking steps to limit exposure."

Bolan considered Grimaldi's words. As usual, the pilot was no slouch in the thinking department, and his values and insights were pretty much on target with the Executioner's.

"You got a way of getting in touch with her?" Grimaldi asked.

"Yeah."

"Then do it," the pilot suggested. "I got clean-up."

"Thanks, Jack." Bolan stood up from the table and pulled on the watch cap and coat. He left the galley and climbed the companionway leading to the main deck.

A cloud of salt-laden mist rolled over *Scarlet Queen*'s starboard side. A motor-driven winch in the boat's stern hauled in one of the nets that had already been cast. Hoarse, excited shouts and curses filled the air.

For a moment, Bolan felt as if he were standing on the deck of a ship in a novel by Herman Melville. It was a good feeling, a clean, strong and certain feeling. But that wasn't where he was going to fight the battles he had coming up. He walked to the fishing boat's prow and took out the satellite phone he'd pocketed.

During the investigation of Saengkeo Zhao and the Moon Shadow's resources, Price and Kurtzman had turned up a number of phone numbers associated with the woman and her family. The soldier punched in the number for the triad leader's personal cell phone.

When the phone rang, Saengkeo considered ignoring the call. She guessed that it would only be Stoddard, and she wasn't ready to deal with the CIA section chief again. She had finally managed a light doze despite the fact that the jet hurtled through the air nearly forty thousand feet above the Pacific Ocean.

She sat fully reclined in one of the spacious chairs at the back of the private cabin that was set up as a conference room. SynTek, she remembered with a pang of loss, had often enjoyed doing business aboard the jet. He had even learned to fly the craft and gotten his license for small planes and small jets. Saengkeo's own interests echoed those of Ea-Han, and under the old man's tutelage she had learned to love sailing ships.

The phone rang a second time, drawing Johnny Kwan from the light slumber he had permitted himself while suspended high above the earth and presumably out of reach of their enemies. No expression touched his face as he gazed at her from behind the black-lensed sunglasses.

Saengkeo tilted the chair forward and lifted the handset. She spoke her name.

A man said, "Do you recognize my voice?"

The image of the man in black filled Saengkeo's head. She had seen him first as her enemy, blurred through the fog that had covered the shower glass. But another image of the man as her rescuer, holding her at arm's length to drop her to the next floor of the hotel while taking a bullet from an opponent, warred immediately. Despite Stoddard's assurances to the contrary, Saengkeo was convinced that the men who had invaded the hotel room would have killed her, as well as the man in black.

"Yes," Saengkeo answered.

Johnny Kwan sat up and reached for the phone on his side of the cabin. He lifted a questioning eyebrow.

Saengkeo nodded and spoke to help cover Kwan's action. "How did you get this number?"

Kwan lifted the handset, covered the mouthpiece and listened while she spoke.

If the man in black heard the click of the second phone being lifted, he gave no indication. Saengkeo thought the man was too canny to miss such a thing and guessed that he chose to ignore the presence of another listener.

"I asked a friend for your number."

"This number is not an easy one to find," Saengkeo countered.

"She's a good friend. With a lot of sources."

She. The word struck an uncomfortable chord within Saengkeo. Thinking of the man in black with a woman hadn't before entered her mind, and now that it did, the concept felt unsettling.

"I'll get another number," Saengkeo promised. "Perhaps we'll see how good your friend continues to be at finding numbers."

"That would be a mistake."

"I don't think so."

"You'll only slow her down," the man in black replied. "You can't stop her."

"You believe she is that good?"

"Yes."

Irritation shifted among Saengkeo's thoughts and felt like sandpaper.

"Besides," he went on, "you may want to keep the line of communication open."

"I don't think so. You and I don't want the same things."

"No," the man in black answered reasonably. "However, I think we're both unwilling to allow some things to happen."

Saengkeo let out a long, slow breath. She thought briefly about breaking the connection, but she didn't. She also felt that the man in black was aware of her decision.

"Let me give you a number where I can be reached," the man in black suggested. "Change your number if you want, but this way you can reach me if you need to."

"I won't need to."

He was quiet for a moment. "Probably not."

"And if I call you, you can track me down through the contact."

"There are ways around that."

"If your friend is as good as you say she is," Saengkeo pointed out, "maybe there aren't."

"I hope that staying in contact with me can be beneficial to you," the man in black offered.

"And beneficial to you?"

"A mutual reward."

"What do you want?"

"To keep the communication open."

"Why?"

"Because we share a common enemy."

"So you say," Saengkeo said.

"Your brother was murdered," the man in black said in a flat voice. "I think it was because of the merchandise we share an interest in. And I think the person responsible for his death was close to him. As close to him as that person is close to you now."

"You could be saying this only to undermine the alliances I have in place."

"Do you have alliances, Saengkeo?"

His use of her name threw Saengkeo off for a moment.

"Or are you just being blackmailed and being led around by the lure of finding your brother's murderer?" the man in black continued.

Saengkeo turned cold with anger. "You're overstepping your boundaries."

"I am. I apologize."

Even connected over the phone and separated by hundreds of miles—although the ghost of trepidation slid through her thinking he might somehow actually only be a few miles away, Saengkeo got the feeling that the apology was real, that the man in black had gone further than he had intended.

"I want to send you a computer file," the man in black said.

"So you can put a virus into the computer network I use? I don't think so."

"Give me an Internet address you feel confident about," he suggested. "These files contain the identities of three men who were involved in the attack on the hotel last night. They were ex-CIA."

"Those files could be forgeries."

"See them. Judge for yourself."

"Why do you want me to see this file?"

"Because I respect what you're doing."

"I didn't get that impression last night."

"I don't want to see you get hurt. Not if I can help it."

The honesty in the man's words was astonishing.

There was no answer for a moment. "I'll have the file put on the Internet." He gave her the IP address, giving her time to punch the information into her PDA. "Look at the files, Saengkeo, then get back in touch with me if you want to." He read off an international number. "Do you have that?"

Saengkeo added the phone number to the PDA information. Johnny Kwan's nod indicated that he memorized the number, as well. "Yes. Am I supposed to believe that number is yours?"

"No, that number is a dead end. Untraceable. But you can reach me through it. When I'm available."

Suspicion darted through Saengkeo's mind as she tried to measure the trick. "When are you going to be available?"

"When I can be. Like you, there are a lot of things I've got to do."

"What things?"

"I'll be in touch."

Saengkeo considered his words. Was it a threat? Or was it a promise?

"Your country has an old saying."

"China has many old sayings."

"The enemy of my enemy is my friend."

"That only works," Saengkeo said, "when you are not surrounded only by people who are your enemy."

"I'm not your enemy," the man in black said. "Let me know what you decide."

Before she could say anything, the phone clicked dead in Saengkeo's ear. She lowered the handset and looked at Kwan.

Kwan remained silent.

"I don't want to trust him," Saengkeo said finally.

"Nor do I." Kwan shifted uneasily in his seat. "But I don't want to trust Stoddard, either."

Unable to continue sitting, Saengkeo stood. The jet's floor felt solid and dependable beneath her, but she still sensed the ghost of movement of speeding through the sky. She crossed to the wet bar and poured herself a glass of apple juice. "Would you like anything?"

"Thank you," Kwan replied. "No."

Hesitantly, Saengkeo raised one of the louvers over the window nearest her. She stared out over a landscape of white clouds that looked like frozen cotton whipped into peaks. The old familiar fear of falling knotted her stomach. But instead of coursing through her with almost unconquerable fierceness, the fear seemed distant. Maybe I'm too fatigued, she thought. But she was certain that wasn't the reason. There were simply too many other things going on, too many questions without answers.

"Has Stoddard been in touch?" Kwan asked.

"No. Not since Vancouver." The question irritated Saengkeo a little. Kwan should have known that if Stoddard had contacted her she would have told him. Besides that, she had hardly been out of his sight.

"If you had to choose who to trust between them, who would you choose?"

"I choose to trust myself," Saengkeo answered. "And I choose to trust you. I'm only doing business with the others, and there is no picking between hungry wolves that will devour you."

A smile flickered at a corner of Kwan's mouth.

"Call and get those files," Saengkeo said. "I want to see them before we land in Shanghai. Use Liu. If they are forgeries, he'll be able to find out."

"And if they're not," Kwan said as lifted the handset again, "you're going to have to choose between Stoddard and Jacy Corbin."

Folding her arms, Saengkeo gazed at Kwan. "I may not. You're overlooking another possibility."

"What?"

"That Stoddard and Jacy Corbin are working this thing together, and that she has only come around me to confuse me further."

Kwan paused, the black-lensed sunglasses expressionless. "I had not thought of that."

"The Moon Shadow triad is an island," she told him. "We have been so since my great-grandfather began his efforts to move the family out of the triad business. It has been our legacy to move apart from the rest of the world. We are alone." Even as she said the words that her grandfather and father had handed down to her, remembered how she had shared them with her brother, she knew she had never before felt the entire terrible weight of the responsibility that had fallen to her.

A pang of sorrow at the loss of her family and that aloneness swept over her. She thought that Johnny Kwan saw the weakness within her and silently cursed herself for permitting herself to falter. Turning back to the window, knowing that Kwan would realize that she was turning away from him and not to the window because there was nothing out there that she wanted to see, she raised the glass of juice in a shaking hand.

The clouds hurtled by, cold and austere and uncaring. She stared through her reflection in the glass, then realized she was keeping an eye on Johnny Kwan talking in a low voice on the phone behind her. Was there no one she trusted?

And for a brief, fleeting moment, she felt again the calm and strong grip of the man in black as he held her above the street. That instant, she realized, only in that instant had she felt the safest since she had learned of her brother's death. She sipped her drink and told herself she was imagining things.

"Liu will retrieve the files and e-mail them to us here if there is time," Kwan said.

"Good," Saengkeo responded.

"Pei-Ling Bao's plane has landed in Shanghai. The men I have with her will hold her there until our arrival."

Consulting her watch, Saengkeo saw that they were less than two hours out from Shanghai.

"She wants to talk to you over the phone," Kwan said.

Saengkeo thought of Pei-Ling, knowing that the woman would be afraid. Especially if she, as Saengkeo believed her to be, was hiding information. But Pei-Ling being Pei-Ling, she would also believe that she could lie and wheedle herself out of Saengkeo's disfavor.

"No," Saengkeo said. "I'll talk to her when I reach Shanghai. There are already too many lies in this thing. I know that if Pei-Ling opens her mouth over the phone, nothing but lies will come out. The time for lies is over."

BOLAN STOOD NEAR the port-side railing as *Scarlet Queen* rolled over the waves. The heavy drag of the net caused the boat to wallow a little in the trough between the waves.

Voice stern and full over the sound of the sea and the boat's rigging, Captain Murdock commanded his crew. Striding quickly along the boat's stern, the captain oversaw the process of dragging the net from the sea.

Bolan punched buttons on the sat phone, dialing up one of the numbers he had for Stony Man Farm. Price answered on the first ring. "What's your take?" the soldier asked the mission controller.

Price had listened to the entire conversation between the Executioner and the triad leader. "She doesn't trust you."

"I'm not asking for her trust," Bolan said. "I'm hoping she keeps a little breathing room between herself and Stoddard."

"Even when she downloads the digital pictures we sent her," Price said, "she may choose to believe you faked them rather than turn against Stoddard."

Scarlet Queen's stern settled into the water as the drag of the net increased, dragging her prow from the ocean and leaving her vulnerable for a moment to the unkind caress of the sea. The diesel-driven winch snarled, coughed and popped as it strained to lift the net. Excitement flared through the fishermen, and Bolan gathered the catch was going well.

"You don't have anything to offer her, Striker," Price went on. "I don't mean to be harsh, but she's in a hard place. She's got an empire—a small empire, to be sure, but an empire nonetheless—scattered across the Western world. If the wheels came off on everything she's doing, and the events in Vancouver give every indication of that happening, she can't defend everything. She's exposed, and she knows it. Even if she has doubts about Stoddard, she may want to ignore them. Those doubts had to have been there before now. But she needs Stoddard. Without Stoddard, a lot of the visa concessions she's been given are in danger. Instant revocation of those visas, especially with the added heat of everything that took place in Vancouver, is going to leave her vulnerable to her enemies among the triads. They'll pick over her bones like vultures working roadkill."

Bolan knew that was true. "Have you been able to verify that Stoddard is working on those visas?"

"Yes." The clacking noise of a keyboard carried over the phone line. "Akira managed to slip into the CIA's files and turned up the information on Stoddard's operation in Hong Kong."

"So the offer of help in exchange for spying on triad and Chinese government business is real?"

"Absolutely. The CIA is bankrolling the efforts under Operation Janus. If you remember your Roman mythology, Janus was a two-faced god that peered into the future and into the past at the same time."

Squealing and screaming, the winch hauled the net from the sea. Morning sunlight shattered against the writhing and gleaming fishes trapped in the net. Bolan didn't recognize the fish, but most of them were longer than his arm. Appreciative comments rolled through the fishermen. Four men grabbed the bottom of the net and hauled the boom arm around to the hatch in the middle of the boat. Water cascaded from the net and the catch.

"We found something we didn't expect," Price went on.

"What?"

"Stoddard isn't just aiding the Moon Shadows. He's also catering to another triad group."

Vague unease filled the Executioner. "Who?"

"The Jade Mantis triad."

Bolan reviewed the events of the past few days since he had first picked up the trail of the missing nuclear weapons. No mention had been made of the Jade Mantis triad.

"Who are they?"

"A smaller, more aggressive triad," Price answered. "The group splintered from the Brass Mist organization in the early 1990s. Their leader is Duk Mok Dahn. I'm getting a package together for you now. He's in his early thirties, putting him in his early twenties when the group split off from the Brass Mist triad."

"Why the split?"

"The same reason the other young protesters stood against the Chinese old-guard government," Price answered. "Only the members of the Jade Mantis were the dark side of the youth movement. Dahn and his group have made it a practice to prey off the tourists who flow through Shanghai, Hong Kong and Taiwan. They also have other groups they do business with spread around the globe. They traffic in illegal immigrants, drugs, weapons and protection rackets. The Jade Mantis triad has even encroached on territory claimed by the Big Circle Society and United Bamboo."

"That seems like it would have been suicide," Bolan commented.

"The Jade Mantis group is ruthless, Striker," Price said. "When the Big Circle Society attacked them, the Mantis group spent a month tracking down Big Circle members, including their wives and children, and killing them. They mailed the heads back to the Big Circle Society leaders."

The wind felt colder now as Bolan imagined the carnage that the young triad group had wrought. So much violence in the outlying parts of the world was covered over. Only the Western world, with its freedom of press, seemed to consistently air its dirty laundry for everyone to see.

"In the end, the Big Circle Society granted concessions to the Jade Mantis triad," Price said. "They've never admitted to those concessions, but they're in place. However, the Jade Mantis organization was also encouraged to locate its business in Taiwan and Macao."

"Did they?"

"To a degree. They haven't vanished from the old neighborhoods, but they have managed a lower profile."

"If you can," Bolan suggested, "cross-check that lowered-profile time frame with their involvement with Stoddard."

"We're already working on it. Getting into the file was hard enough. Managing to extract concrete data from the encryption is harder, and the process is time-consuming."

Once the fishermen had the net in position, one of the men loosened the net. Tumbling and flashing in the morning light, the fishes dropped into the boat's live well belowdecks with a cascade of liquid smacks.

"How did Stoddard sell the Jade Mantis triad to the Agency?" Bolan asked.

"I don't know."

"And what did they stand to gain by a partnership with Stoddard? What did Stoddard have that they wanted?"

Price let out half a breath. Bolan knew from the exhalation that she was growing frustrated, too. "It doesn't make sense, Striker. Getting approval to open negotiations with one possible triad family would have been difficult enough, but getting two should have been impossible."

"Only it wasn't."

"Apparently not."

Bolan paced the rolling boat's deck restlessly. The fishermen were preparing the nets for another set. "Two spies within the Chinese government and among the triads would offer a built-in check for information Stoddard and his group acquired."

"But it would increase the risk of discovery of one of the triad leaders exponentially," Price pointed out. "There is one interesting facet we may have discovered about the Jade Mantis triad."

"What?"

"They may have been affiliated with the Green Ghosts."

Bolan turned the information around in his head, prying and

pulling at it. "I thought the Green Ghosts were tied in with United Bamboo."

"They are," Price agreed. "The Brass Mist is still affiliated with United Bamboo. But that doesn't mean that the Green Ghosts are adverse to working with the Jade Mantis group."

"Stoddard seems to know where the nuclear weapons are," Bolan mused.

"Or he has a way of finding out."

"The Green Ghosts were planning on selling the weapon back to the Russian *mafiya* in New York." Bolan stared at the green-gray swells of the ocean rolling into the boat's side. Pieces fit together in his mind quickly. "Syn-Tek was killed getting one nuclear weapon from *Jadviga*. The Green Ghosts believed they had one of those."

"By way of the Jade Mantis?"

Bolan rubbed his stubbled chin. "Maybe. It fits."

"But where does Stoddard come in?"

"We're going to find out," Bolan said.

"He could be using the black-bag team in an effort to recover the third nuclear weapon."

Bolan shook his head. "Speculation isn't going to get us anywhere, Barb. We've got to keep the pressure on, keep hammering everything we can to see what shakes loose. The clock is working against us, but it's working against everyone. How soon before Jack and I can get started for Moscow?"

"Within the hour. I've arranged for a seaplane to pick you up there, then ferry you in to Sea-Tac. From there, I can get you aboard a commercial flight out of Seattle to Moscow with one layover in Chicago."

"How long is the flight?"

"Over seventeen hours."

Bolan gazed out at the sea, feeling the cold plastic of the sat phone pressed up against his cheek. "Even with a private jet, Saengkeo has a twenty-hour flight ahead of her."

"Yes."

"She has a nine-hour lead."

"I can't make that up," Price said. "Not and provide you a low profile. However, once you get into Moscow, I can arrange a supplier to get you outfitted."

Bolan pushed his breath out. "That's fine, Barb." His thoughts turned to Saengkeo Zhao, remembering how she had looked in the hotel bathroom, draped in shower spray and hot mist, remembering how small she had felt hanging at the end of his arm. He'd gotten her clear of the hellzone a step ahead of the ex-CIA shock troops, but she wasn't any safer because of it.

"She'll be fine, Striker," Price said in a gentler voice.

Bolan felt a little uncomfortable that Price knew his thoughts, but the mission controller knew him intimately, and more thoroughly than most. "She's in a hard place."

"She's handled it so far."

"Maybe. Tell Hal I need to talk to him when he's available."

Brognola stayed busy as liaison for both Stony Man field teams, Able Team and Phoenix Force. But he was hardwired into the office of the President of the United States, supporting several of the Middle Eastern operations currently in operation.

"I will," Price said. "The plane will be there within twenty minutes."

Bolan said goodbye and broke the connection.

NEON LIGHTS STRETCHED long fingers into the night that hung over Shanghai. Saengkeo rode in the back of a black Mercedes sedan from the airport and looked out over the city. More lights gleamed along the banks of the Whangpoo River as the car passed, shining brightly from the watercraft that trolled the river's gentle currents and from the bars, warehouses and docks that littered the mud flats. If she rolled the window down, Saengkeo knew she would hear the voices and clangor of the docks crashing up against the street noises of the traffic starting only a few feet from the river.

When the British had arrived in the city early in the nineteenth century and brought with them the opium trade that consumed so much of China for so long and sparked two wars named after the drug, Shanghai had been a veritable wilderness, little more than a small fishing village with a sideline in trade. With their usual take charge attitude whenever profits were in the offing, the British architects and engineers had made changes and adaptations that reclaimed some of the land that would have otherwise remained inaccessible. The city came into being practically overnight, infused with sailors, immigrants and entrepreneurs from Great Britain, France, the United States and other countries.

Spurred by profits from the drug trade, as well as the mixed blessings of becoming an overnight international port, Shanghai continued to grow despite wars between businesses and nations.

Tall buildings stood on supports driven deeply into the mud. Despite the sophistication that came with being a cultural and trade center, pockets of decadence and slum life remained in the rows of poverty-level housing that thronged the riverbanks on either end of the docks. A city's success didn't lift everyone from the harsh life, and many remained in squalor at Shanghai's feet.

Johnny Kwan talked quietly over a phone headset that dangled from one ear. From bits and pieces of his conversation, Saengkeo knew Kwan was checking in with the men who held Pei-Ling Bao.

Saengkeo's own thoughts stayed full of her family's history. Her great-grandfather had held her great-granduncle as he died not far from the area they were presently in. Nanking Road remained a center of entertainment in Shanghai. While newer businesses and sophistication had been layered into the neighborhood, many of the old businesses remained in one incarnation or another.

One hundred fifty years ago, Nanking Road had boasted marketplaces and operas, taverns and upscale restaurants offering cuisine from around the world. Shoehorned between those businesses, singsong houses and opium dens operated around the clock.

Jik-Chang's first wife had been a singsong girl. His second wife, taken in Hong Kong after his first wife had died of illness, had been a schoolteacher. Saengkeo's family traced back to the first wife, but the second wife, whom he said had never quite captured the heart of Jik-Chang as the first wife had but who had been a very loving woman, had raised Saengkeo's father.

And that, Saengkeo thought, was the dichotomy of the Zhao family. Born of the gutter and raised into success by ambition, but tempered by desire into something better than they had started out.

She remembered the man in black's words. *"Because I respect what you're doing."* Was it the truth? She still didn't know, and she prayed that the decision to believe or disbelieve those words would be taken out of her hands. Aboard the Russian freighter, he had shot her. Only her Kevlar vest had saved her life. The previous night, he had saved her, risking his own life in the process.

The car glided to a stop in front of a row of buildings. Three men stepped from the shadows and approached the Mercedes.

Johnny Kwan raked the men with his gaze. "These are our people," he announced.

Saengkeo noticed that Kwan didn't take his hand from beneath his coat.

She waited while Kwan got out of the car. The Mercedes was

bulletproof, rolling armor, and the driver was trained in evasive maneuvers.

After a brief conversation with the men, Kwan opened Saengkeo's door. She got out, dressed in American jeans, a midnight-blue blouse, boots and a long black rain duster that concealed the Walther Model P-990 QPQs. She reached back into the car for the PDA she'd had Liu set up for her. It had been delivered to the Shanghai airport.

The three men nodded in deference to Saengkeo. All of them were young and hard, men who used their bodies as weapons and their honor as fuel. They were representative of the best that Johnny Kwan expected from his troops. They wore Western casual wear, slacks and pullovers under light jackets marked with sports teams colors. In Shanghai, they would fit in anywhere.

Kwan led the way up the wooden staircase built against the side of the apartment building. Saengkeo followed, listening to the creak of the steps. The three men remained below while the Mercedes glided into a nearby alley. The lights dimmed and the vehicle seemed to become part of the darkness.

At the third-floor landing, the door opened and another young man gazed at Kwan, then at Saengkeo. He stepped back, revealing a small, modestly outfitted flat.

"Where is the woman?" Kwan asked.

The young man closed the door after they had entered the flat. He nodded toward the back room. "There. In the bedroom. There are no windows. No one can see and she has no way out."

Kwan nodded. He reached out and touched the man's chin, tilting his head back to reveal three parallel scratches that ran from his jaw down his neck. "Were there any problems?" Kwan asked.

The man left his head tilted and his neck exposed. "She discovered that we were under orders not to harm her. We had to restrain her to the room. Doing so without hurting her was difficult."

A spark of compassion for Pei-Ling ignited inside Saengkeo, but she quickly extinguished it. The furrows on the man's neck still appeared bloody and inflamed. Once Pei-Ling had discovered her guards' weakness, she had used it against them.

"She is unharmed?" Kwan asked.

"Yes. As you asked, Mr. Kwan."

Saengkeo looked around the room. Two other men sat at a small table and watched an anime cartoon on a portable television. Plates of rice and broccoli and beef sat before them next to bowls of bird's nest soup and a basket of eggrolls. They had put away their chopsticks and now waited expectantly. One of them had an eye that was swelled nearly shut.

Saengkeo's sympathy for Pei-Ling dissolved and re-formed as anger. Pei-Ling had always been petty and demanding, more so among people that she didn't like than among people she expected to be her friends.

"She has been well cared for since we took her into our custody, Miss Zhao," the young man with the scratched neck said. "I can assure you that no harm came to her through us."

Saengkeo flicked a glance at Kwan.

"Billy Chu," Kwan said.

Inclining her head toward the young man, Saengkeo said, "I will remember your name, Billy Chu. For now, you have my thanks."

"It was our pleasure, Miss Zhao."

Not a pleasure, Saengkeo thought.

"Saengkeo!"

Turning, hearing the sound of Pei-Ling's little-girl voice that she used when she knew she was in trouble or when she wanted something, Saengkeo looked at the door at the end of the room. A chain held the door nearly closed, leaving a gap of less than three inches.

Pei-Ling stared through with one eye. "Saengkeo! You have come to save me from these barbarians! I am so glad to see you! You would not believe the things they have done to me since I have been locked up here!"

"I have to apologize for the way we have kept her, Miss Zhao," Chu offered.

"No apologies are necessary," Saengkeo said. She shrugged out of her duster and left the garment lying on the back of an empty chair as she passed.

"Oh, Saengkeo," Pei-Ling said, "I thought for certain that I would not see you again this time."

Quietly, Saengkeo reached into her jeans pocket and took out a band. She pulled her hair back in a ponytail and bound it.

Pei-Ling's eye widened in surprise. She turned her head so that the light inside the room showed the fresh tears on her cheeks.

Saengkeo wasn't impressed; Pei-Ling had always been able to cry whenever she wanted to.

"They've kept me locked in this room like some beast since this morning," Pei-Ling said. "They haven't even let me out to go to the toilet."

"We gave her a bucket," Chu said. "Every time we tried to take her, she fought us."

"It's all right," Saengkeo said. She took the chain from the door and pushed it open.

Pei-Ling stepped forward, throwing a finger into Chu's face. "You bastards are really going to get it now! I told you that my friend was the leader of the Moon Shadows! But you didn't believe me! You didn't—"

Without warning, without mercy, Saengkeo backhanded the woman across the face.

Caught off guard by the unexpected blow, Pei-Ling Bao stumbled backward three steps, twisted and fell in a heap to the floor. She yelped in pain, then cursed harshly enough to make a sailor blush, and folded her right arm protectively behind her head.

During her years as a prostitute and because of the lifestyle she'd chosen and her own disagreeable nature, Pei-Ling had learned to take a beating. Saengkeo remembered that as she stepped toward the woman who had been her friend nearly all of their lives.

"What are you doing, you damn bitch?" Pei-Ling squalled. She raked a handful of fingernails at Saengkeo's face.

Effortlessly, Saengkeo riposted the blow with her own wrist, striking again with bruising force.

Pei-Ling yelped and drew her arm back. "Stop, Saengkeo! Stop! You're scaring me!" She coiled into a fetal ball.

"I want the truth from you, Pei-Ling," Saengkeo stated coldly.

"What truth?"

"I want to know what you saw that caused my brother to give you to the snakeheads."

"I told you. I saw Syn-Tek with the CIA agent. Stoddard."

Saengkeo hunkered down, resting easily on the balls of her feet. She rested her forearms on her knees, staying within easy reach of Pei-Ling. "That isn't everything you saw."

"It is. I swear." Gaining confidence, Pei-Ling moved her arm to reveal her tear-streaked face. She wore bright green contacts, and the color set squarely in the middle of her features served only to remind Saengkeo how false she could be.

Saengkeo backhanded the woman again, catching her full in the mouth and splitting her lips.

"You fucking bitch!" Giving way to her anger, Pei-Ling surged to her feet.

Saengkeo rose easily and turned to present her profile to the other woman. She kept her left hand low, her right hand back and ready.

Blood trickled down Pei-Ling's chin, splashing across the tops of her breasts. She launched a snap-kick, showing more skill than Saengkeo would have believed. Evidently somewhere along the way Pei-Ling had taken up martial arts. Maybe she had chosen to get involved on her own, or maybe she had spent time with a man or men who had such interests. Pei-Ling was a quick study and could learn anything that would attract the attention of a man. Where a man went, Pei-Ling had often told Saengkeo, so went his wallet.

Moving her right hand only slightly, Saengkeo intercepted the kick and deflected Pei-Ling's foot from her body. Before the other woman could react, Saengkeo slapped Pei-Ling in the face. Her palm smacked into Pei-Ling's nose hard enough to cause considerable pain but not hard enough to break cartilage.

Stung, barely able to keep her balance, Pei-Ling clapped both hands to her face, yelped, cursed and hobbled backward. She feinted with her hands, then tried to kick Saengkeo again.

Smoothly and efficiently, Saengkeo turned away from the kick and slapped Pei-Ling again. This time, Pei-Ling managed to get her hands up in front of her face, but Saengkeo swung hard enough to snap her head back all the same.

Pei-Ling directed a flurry of blows with her fists. Calmly, walking forward slowly to take away all room to maneuver, Saengkeo deflected the blows, seizing opportunities to slap Pei-Ling in the face three more times. Each time, the young woman howled and screamed curses, stepping back toward the sagging single bed. When the backs of Pei-Ling's legs touched the bed, Saengkeo swung suddenly and thrust her left leg out.

Saengkeo's kick caught Pei-Ling's upraised arms, jolting the other woman's wrists and hands back into her face. Driven by the kick, Pei-Ling fell back onto the bed. Before the woman could get to her feet, Saengkeo dived on top of her, straddled her facedown on the bed and grabbed a fistful of her hair.

Mercilessly, Saengkeo tightened her hold on Pei-Ling's hair and yanked upward. Pinned, Pei-Ling's head pulled back. She yowled in pain and terror. Saengkeo didn't worry about the noise; the neighborhood they were in had trained for generations to ignore anything that didn't directly involve the people who lived there.

Bending low, her lips almost touching Pei-Ling's ear, Saengkeo spoke calmly and coldly. "You will tell me the truth, Pei-Ling. People have died because of what you know. I think Syn-Tek died because of what you know. You know me as a sister, and you know that I will never forgive or forget that."

"Please! You're hurting me!" Pei-Ling's blood stained the spread that covered the bed.

"I will hurt you more," Saengkeo said. She was conscious of Johnny Kwan standing in the doorway. "I swear this to you, Pei-Ling—if you lie to me now, you will regret it."

"Okay," Pei-Ling replied. She pushed herself over on one side and reached for the clump of hair Saengkeo held. "I will not lie to you. Please stop."

Saengkeo relaxed her grip on the woman's hair, feeling as though she were making a mistake. In order to get the truth, she felt certain that Pei-Ling had to be in fear for her life. Pei-Ling had always kept her own secrets while spilling those of others, or bartering them out for still other secrets.

"What did you see that night?" Saengkeo asked.

"Stoddard. I saw Syn-Tek with Stoddard. I guessed that they were doing some kind of business. I tried to find out what it was. The next thing I knew, Syn-Tek had sold me into slavery."

It was partially the truth, Saengkeo knew. Enough of the truth to have satisfied her if Jacy Corbin hadn't pushed her paranoia to fever pitch. Even then, Saengkeo had to admit that the man in black might have been enough to cause her to doubt Pei-Ling's words. Syn-Tek had sold Pei-Ling to the snakeheads, something he would never have done if the stakes weren't so high. Merely knowing Stoddard was talking to Syn-Tek hadn't been enough of a threat. Pei-Ling tied all of them together: Syn-Tek, Stoddard, the man in black and Saengkeo. There was no way she couldn't be involved. And if the man in black had learned of Pei-Ling while he was in New York, and Saengkeo believed him, the truth had to be something more.

Dispassionately, Saengkeo yanked on Pei-Ling's hair again. Some of the hairs pulled out and left bloody dots behind.

Pei-Ling screamed.

"Tell me the truth, Pei-Ling," Saengkeo said, "or I will tear all of the hair from your head."

"I am!" Pei-Ling yelled. She kicked and screamed, arching her body against the bed and trying to throw off Saengkeo. The triad leader managed to stay on top of the other woman, yanking her hair again to control her. Pei-Ling raked her nails backward, catching them in the back of Saengkeo's hand and carving shallow divots from her flesh. Saengkeo slapped the hand away.

Johnny Kwan started forward.

"No," Saengkeo told him.

He stopped. "I can—"

Glancing over her shoulder, Saengkeo agreed. "You can, but I will."

Nodding, Kwan stepped back to the doorway. He stood in a relaxed fashion, his face impassive and his hands clasped in front of him.

Pei-Ling reached back again.

Saengkeo captured the woman's hand. Blood ran from her own hand, making her grip on Pei-Ling's slippery. "Tell me about Sebastian Cain."

Pei-Ling started to make no reply, but Saengkeo twisted the woman's fingers, bending them back. Pei-Ling cried out shrilly. "He is a client!" Pei-Ling shouted. "Dammit, Saengkeo, he is a client!"

That would be simple enough to investigate, Saengkeo knew. There were people who kept up with Pei-Ling, hotel managers who arranged rooms for her trysts and services in exchange for a fee.

"How long has Cain been a client?" Saengkeo asked.

"Three years. Maybe four." Pei-Ling tried crying again. Her body shook and quivered with her efforts.

"Something you knew made you dangerous to someone," Saengkeo said. "Tell me."

Pei-Ling shook her head stubbornly. "Nothing. Nothing,

Saengkeo. You're imagining things. Seeing Stoddard with Syn-Tek was enough."

Shifting her hand quickly, Saengkeo caught Pei-Ling's little finger. Cold fear filled Saengkeo as she thought about what she was going to do, and she knew with certainty that she was going to do it because she couldn't back away from the threat once she had made it. And she knew Pei-Ling would force her to do it.

"Tell me," Saengkeo demanded. "Tell me about Sebastian Cain."

"He is a client," Pei-Ling said. "He—"

Without warning, Saengkeo broke the woman's little finger. The snap popped like a pistol shot inside the tiny room. Then the screaming started in earnest.

Saengkeo fought her own emotions as she remained straddling the writhing woman. If it had just been her, Saengkeo knew she would never have harmed Pei-Ling. But it wasn't just her. Pei-Ling had somehow endangered all of the Moon Shadows, all of Saengkeo's family.

And perhaps it had been Pei-Ling's actions that had gotten Syn-Tek slain. Even after all the years that they had been friends, Saengkeo couldn't forgive that. In spite of the anger and fear that throbbed inside her, she was surprised to find tears in her eyes that pooled and ran down her cheeks.

Johnny Kwan started forward again. "Please, Miss Zhao, let me."

"No." Saengkeo's voice was hoarse, raw, thick to get out.

"Please," Kwan said.

Saengkeo turned and glared at him through her tears. She was angry with herself for showing the emotion, for feeling the emotion, and she was angry at Kwan for deflecting her. "Stay back or I will ask you to leave."

Chastened, Kwan stepped back. Despite the blank expression on his face and the dark lenses of the sunglasses, Saengkeo felt that he was afraid for her.

Pei-Ling cried and shook and cursed, mewling like a small child and trying to draw herself up into a fetal position. Blood from her nose coated the bedspread now, and her tears thinned the blood so the stains spread farther and faster.

Saengkeo kept hold of Pei-Ling's injured hand. The little finger hung crookedly in her grip. She wrapped her fingers around Pei-Ling's ring finger meaningfully.

"Tell me," Saengkeo ordered.

Pei-Ling cried louder. "I didn't know, Saengkeo! You have to believe me! I didn't know!"

"Tell me."

"Sebastian Cain is—*was*—one of my clients," she said, halting and crying as a child would. "I didn't know he knew Stoddard."

"And Syn-Tek?"

Pei-Ling shook her head tiredly. Her shoulders shook with the crying jag. Her hand trembled in Saengkeo's. "I don't know if Syn-Tek knew Cain."

"If you lie to me—"

"Please, Saengkeo! I am not lying!"

Saengkeo waited, feeling her tears cool on her flushed face and studying Pei-Ling's own makeup-smeared features. "All right," she said after a moment, "I believe you."

"Cain is an asshole," Pei-Ling declared in her broken voice. Saengkeo knew the way the other woman spoke was designed to give them a common enemy they could both agree on. It was a game Pei-Ling had played since she was a child. "It was Cain's fault I was there. If he hadn't taken me there, I wouldn't have seen anything."

"Where?"

"In the office at the Bank of China Tower."

"Whose office was it?"

Pei-Ling shook her head and looked miserable. "I don't know."

Saengkeo believed Pei-Ling was telling the truth, but she also knew she could show no mercy. Steeling herself, she twisted the woman's broken finger.

Pei-Ling squealed in pain and bucked fiercely.

Holding on to Pei-Ling's hair, Saengkeo shoved the other woman's face into a pillow. Remember Syn-Tek, she told herself. Remember that Pei-Ling might have helped you save him. She distanced herself from Pei-Ling's screaming, remembering the whole time how Pei-Ling had gotten hurt out on the playground and had always come to her first. But Pei-Ling had also kept crying to get the attention of the teachers and had gladly gone to them, as well. Saengkeo had always been the first and greatest safe harbor for her.

Now, though, Saengkeo knew, Pei-Ling would never again think of her like that. The realization cut deep. Without speaking, she relaxed her hold on Pei-Ling's hair and let her head come up.

"I swear to you, Saengkeo," Pei-Ling gasped. "I swear to you that I am telling you the truth." Her eyes were bloodshot, wide with fear.

Calmly, Saengkeo said, "I believe you."

"You hurt me," Pei-Ling accused.

Saengkeo maintained her grip on the broken finger. "Yes. And I will hurt you again if you lie to me."

"You would never have done this before." Pei-Ling sniffled theatrically and searched Saengkeo's face. "You have changed."

"Yes."

"You would have never hurt me before."

"No. But things have changed. I can no longer only think of myself." Saengkeo kept her voice neutral and her eyes level. "And I can no longer think only of you. I have to think of my family. You have endangered them. You have caused my brother to be killed." The last was a guess, but even if it wasn't true, it was enough of a self-contained threat to give Pei-Ling further notice.

"I am your family, Saengkeo," Pei-Ling said. "You swore to me that we would always be family."

"We will be."

"You broke my finger."

"I will break another," Saengkeo said, "if you lie to me again."

Pei-Ling tried to withdraw her hand from Saengkeo's grip. Saengkeo kept her hand in place. "I won't lie."

"Tell me about the office," Saengkeo ordered.

"It was an office, Saengkeo. That's all. A business office. I don't know whose it was."

"What do you know about it?"

Pei-Ling's eyebrows knitted in concentration. "It was near the top of the building. I think it was an American office. There were newspaper stories and papers on the walls that were in English."

Saengkeo nodded. If the office were American, that would be easy enough to check out. "Cain took you to the office?"

"Yes."

"Why?"

"We went there after."

"After what?"

An uncomfortable look creased Pei-Ling's face. "After we left the hotel."

Saengkeo felt a little uncomfortable herself. During their years together, Pei-Ling had often bragged of her sexual conquests, but there had been no mention of the money involved or the fact that she conducted her services for pay. She had always talked of her work as having a succession of dates, and her foray into sex films as becoming a star.

"Why did you leave the hotel?" Saengkeo asked.

"Because Cain had business at the office building with Stoddard."

"What business?"

Pei-Ling bit her lower lip and looked at her broken finger nervously. The finger had already started swelling and had turned purple around the knuckle. "I don't know." Her voice sounded hoarse and desperate. She tried to clench her hand into a fist but couldn't. "I swear to you, Saengkeo. I don't know. Stoddard got upset and yelled at Cain."

"About what?"

Hope dawned in Pei-Ling's eyes. "Stoddard said I should not have been there."

"Stoddard knew you?"

"He has been my...client before. Cain became upset, as well."

"Stoddard was upset because you saw the two of them together?"

"I don't know. There was someone else there."

"Who?"

"Duk Mok Dahn. The leader of the Jade Mantis triad."

The announcement staggered Saengkeo. She glanced over her shoulder at Johnny Kwan. His head shook almost imperceptibly. Saengkeo's thoughts scattered, trying to make sense of the news.

The Jade Mantis group was small but violent, a young organization by the standards of most triads. Still, Dahn was aggressive and ambitious, a bad combination for most triad leaders. But his followers supported him to their deaths. They had to. Dahn marked his men with facial tattoos, leaving them no chance of blending into other triads, no chance of being mistaken for anything other than what they were.

She didn't know why Stoddard or Cain would have anything to do with the Jade Mantis triad, but she also believed Pei-Ling's statement was true.

"It's true, Saengkeo," Pei-Ling pleaded. "I swear to you that it is true."

Saengkeo looked at her. "I believe you."

Tears still ran from Pei-Ling's eyes as she shook her head. "I won't lie to you anymore. I swear I won't."

"What did you see at this meeting?" Saengkeo asked.

"Only that. Only the three of them." She mewled and her hand crabbed again in Saengkeo's as she tried to pull it away. "That's all I know."

"What happened at the meeting?"

"I don't know. I was taken from the building."

"Then why did Syn-Tek sell you to the Soaring Dragons?"

Another wave of fear shivered through Pei-Ling. "I did something stupid, Saengkeo. You know how I get when I get too smart for my own good." She held up her broken finger in mute testimony.

"What did you do?" Saengkeo asked in a softer, more sympathetic voice.

"The day after the meeting—" Pei-Ling sipped a quick gasp of breath that made a rattling noise in the back of her throat "—I called Cain. I threatened to tell that I had seen him there with Dahn and Stoddard."

"You blackmailed him?" Saengkeo couldn't believe it. Even after she'd seen what Pei-Ling was capable of, she couldn't believe the woman would have the audacity to do such a thing.

"Yes," Pei-Ling said. "It wasn't that much. He could have easily afforded to buy my silence."

But Saengkeo knew that Cain had known he would have to buy her silence again and again. "You can't blackmail a man like Cain. He has too much power, too much wealth."

"You can't get anything by blackmailing people too poor to pay you."

Feeling dazed and worn, Saengkeo released Pei-Ling's hand and crawled off her. She stood by the bed and watched as Pei-Ling cautiously pulled herself into a sitting position on the bed while cradling her injured hand against her breasts.

"You can't go back to Hong Kong," Saengkeo said. Her thoughts came furiously. "If Stoddard finds you there, or if Cain finds out you have returned, they will have you killed."

Pei-Ling nodded. "I know."

"Have you been in touch with anyone in Hong Kong?"

Pei-Ling hesitated.

"Who?" Saengkeo demanded sharply.

Pulling her knees up to her breasts, Pei-Ling looked sullen. Her nose had swelled and drying blood crusted her nostrils and upper lip. "Someone I knew could get a message to Cain."

"Why?"

"To let him know the price for my silence had gone up," Pei-Ling declared.

"Fool," Kwan spit. "You'd save yourself some time if you put a pistol inside your mouth and blew your brains out."

Pei-Ling flinched at the thought and ducked her head lower behind her knees.

"Did you talk to Cain?" Saengkeo asked.

"No. Only the acquaintance we have in common."

"When?"

"Before I left California."

Kwan looked at Saengkeo. "Miss Zhao, you have to assume that this person contacted Cain, and that Cain contacted Stoddard. By now, they know that Pei-Ling didn't arrive in Hong Kong. They will, unfortunately, also assume we know more, as well."

"But what do we know?" Saengkeo asked.

"For one, that Stoddard planned on betraying you," Kwan said. "If we can believe this woman—"

"I told the truth," Pei-Ling interrupted.

"—the Jade Mantises were there," Kwan continued smoothly. "We have had problems with them in the past."

Saengkeo remembered. Syn-Tek had been forced to kill some of the young triad members when an attempt was made to extort protection money from Moon Shadow holdings. The Jade Mantises already had a grudge against the Moon Shadows, as did every other young triad that tried to muscle in on protected territory.

"It's not safe for her," Kwan went on, "and it's probably not safe there for you."

"I'm going back," Saengkeo said.

"Waiting might be the best thing."

Saengkeo returned Kwan's black-lensed gaze full measure. "No. I'm tired of being lied to. It ends now. I'm going back to Hong Kong, and I'm going to find my brother's murderer." She glanced back at Pei-Ling. "Get cleaned up, and do not try to leave this flat."

"I won't."

Saengkeo stepped to the doorway beside Johnny Kwan. She peered out at the men gathered in the room beyond. "Billy Chu."

"Yes, Miss Zhao." The young man stood up from the couch where he had been sitting with a plate of food.

"See that Miss Bao gets cleaned up. Splint her finger. But don't let her out of your sight."

"Of course, Miss Zhao."

Saengkeo started for the door. She took her duster from the back of the chair where she had left it. Dozens of thoughts swam in her head like the minnows she and old Ea-Han used to feed bread crumbs to off the back of the fishing boat. Those thoughts darted and twisted against each other in the same fashion as the fish had.

"Saengkeo?" Pei-Ling stood in the doorway to the bathroom. "Are you leaving?"

"Yes."

A hurt and fearful look twisted Pei-Ling's blood-smeared features. "When will I see you again?"

"I don't know."

"But I will?"

"Yes."

Contritely, Pei-Ling crossed the room and threw her arms around Saengkeo's neck. She hugged Saengkeo fiercely, like a child would. Moved by the other woman's emotion, Saengkeo put her own arms around her friend and hugged her back.

Pei-Ling cried, heaving against Saengkeo for a moment. Saengkeo rubbed her back.

"It will be all right," Saengkeo said.

"I'm scared," Pei-Ling whispered hoarsely.

"I won't let them hurt you," Saengkeo replied. "I promise."

"I'm not afraid of them," Pei-Ling whispered. "I'm afraid because I don't want to lose you as my friend. You are my only true friend, Saengkeo."

With more ease than she would have expected under the circumstances, Saengkeo put aside her anger. "I will always be your friend, Pei-Ling. Just as I have promised you." She took the woman's arms from her and pushed her back. "Now go. Clean up. You know you always feel better when you look pretty. Take a long, hot bath and you will feel pretty again in no time. I will have clothes sent to you."

Tentatively, Pei-Ling smiled through her tears. She wiped at her flushed cheeks with her good hand. "Thank you, Saengkeo. You are the best friend anyone could ever have."

Saengkeo stepped through the door Johnny Kwan held open. She headed down the stairs without a backward look. The Mercedes glided from the alley across the street.

"I want her moved," Saengkeo said to Kwan. "I want her in a nice hotel here in Shanghai. And under guard. I don't want her leaving, and I don't want anyone to see her or know where she is."

"All right."

"I know you believe her to be a waste of time, but she is my friend."

"I will see that it is done."

The Mercedes came to a stop at the foot of the stairs.

"You should not feel guilty for what you had to do up there, Miss Zhao," Johnny Kwan told her.

"I don't."

"You will. I know you. It had to be done." Kwan opened the Mercedes's door.

"I know." Saengkeo slid into the car.

"You should have let me do it." Kwan closed the door and walked around the car. The stiffness of his movements testified to the effects his wounds still had on him. He got in on the other side.

"I had to be the one that did it," Saengkeo said. "She would have expected such harsh treatment from you."

"Perhaps."

The Mercedes slid through the narrow street.

Saengkeo raised her voice and told the driver to take them back to the airport.

"What will you do if she helped cause Syn-Tek's death?" Kwan asked.

After only a moment's reflection, Saengkeo said, "She did not kill my brother. If she inadvertently helped cause Syn-Tek's death, I will do my best to forgive her."

"I wouldn't."

"I know. But as I broke Pei-Ling's finger, and as I hugged her goodbye at the door, I couldn't help remembering that she is part of my family, Johnny. And I am trying desperately to save my family. As she hugged me, even with all the pain and hurt between us, I remembered that she is one of the people we are working so hard to save." She paused, looking at the side window and at Kwan's reflection in it. "I want you to remember that, as well."

"I will."

Saengkeo looked past his reflection then, staring out at the neon lights of the city. She couldn't help thinking how at home the man in black would have been in the shadows, and wondering what he was doing now. She wondered if he had family. She knew he had lost family. He had told her that. So what kept him anchored? Reluctantly, she turned her thoughts from the man.

"Get hold of our people in Hong Kong," Saengkeo said. "I want to know where Stoddard is. And I want to know where his agents are. I want one of them to question, but I do not want him taken until we are ready."

Kwan took out his phone.

Saengkeo laid her head back and closed her eyes. Although she couldn't go to sleep, she worked on her breathing, relaxing and letting go the rampant thoughts that slammed inside her head. She didn't know how many lies she had been told, nor which one had gotten Syn-Tek killed.

Traffic from Sheremetyevo International Airport delayed Bolan's arrival at the Aerostar Hotel by seven minutes longer than the travel brochures advertised. The local time was almost half-past one in the afternoon.

Slanting in slightly from the west, the sun painted shadows of the trees lining the street leading up to the building across the pavement and the narrow islands of grass. Aerostar Hotel was written in the Cyrillic alphabet in freestanding letters above the canopy over the entrance. Below that, Aerostar Hotel rendered in English stood out on the canopy's edge. The four-star hotel was a joint Canadian and Russian effort that had opened in 1991.

Several cars, most of them rentals from the airport, as well as service vehicles used by the hotel staff, occupied parking areas in front of the building. Groundskeepers stayed busy with the neatly trimmed grass.

Moscow, Bolan knew from visits during the past years, remained a city in transition. The fall of the Berlin Wall and the move toward democracy from the Communist way of government had taken a toll on the citizens and the city. Several metro areas Bolan had passed on his way to the Aerostar Hotel were in the process of being gutted and reclaimed, but the businesses or agencies responsible for tearing down or gutting the interiors of those buildings often found themselves without financial resources or continued belief in whatever vision had led them there to continue. Dreams lay broken and abandoned in places, wrecks that the government had to schedule to be cleared away by overworked sanitation crews. Still, the work continued in many other places, and the magnificent history of the area showed in the onion domes that mixed with tall buildings against the skyline.

Bolan sat in the back of the Chaika GAZ-13 limousine. The soldier wore a heavy coat and a fur-lined cap that made him look like any of several foreign and domestic businessmen that operated out of the offices in Aerostar Place, which was adjacent to the hotel. He could have been a native or a visitor, and, ten minutes out from the Kremlin at the Aerostar Hotel, either was accepted.

The limousine driver was an NSA agent who believed Bolan was a fellow agent. Bolan had possessed all the proper credentials when they had met at the airport. Huge and compartmentalized, funded through slush accounts that never showed up anywhere in a budget proposal that passed through both Houses of Congress in the United States, the NSA was a giant conglomeration. Price had taken advantage of that fact by hacking into the agency network and creating a false set of orders, as well as identification for Bolan. The agents who worked for the intelligence agency were used to operating in the dark.

Agents like the man driving the Chaika were especially used to knowing nothing about the men they worked with. He was young and lean. His pale green eyes moved restlessly, and the easy smile he favored never quite reached them.

He guided the limousine to the curb, got out smartly and opened Bolan's door. "I'll be watching for you, sir," the man said in flawless Russian.

Bolan nodded. "If there's trouble," the soldier replied in the same language, "get clear. I'll find my own way out. It won't be the first time."

"Yes, sir."

Together, they removed the slimline briefcase from the limousine's trunk. Electronic locks secured the case and the half-million U.S. dollars inside.

Under the coat, Bolan wore a double shoulder rig that boasted two silenced Yarygin pistols. Chambered in 9 mm ammunition designated as the 7N21 by the Russian military, the Yarygin carried a significantly more potent punch than 9 mm Luger rounds. The double-column magazines carried seventeen rounds, providing plenty of immediate firepower. The sound suppressors had come with the pistols.

"Good luck, sir," the young agent stated as Bolan started toward the Aerospace Center, which housed offices and apartments.

"Stay frosty," Bolan replied. He gripped the briefcase and moved easily. His combat senses wrapped a protective cocoon around him, mapping the movements of the people and vehicles around him.

Barbara Price and Aaron Kurtzman had pinpointed where Ivar Torvitch kept his offices on the third floor of the building. CIA files had been up-to-date on Torvitch's whereabouts since they used the man to move cash around on a regular basis.

Bolan's footsteps cracked against the pavement in the cold, still air. His thoughts ranged from Torvitch to Saengkeo Zhao. The Stony Man mission controller had let him know the Moon Shadow triad's leader had landed in Shanghai instead of Hong Kong, but didn't know why. Shortly after that, Saengkeo had made the trip to Hong Kong. The woman had been there nearly ten hours, but Price hadn't been able to keep tabs on her. But Saengkeo stayed around Moon Shadow holdings.

Every tick of the clock, the Executioner realized grimly, pushed them all closer to the point of no return. Doomsday lurked just around the corner in the form of the third missing nuclear weapon.

He pushed through the Aerostar's main doors. The glass reflected the surrounding cityscape, complete with multicolored onion domes and statues. Warm air pushed at Bolan as he crossed the vestibule and stepped onto the polished tile floor.

The Aerostar logo was printed on the floor only a short distance ahead, again in Cyrillic and English. A maze of beige and off-white tiles twisted across the main foyer. Security cameras hung from the high ceiling, only partially hidden by the beams. Bolan knew where all the cameras were from Price's information.

Large pots held young trees in the foyer. Mirrored columns enhanced the open feeling of the area and provided reflective surfaces that the soldier used to keep track of pedestrian traffic as he turned toward the elevators. He caught a cage going up and stepped into a small group of businessmen speaking German and Hungarian.

Quietly, Bolan watched as the digital floor counter changed to 2. He was the only person off the cage. Torvitch had the rooms all the way to the right at the end of the hallway.

Two young hotel maintenance men in uniforms stood near a wheeled trashcan talking and listening to American rap music on a small radio. Without looking at Bolan, they turned the radio down and pushed the trashcan into the nearest conference room.

Bolan swept the conference room with his gaze as he passed. No one was inside except the maintenance men. He continued on, stopping at the door and knocking. Calmly, aware of the small security camera in the left corner where hallway wall joined the ceiling, he waited, both arms crossed in front of him as if he were holding the briefcase with both hands.

A moment passed, then the door opened to reveal a broad man dressed in American Levi's jeans and a turtleneck sweater under a jacket that had been tailored to conceal the shoulder holster from the casual observer. The Executioner wasn't a casual observer.

The man made no move to step aside. He wore a goatee and had a scar that pinched his right cheek, drawing down the lid slightly over his right eye. "You are Mr. White?" he asked in accented English.

"Yes," Bolan replied. During the flight, he had made arrangements through one of Torvitch's contacts, again passing himself off as a CIA agent. According to the cover story he had in place, he was hiring Torvitch to pay off some informers within the Russian government offices. The assignment seemed routine, and Torvitch had been used for such operations before, taking his cut as a percentage.

"You have the money?"

Without speaking, Bolan held up the briefcase, flipped the electronic locks using the sequence of hidden pressure points to bypass the built-in security measure, and revealed the stacks of banded American currency.

Hypnotized by the cash, the man started to reach.

Bolan closed and locked the briefcase.

"Come in," the man said.

Maintaining his stance outside the door, Bolan made a show

of peering into the office around the man. The office was simple, clean and efficient. No personal stamp or any indication of what business was done there existed anywhere. The small desk sat empty except for a copy of *Maxim* magazine and a rectangle of security camera screens that monitored the hallway outside from three different angles.

"Where's Torvitch?" Bolan asked.

The man jerked a thumb over his shoulder. "In back."

"He's expecting me."

"Yes."

Two other men stepped through the door at the back of the reception room. Both of them bore marks of a grim and savage life and looked out of place in the jackets they wore.

"I want to see Torvitch," Bolan said.

"Mr. White," the big man said with a sigh. "I assure you that your apprehension is—"

Bolan cut the man off. "I'm not apprehensive. I'm careful. I haven't done business with Torvitch before."

"Many of your associates have done business with *Mr.* Torvitch. Otherwise you would not be here now."

Bolan showed the man a thin grin. "Money's getting me in through the door. No guarantees about getting back out."

The big man manufactured an innocent expression. It didn't wear well. "You do not trust us."

"I don't know you," Bolan countered.

The big man nodded at one of the others, who opened the rear door and said, "Mr. Torvitch."

A moment later, Torvitch stepped through the door with a quizzical expression. The recessed lighting gleamed against the piercings in Torvitch's face. Cool and calm, he looked at Bolan. "Is there a problem?" His English was flawless.

"I like to see the guy I'm doing business with," Bolan replied.

"So do I." Torvitch turned and spoke in Russian to the big man who had been watching the door. "Is he alone?"

The big man glanced at the security monitors on the desk. "No one is in the hallway. He came from the elevator by himself."

"And I know the language," Bolan interjected in Russian. He extended his arm, exposing the watch. "Time is money, Mr. Torvitch. We're on a deadline here."

"You're an impatient man, Mr. White." Torvitch looked sour.

Bolan didn't bother to disagree. "I'm also punctual."

"Come on back," Torvitch said. He waved to his men, motioning them out of Bolan's way.

Conscious of the stares boring into his back, Bolan followed Torvitch into the rear office.

"Are you armed?" Torvitch asked.

"Yes," Bolan replied. "And I'm going to stay that way."

"Then you don't mind if we have company," Torvitch said, waving to the two men by the door. They entered behind Bolan. "You see, I'm every bit as careful as you seem to be."

"Fine," Bolan replied.

The two men took up positions just inside the doorway. Both of them drew pistols from beneath their jackets and held them at their sides.

The rear office held a desk at the back, but the long rectangular conference table took up the length and breadth of the room. A notebook computer was interfaced with a console built into the table. A cube screen hung from the ceiling, showing stock market listings.

"I'm something of a techno-geek," Torvitch confided. "The display is a toy that impresses a number of...legitimate clients I do business with."

Bolan studied the figures, knowing Torvitch would expect him to. But the Executioner's eyes mapped the room with the eye of a tactician.

"The New York Stock Exchange shut down twenty minutes ago," Torvitch explained. "I'm analyzing the results of properties I've been interested in, trying to spot the trends that may occur after opening and during the day tomorrow."

"I was told playing the stock market was a bad thing to get interested in now."

Torvitch shrugged and grinned. "I like to gamble. And profits are always there to be made for a man willing to risk capital. The only true problem in dealing with the current situation in the United States is being able to move around and repackage investments quickly. That's why the big investment firms are posting losses. They can't move as quickly as I do." He shrugged. "Still, the profits I manage to eke out of the stock exchange are certainly smaller than anything else I do." He dropped his eyes to the briefcase Bolan held. "And, as you pointed out, time is money."

Bolan placed the briefcase on the table and recited the lock code.

Torvitch took a seat at the head of the conference table and grinned. "I think not. You open it, then I'll look."

Using the secondary code that opened the briefcase and set the timed detonator, Bolan flipped the lid back to expose the stacks of money. Torvitch's eyes glimmered instantly with greed.

"A half million?" Torvitch asked.

"Yes." Bolan pushed the briefcase down to the man, then followed it down. He felt loose and ready. The weight of the Yarygin semiautomatics felt comforting in the double shoulder rig. He kept a mental countdown going inside his head.

"And I get my usual fifteen percent?"

"Unless you choose to lower it." Bolan stopped at the wall almost ten feet from Torvitch.

"I don't think—"

The blast of the briefcase blowing up cut off Torvitch. Crimson liquid deluged him, bursting forth from the well created in the briefcase's lid, spraying past him to paint the desk and the wall behind him. Money, blown clear of the briefcase by an immediate secondary explosion, erupted into the air and whirled into a cloud of confetti.

"WE CAN DO THIS without you."

Saengkeo Zhao chose to take no offense at Johhny Kwan's words coming to her over the electronic earbud tucked into her left ear canal. "I know," she replied. "I'm only doing this because I also know you can do this with me."

She eased from her car and stepped onto the sidewalk in Kowloon's Temple Street market area. The sun had gone down promptly at six, and the time was now almost 7:00 p.m. By local standards, the evening was still young. The actual frenzy of business wouldn't begin in earnest until eight and would run to eleven. Darkness was held at bay in places by neon lights and signs that advertised food, beer, drinks, tattooing and massage parlors.

Temple Street Night Market ran nearly a kilometer long between Yau Ma Tei and Jordan Road. The area had hardly changed at all in the past few decades. Seafood was served in several full-service restaurants, as well as walk-up kiosks that bundled rice and fish in rice paper and cups. Small shops specialized in fake brand-name clothing, watches and black market DVDs and electronic games. The place was never quiet, always thrumming with the sound of partiers or tourists haggling over the prices of goods. Fortune-tellers and soothsayers shilled for attention from stalls and small tables that lined the street.

Saengkeo passed shops that held shelves of T-shirts, incense and ersatz jade Buddhas. Shopkeepers bellowed at her from in front of their businesses or carts. A man and his son offered fresh fish from a small pushcart filled with ice. A little farther on, two girls that were probably sisters and not over the age of nine tried to sell nightingales in tiny cages.

"Where is he?" Saengkeo asked.

"He's just leaving the building," Kwan responded.

Saengkeo lengthened her stride. Her heart sped up slightly. She still hadn't slept well. Even after returning to Hong Kong and putting her teams into play, she hadn't been able to rest. Every time she closed her eyes, she saw Pei-Ling Bao's blood-smeared face, heard the woman's shrill cries for help, heard again the pistol snap of her finger breaking.

A cold distance dwelt in Saengkeo now. She had felt its resonance even when she had gone to the Moon Shadow school. Ea-Han had been lying down and she had told the teachers to leave him be. For a time, Saengkeo had watched the children play, but she hadn't been able to forget about the world outside the walls as she usually did. She knew the wolves were there, waiting to tear into the school and destroy everything she and her family had worked so hard to defend and build.

And Stoddard had helped allow that to happen.

She still hadn't guessed what the Jade Mantis triad was doing at the meeting Stoddard had with Sebastian Caín, nor what Cain himself was doing meeting with the CIA agent. But suspicions had formed quickly.

Sebastian Cain had a vested interest in the Taiwan situation. If Taiwan agreed to again become a subject of the Chinese government, or if China seized the island country by military force, a number of international corporations would lose money. Western nations also wanted possession of, or an agreement with, the island government that would allow the presence of troops and equipment, as well as spy outposts.

"Hey, lady," a young boy called from a stall. "We have watches. Lots of watches. You need a nice watch."

Saengkeo smiled and shook her head, watching the boy break away immediately to give his attention to a young couple behind her. Their white skins and clothing marked them as probable tourists.

At the corner, Saengkeo waited near a pushcart filled with cut flowers. Carnations, gerbera, lilies, and roses sat in buckets.

"Do you see him?" Johnny Kwan asked over the earbud.

Saengkeo peered down the street and spotted the man they had targeted. Once Syn-Tek had started dealing with Stoddard, Kwan had been assigned to find out as much about the CIA section chief and his team as possible.

David Kelso was Stoddard's unofficial second in command. He was overweight and had thick black hair. His half-Chinese ancestry marked his features and olive skin, the epicanthic folds of his eyes. He wore a tailored suit.

Standing at the top of the steps leading to the small hotel that specialized in meeting the needs of the prostitutes who worked the market area, Kelso reached into his pocket and took out a cigarette pack. He lit up, then exhaled and continued down the steps.

"I see him," Saengkeo said, watching as the CIA agent approached her position at the corner.

"We could take him," Kwan said.

"You will," Saengkeo replied. "I just want to know what he will tell me."

Kelso continued down the street. He ignored the clamoring street vendors and waved to a couple of the prostitutes. In short order, Kwan had discovered Kelso's weakness was women. He drank and he sometimes partied with tourists, passing himself off as a Buddhist monk or a Chinese action-film star or whatever he took a notion to, but never in excess. But the women—the women were definitely an excess.

However, Kelso's budget didn't reach to Pei-Ling's range. He contented himself with the street girls, the younger the better.

When the CIA agent drew even with her at the corner, never really taking notice of her probably because she looked like another young Chinese woman standing on a Kowloon corner, Saengkeo said, "David Kelso."

He turned toward her, the purple light of a nearby bar falling across his face. He squinted against the light. "Do I know you?" he asked in Chinese.

Saengkeo stayed with English. Only a few people understood more than rudimentary English in the market area. "You know me," she told him. "I am Saengkeo Zhao."

"I don't know anyone by that name."

"Of course you do," she replied. "You're one of the CIA agents who work for Rance Stoddard."

Kelso's eyes narrowed. He took a hit off his cigarette to cover his surprise and give himself a little more time. He put it together that she had known exactly where and when to find him. "What are you doing here?"

"I wanted to talk to you."

"I don't think this is such a good idea." Kelso glanced around them. "And you shouldn't be out here alone with the Black Swans gunning for you."

"I'm not alone." Saengkeo's statement was simple, but she knew her words carried a plethora of threat.

Kelso turned, more obvious in his visual search now. "I don't want any trouble."

"Neither do I."

Kelso began walking, trying to put distance between them. He disrupted the flow of the pedestrian traffic in his haste.

After Kelso opened the way through the crowd, Saengkeo followed him easily. Her hands never left the pistols in her duster. "Agent Kelso, I want to know who killed my brother."

"I don't know," he said over his shoulder.

"I want to know why Stoddard is meeting with Sebastian Cain."

"I don't know anything about that." Kelso stepped off the curb and hurried across the street. A driver had to step on his brakes quickly to prevent a collision. Rubber shrilled briefly. The driver leaned out the window to curse at Kelso.

Saengkeo followed, jogging easily, moving behind the stopped vehicle. She reached the opposite side of the street at the same time Kelso did. He was so intent on his escape and thinking he was ahead of her that he turned and almost ran into her.

"Get away from me," Kelso ordered raggedly. Fear tightened his features.

Moving quickly to intercept him, Saengkeo jammed the barrel of the Walther in her right hand into Kelso's stomach. Even though her duster disguised the weapon, the CIA agent recognized the touch immediately.

"What are you doing?" he demanded in a strained voice.

"For the moment, I'm talking," Saengkeo said. "Shooting is much louder."

"Why are you doing this?"

"Someone is lying to me, Agent Kelso," Saengkeo stated evenly. "I want to know who, and I want to know why."

"You're crazy."

Saengkeo shrugged but the Walther never moved. "Will it help to think of me that way?"

"You can't do this."

"Of course I can." Saengkeo scowled slightly. "I'm a criminal. In my country, as well as your own and a half-dozen others. That's why Stoddard chose to work with my brother and me."

Struggling to regain his composure, Kelso tried to stand a little straighter, a little taller. He towered over her, but he couldn't stand straight against the pistol hidden in the duster's folds.

"You're jeopardizing your standing in this operation, Miss Zhao." He tried to sound officious. He came across as scared.

"I think my position in this operation is already jeopardized," Saengkeo said coldly. "I began thinking that as I looked at my brother's body nearly two weeks ago. That thought hasn't left me. When I found out a few short hours ago that Stoddard had held secret meetings with the Jade Mantis triad, I suddenly realized that jeopardy didn't get any deeper." She paused, pushing the Walther against the man's ample stomach. "And I decided to share that jeopardy."

Perspiration dotted Kelso's face. "Look, you got the wrong guy. I don't know anything about that. If you say Stoddard was there, and I believe you, then you need to be asking him these question, not me."

"I will," Saengkeo said, "if you don't have any answers."

A large sedan glided to a halt at the street, moving quickly enough to frighten away the hawkers and the pushcart people. The vehicle's rear door snapped open. One of Johnny Kwan's men stepped out with a cut-down shotgun in one hand. He grabbed Kelso's shirtfront and slapped the shotgun's muzzle under the man's chin.

"Into the car," the shotgunner growled.

Kelso hesitated, looking desperately at Saengkeo. "Miss Zhao. Please."

Moving with an amazing economy of motion, the shotgunner slammed his weapon's barrel into Kelso's forehead. A cut opened up and blood trickled down into his face.

For a moment Saengkeo saw Pei-Ling's face instead of the

CIA agent's. She started to speak, to tell the shotgunner to release Kelso.

Then Johnny Kwan was at her side, taking her by the elbow and pulling her gently away. Kwan gave orders to the man with the shotgun and the driver, telling them to get Kelso out of the area.

Feeling afraid and confused, Saengkeo watched the sedan pull away and disappear around the next corner. Kwan kept her moving. People along the street hurried away from her. Some of them, she was certain, would remember her. They would know her, and by morning news of the kidnapping perpetrated by the Moon Shadows would hit the streets, enhancing their reputations.

Stoddard, of course, would know long before that.

"Where are you taking him?" Saengkeo asked.

Another car stopped along the street. Johnny Kwan opened the rear door and ushered her in.

"I will tell you," Kwan said. "After."

"No. You will—"

Kwan leaned in and whispered so that only they could hear. "Remember the family, Miss Zhao. Hold that thought. This thing that has to be done is hard. You do not need to be there. Even Syn-Tek could not be present during such things. Your father knew that. That is why he had me trained as he did."

"If I let you go with this man," Saengkeo said, feeling how dry and tight her throat had gotten, "it will be the same as if I were there."

"But you won't be, and that will make all the difference." Kwan paused. "Please." He looked at her through his sunglasses. "Don't put yourself in a position where you will falter. We know there is one more nuclear weapon out there. We might be able to save many lives. This needs to be done, and it will be better done quickly."

"Give me your word that you will not kill him."

Without hesitation, Kwan said, "I give you my word, Miss Zhao."

Drawing a deep breath, knowing she was taking on a burden of guilt that she might not ever be rid of, Saengkeo nodded. Before she knew what Kwan intended, he closed the door and stepped back from the car. He rapped his knuckles against the car's top. The sedan shot forward.

Saengkeo turned in her seat, watching as Kwan turned and walked away, seeming to melt into the shadows between the neon lights of the marketplace.

Neither of the explosions from the briefcase was loud enough to carry past the room, but they would alert the man in the front office.

Bolan drew both of the Yarygin pistols and brought them up, centering them on the two men facing him at the other end of the room. "Don't," the Executioner commanded in a graveyard voice.

Both men raised their weapons.

Squeezing through the double-action pistols, the Executioner targeted both men. The low chuffs that escaped through the sound suppresors were hardly noticeable. Caught by the 9 mm loads, the men twisted and went down.

One round exploded, sounding stark and surreal against the background of Torvitch screaming. Bolan knew the crimson dye would confuse the man, make him believe he had been severely wounded. The dye also carried a pepper irritant that would prove nearly incapacitating.

The third man came around the door, spotted Bolan and dodged back with his pistol in his hand.

Without pause, the Executioner lifted the pistols and opened fire on the section of wall where the man had ducked. The 9 mm hardball ammunition chewed through the thin wall, caught up with the man and knocked him to the floor.

Bolan moved forward quickly and fired a round into the back of the man's head as he struggled to raise his own weapon. The corpse dropped back to the floor in a spreading pool of blood.

After making certain both the other men were down, the Executioner recharged the pistol in his left hand and slid it into leather beneath his coat as he marched back to Torvitch.

The Russian was only starting to realize that he had been hit with a dye bomb and hadn't been ripped to shreds. The pepper irritant stinging his eyes, nose, mouth and exposed skin had helped carry over the illusion. He started for his desk, lunging to his feet.

Bolan fired once, putting a round through Torvitch's right knee.

Screaming in pain, the man went down, rolling and grabbing his wounded leg.

Bolan stood over the man and pointed the Yarygin at his head. Reaching into his coat pocket, the soldier took out one of the two satellite phones he carried. He punched the redial button and pushed an earbud into his ear.

Barbara Price answered immediately at the other end. "Go."

"What's the sitrep?" Bolan asked.

"You're clean and green, Striker," the mission controller reported. "None of the alarms have been tripped." She and Kurtzman had hacked into and were monitoring the on-site and off-site security systems.

Torvitch curled into a fetal position on the floor. He moaned and cursed and cried. Tears streaked the wet red dye coloring his face. Burned fragments of U.S. dollars littered the carpet around him.

Bolan placed the Yarygin squarely between Torvitch's eyes on the bridge of his nose. He pressed hard enough to hurt. "Listen."

"Damn you!" the man croaked. "My eyes are on fire!"

Bolan took a bottle of neutralizer from his coat pocket, popped the cap and splashed the contents over Torvitch's face. Red dye streamed to the carpet. As he poured, he kept the pistol barrel jammed tightly against the Russian's head. The soldier threw the empty bottle away.

"Time," the Executioner said in a graveyard voice, "is now your life."

Torvitch blinked in pain. His pupils dilated and tried to focus. Red streaks flamed the whites of his eyes. "What do you want?"

"Information."

"What kind of information?"

"About a buy you set up on behalf of the Green Ghosts in New York City. A nuclear weapon that went missing after the *Kursk* was salvaged."

Glaring up at Bolan savagely, Torvitch snarled, "I don't know what you're talking about."

"Then you're dead," Bolan said.

The clear promise in the Executioner's words cut through Torvitch's resistance like a razor blade, sliding across the bones of fear that held the man together. "What do you want to know?"

"I want you to give me the accounts you used to set up the buy," Bolan said.

"If I do that—"

Bolan cut him off, bumping the Russian's head with the pistol meaningfully. "If you don't..."

"You're not a CIA agent, are you?"

"No."

"I didn't think so. You knew they were involved in this, didn't you?"

Bolan covered the little surprise that stirred within him. "He couldn't keep everything together."

"I told him he was being foolish. There was too much exposure. How did you get onto him?"

Bolan grabbed Torvitch's collar and yanked him to his feet. The Russian cursed bitterly for a moment as his wounded leg buckled and threatened to completely go out from under him.

The Executioner pulled Torvitch over to the notebook computer. "Can you reach the information you need from this computer?"

A shadow passed through Torvitch's pain-filled eyes, letting the soldier know that a lie had been considered. He exhaled, giving up. "Are you going to let me live?"

"If you give me the information I need, yes."

"Can I believe you?"

"You don't have a choice. Do you believe me when I say that I will kill you if you don't cooperate?"

"Yes."

"Then let's start there," Bolan suggested.

Torvitch nodded. He started for the keyboard.

"Wait," Bolan ordered. He reached into his coat pocket and brought out another sat phone. He disconnected the computer's phone line, then reconnected using the sat phone. "Reboot."

Quickly, Torvitch rebooted the computer. After a moment, the hard disk came back online again. He connected to the ISP through the sat phone.

The sat phone guaranteed that Kurtzman and his cyberteam at Stony Man Farm would have no problem hacking into the ISP connection. Screens full of indicia and figures came and went in flickers of movement. Finally, the view stopped on the Web page to a bank in Switzerland.

"Base," Bolan spoke over the pencil-mike attached to the sat phone headset, "do you have contact?"

There was a momentary pause. "Affirmative, Striker. Base has contact. Have your party enter the passwords."

"The passwords," Bolan said to Torvitch.

Reluctantly, the Russian tapped the passwords into the appropriate grids. His fingers left red dye scattered across the keys. When he finished, he watched anxiously.

A moment later, another screen popped up, prompting Torvitch to enter a new password. He reached for the keyboard.

"No," Bolan said.

Torvitch lowered his hands as the flashing cursor took on a life of its own and darted across the grids on the monitor, filling them out in quick succession. The new pass codes appeared as a series of asterisks. When the grids were filled out, the cursor clicked a final button and the window closed down.

"We're done," Price told Bolan.

"I'll talk to you soon." The Executioner pocketed the two sat phones while keeping Torvitch covered.

"Who are you after?" the Russian asked.

"Be glad it's not you," the soldier advised him. "But if this information is wrong, or if the people I am after suddenly find out I'm onto them, I'm going to come back."

"I won't be here," Torvitch replied sullenly.

"You'll stay in business," Bolan said. "And when you do, I'll find you. I knew you were here to begin with. You're not invisible." Before the man had a chance to avoid it, the soldier used the tranquilizer from his coat pocket, slamming it home into the man's neck and shoving the plunger down.

The anesthetic worked quickly. Racing through the neck, the drug crashed into Torvitch's brain in the space of a drawn breath. The fear that had flooded the Russian's features suddenly relaxed. Overcome, he sprawled across the floor.

Bolan turned and walked from the offices. He made certain the hallway beyond was empty, then hung a small sign on the door that announced the office was temporarily closed. Evidently Torvitch kept his own hours.

The Executioner reached the elevators without drawing attention and went down to the ground floor. Outside the Aerostar Hotel, the cold air hammered him, raking frigid fingers at the heavy coat. He used the sat phone again as the NSA agent rolled up to the curb. Bolan signaled the man to stay behind the wheel and let himself inside the vehicle.

"Me," he said as he opened the door and Price answered.

"We're working the files now," Price responded. "They look good. This isn't all of the networks our guy used, of course, but we didn't expect that. We'll know something soon."

"This is the real buy?" Bolan slid into the limousine's rear seat. He nodded at the NSA agent and they got under way.

"The account numbers match up with the ones that turned up through New York. I don't see why there would be a dummy set, and there was no reason for our guy to protect them. He's already taken his cut from this deal."

"What about the lady?"

"She's still in Hong Kong."

Bolan considered his options. What he knew limited what he could do, where he could go. "Can you get me there?"

"A plane's waiting. You'll be there in a matter of hours."

Bolan stared out at the onion domes of the buildings throughout the city.

"We also intercepted some interesting news while monitoring the Agency in that area," Price went on. "Apparently, one of their people has gone missing."

"The major player at that end?"

"Negative. One of his main constituents, though. The interesting thing is that witnesses have linked his kidnapping to the lady."

"How?"

"She was seen."

Bolan took a deep breath. He still smelled cordite on his clothing, and only noticed then that the red dye that had hit Torvitch had spattered his shoe. "Why would she do that?"

"Desperation," Price replied. "She's either trying to cover her tracks, or she's trying to figure out where she stands."

"Does the section chief know?"

"Yes."

"What's he doing?"

"According to the reports he's filing, he's looking for his missing man."

"Any idea of where our target might turn up?"

"Not yet. These files will tell us something, Striker."

"I know," Bolan replied. He thought about Saengkeo and the missing CIA agent she had evidently kidnapped. Guilty or innocent? He still didn't know, and so much was hanging in the balance. "But we're running a short fuse here."

"I'll get back to you," Price promised, "as soon as we have something."

Bolan punched the phone off and shoved the device deep in his pocket. His thoughts kept turning to Saengkeo, remembering how she had stared across her pistol barrel while standing naked in the shower. She'd been afraid, but she hadn't backed down. Maybe that was what the move in Hong Kong had been about.

He tried to relax, but everything in him wanted to be up and moving. He had been behind since he had stepped into the play in New York. If something didn't break, the warrior had the distinctly unpleasant feeling he was going to arrive on time for the train wreck.

"YOUR LITTLE CHINA DOLL took Kelso off the streets in Kowloon just after he got his ashes hauled a short time ago. Inquiring minds want to know what you're going to do about it."

Irritation grated Stoddard's nerves as Jacy Corbin's sarcastic words mocked him. Without turning to face her, he swirled his drink and stared through the window over the darkened streets of Hong Kong. Only minutes after hearing the news about Kelso while dining at a favorite restaurant, he had returned to the communications center on the twenty-seventh floor of the Bank of China Tower.

Jacy Corbin had been waiting, sitting in the darkness.

Stoddard hadn't turned on the lights. He knew the room intimately and could get around easily even with his eyes closed. Cool blue-white light filtered through the vertical blinds that covered the broad windows. He stood at the slanted edge of the rectangle of light that stood out against the floor.

"You seem to have gotten to know the Zhao woman lately," Stoddard said in a neutral voice. "What would you suggest I do?"

"Have you tried calling her?"

"She's not answering."

Corbin lit a fresh cigarette. The flames danced over her beautiful face.

Stoddard felt the distance between them now. He knew the woman had been suspicious of him for some time. For most of that time he had believed it was only jealousy, that she was blind-sided by her fixation on Saengkeo Zhao. She didn't love him and never would, but she had believed he could help her ambitions in moving her career with the CIA along. And now, he wondered, what did she believe now?

"If I was in charge of this operation," Corbin said, breathing out a cloud of blue-gray smoke, "I'd want to know what Saengkeo Zhao hoped to achieve by kidnapping Kelso. She is obviously making a statement."

Stoddard sipped his drink. "The first thing that comes to mind with any kidnapping is ransom."

"This isn't just any kidnapping," Corbin countered. "This is the kidnapping of a United States Central Intelligence Agency operative. A man who was supposed to be part of a team that was helping the Moon Shadows get out of Hong Kong and into better lives. Though I've seen some of the sweatshops those people are willing to work in once they arrive in the promised land, and I question that assessment."

"They're their own people in those places."

"Maybe."

Stoddard sipped his drink and looked out over the city. Even in the darkness he could feel her eyes on him.

"So why do you think she took him?" Corbin prompted.

"I don't know."

"Damn," Corbin stated sarcastically, "it's not like you to not know, Rance. You've always been the man with the answers. And when you didn't have answers, you could usually be counted on for some damn fine guesses."

"Yeah, well, I don't have them in this instance."

"Let me try something on you."

Stoddard waited, not knowing how deep the situation was going to go.

"I put myself in Saengkeo Zhao's shoes," Corbin said, "and I tried to figure out what she was thinking. She kidnaps Kelso in front of everyone, even taking care to be there and do the job her-self so she's seen. She has Johnny Kwan, a very dangerous man by anyone's standards, at her disposal and could have made Kelso disappear anywhere without anyone knowing who had taken him. So why not do that?"

"It's your story, Jacy. Run with it."

Corbin leaned forward in her chair. The computer lights blinked red and green from the desk units that covered the tables around her. Smoke swirled around her head. Her face remained concealed in the shadows.

"Saengkeo wants to make a statement," Corbin said. "To the other triads. To you. She's putting all of you on notice. But we're the good guys, right? We're here to help her get a better life for her family. Why would she turn on us?"

Stoddard waited, wondering how much of the story Corbin knew and how much the woman was guessing at.

"The only reason she would turn on us," Corbin said, "is because she thinks someone double-crossed her. That maybe we turned on her. My question is, would we do that? And if so, why?"

"Do you think she suspects Kelso?" The attempt at diversion was halfhearted and Stoddard knew it, but he had never been good at being passive.

"Kelso doesn't make a move without you knowing it," Corbin said.

"Which leaves me." Stoddard hoisted his glass in a salute.

"Or me," Corbin said. "I know enough about things to screw up the operation. Only I know I didn't do it. Which leaves you. So how did you break trust with her?"

"I didn't have a choice. Her brother broke trust with me."

"Syn-Tek? How?"

Stoddard sipped his drink. He kept his stance open and relaxed. He'd shared a bed with Corbin dozens of times since they had become casual lovers; she would know the changes in his body posture in a heartbeat. Women, he knew, were like that. All that was required was sex to fine-tune that personal radar.

"You remember *Kursk*? The Russian submarine that went down with the crew aboard?"

"Yeah."

"The sub carried a nuclear payload. When she was salvaged, three of the warheads went missing."

"That's what this is about? Missing nuclear weapons?"

Stoddard nodded. "I was given information about the missing nukes."

"You didn't tell us."

"I was told not to spread it over the team in place here. Kelso knew." Stoddard almost smiled at the look of jealous surprise that touched Corbin's eyes and the corners of her mouth. But the emotion was only there for an eye blink. "I was told to operate on a need-to-know basis."

"You cut me out."

"Only Kelso knew." Stoddard approached the bar and made himself a fresh drink. "Get you something?"

"No. Why tell Kelso?"

"Because he's been with me the longest. Because he doesn't have the ambition that you do. Because he can sit behind a desk for days watching a computer monitor if he needs to. You can't. You're too antsy. That little soiree you made into the United States after Saengkeo Zhao proves that."

"I knew you were hiding something."

"Sometimes," Stoddard said, "I'm supposed to hide things. My prerogative, and my job. You're a loose cannon, Jacy, and your actions these past few days have proven that." He shrugged. "That's all in my report. Don't be surprised if you get reassigned." He knew the cold, offhand way he delivered the message got to her. Even in the darkness he could see her shoulders draw up a little tighter. Defensive posture, he thought. He'd learned a thing or two while they'd shared a bed, as well.

"How did Syn-Tek betray you?" She stepped closer and the ambient glow of the city lights outside the window raised her features from the darkness like a volcanic island rising from the ocean's floor.

And she was tenacious, too. Stoddard had always appreciated that about her. If she hadn't asked, he would have found a way to feed her the information and make it seem natural.

"I was careless," Stoddard admitted. "Familiarity breeds contempt. I thought we had Syn-Tek right where we wanted him. I was mistaken. Syn-Tek got his hands on the file about the nuclear weapons. You know yourself that the Moon Shadows, especially Johnny Kwan, try to keep watch on us. Syn-Tek knew the Russian *mafiya* was shipping the weapons to a Middle East buyer on a ship called *Jadviga*. I was put on alert."

"And you, in turn, alerted Kelso."

Stoddard nodded. "Syn-Tek intercepted the shipment and took the weapons before the CIA strike force teams could get there. The strike force teams had planned on taking the shipment at sea right before the freighter reached Singapore." The reports he had filed would corroborate that information.

"Syn-Tek is dead."

"He was killed during the attack," Stoddard said.

"But his body was found in Hong Kong."

"Syn-Tek's body was brought back to hide Moon Shadow involvement in the attack on *Jadviga*."

"By whom? Not Saengkeo. She's looking for her brother's killer." Suspicion arched Corbin's brows.

"Someone close to the Moon Shadow operation," Stoddard said. "Someone who knew everything that went on in that family. Someone who Syn-Tek could trust and someone that could lie to Saengkeo Zhao." He sipped his drink. "Do you know someone that could fit that bill?"

Corbin didn't hesitate. "Johnny Kwan."

Stoddard could almost see the gears spinning and twisting in Jacy's head. "Bingo," he said.

"So Kwan covered Syn-Tek's death?"

"And took control of the two remaining nuclear weapons."

"Two?"

"One was lost overboard when *Jadviga* was attacked."

"How do you know this?"

"One of the men who sailed with Syn-Tek to take the weapons is an informer."

Corbin took another hit on her cigarette and waited. Smoke curled in a rush from her lips.

"I informed the Agency about the loss," Stoddard said. "They contacted the U.S. Navy and arranged a pickup from a sub."

"That hasn't been in the news."

"Put that in the news," Stoddard countered, "and you also have to mention that two nuclear weapons were missing. The Agency and the President chose not to deal with that. I thought it was a wise choice." He crossed to one of the computers and brought up a file.

Pictures of the attack aboard *Charity's Smile* opened up on the screen. Saengkeo Zhao, Johnny Kwan and several other Moon Shadow soldiers were immediately apparent.

"Only a few days ago," Stoddard said, cycling through the succession of shots of the attempted boarding of the Russian freighter, "this ship, *Charity's Smile*, was attacked by the Moon Shadows, led by Saengkeo Zhao. There was another nuclear weapon aboard it awaiting shipment to a buyer in the Middle East."

"I heard about that one," Jacy said. "It sank. The CNN and FOX reports said that pirates were responsible."

Stoddard used the mouse to inscribe a yellow circle around Saengkeo Zhao's head. "Here are your pirates."

Corbin was quiet for a moment. "What happened to the nuke?"

"It was lost at sea. Another Navy team managed the salvage."

"That's two out of three. Where's the third?"

Stoddard closed down the file. He turned to look at Corbin. "No one knows, but I think Saengkeo Zhao knows. I think she's setting up a buy."

"With who?"

"I've been trying to find out."

Corbin lit another cigarette from the butt of her first. "If Saengkeo has the third nuke, why did she go haring off to the United States and Canada?"

"Perhaps it was to set up another buy." Stoddard stood his ground, watching the tension on Corbin's face in the glow of the monitor. She knew something she wasn't telling, but the CIA section chief had no idea what it was. For a moment, the silence deepened the distance between them.

"I've been checking around, too," Corbin said. "I'd heard that Syn-Tek kidnapped Pei-Ling Bao and turned her over to the Howling Dogs triad, which in turn sold her to the Soaring Dragons for use in one of the brothels. I was also told that Syn-Tek sold Bao because she saw you and Sebastian Cain together."

The statement almost caught Stoddard by surprise. Still, working with Corbin had taught him that the woman was nothing if not resourceful. "Why would he do that?"

"I don't know."

"Makes no sense to me."

"Do you know Sebastian Cain?" Corbin asked.

"Of course. The man is in the news all the time. He's also one of the most powerful lobbyists in Washington regarding the Taiwan situation with China."

"A free and independent Taiwan."

Stoddard nodded.

"I've been doing my homework," she said. "How did you get to know Cain?"

"He came looking for me," Stoddard answered. "Cain offered to hire me as a security consultant for his Asian-based businesses. I've definitely got the credentials and the experience." The lie rolled off his tongue with such guile that he was impressed with himself. "I'm thinking about it. The employment package he gave me is impressive. I would more than equal my present salary, with benefits the CIA would never think of offering."

Corbin let out smoke and shook her head. "You'd be a toady to Cain if you took that position."

"I'm a toady now. You're fighting against the same thing."

"You wouldn't be happy there," Corbin argued. "You like getting your hands dirty."

"Maybe I'm ready to find out," Stoddard suggested. "I've spent all this time and goodwill trying to get the Moon Shadows jockeyed into a position to help the United States." He gestured to the picture frozen on the computer monitor. "How do you think I felt turning in this report that shows our number one candidate for getting as a double-agent within the Chinese government trying to get one of the nukes."

The phone rang.

Stoddard crossed the room and lifted the handset. "Yeah," he said.

"We're set," a man's voice answered on the other end.

Stoddard listened a moment longer, even after the phone hung up on the other end. Then he said, "Okay, I'll be right there," and hung up the handset. He looked at Corbin. "That was McElway. They've found Kelso's body. I've got to get over there."

She straightened, suddenly realizing she had been sleeping while sitting on the stone bench near the parasol tree at the Moon Shadow school. It was the only place she had felt safe tonight while waiting for the calls she expected. So far, neither Johnny Kwan nor Rance Stoddard had checked in.

Ea-Han, bundled in robes against the night's chill that blew in from the ocean, sat at the other end of the bench. He had a pipe clenched between his teeth, but the tobacco was unlit. Turning, he looked at her and smiled.

"You should have let me know you were coming, daughter," he said gently.

"And you should have awakened me," Saengkeo said. Someone, and she suspected Ea-Han, had draped a blanket over her. She didn't know how she had slept through that, but the offered comfort also left her feeling incredibly vulnerable even with Johnny Kwan's men surrounding the perimeter of the grounds.

Thin moonlight glinted from the circles of razor wire atop the high walls. Traffic noises echoed all around them, as well as the sounds of the boats out in the bay.

"You were tired," Ea-Han stated.

"I worry about you, Saengkeo."

"Everything is all right."

"That's why you're here instead of in your home?"

Knowing she couldn't lie to the old man who had spent so much time raising her, Saengkeo said, "It's not safe there."

"But you feel safe here?"

"Yes."

Ea-Han carefully crossed his legs, using his walking stick to lever the left onto the right. "You've only forestalled the trouble."

Guilt swirled within Saengkeo. "I am working on things."

"I heard that the Moon Shadows captured a CIA agent in Kowloon earlier." Ea-Han looked at her. His eyes were soft and gentle, but they carried the wisdom she had always known in him. "And I heard that the Moon Shadows were responsible."

"Yes." Had Ea-Han been another person, Saengkeo would have been defiant. "I have been lied to."

"By Rance Stoddard? The CIA section chief who is here in Hong Kong?"

Surprise washed over Saengkeo. So often she thought that Ea-Han knew only of the things that occurred at the Moon Shadow school. "You know about Stoddard?"

The old man nodded. "Those people I talk to in Kowloon know many things."

"Do they know who killed Syn-Tek?"

"No. If they had, I would have told you."

Saengkeo wrapped her coat more tightly about herself. "What all do you know?"

"Only that Syn-Tek did not trust Stoddard either. Your brother felt like he was being betrayed by the CIA man."

"Syn-Tek told you this?" Saengkeo felt even more guilt at her absence during the time her brother had been murdered.

"No." Ea-Han waved the possibility away. "Your brother never confided in me, daughter. Nor did your father seek my counsel while he was alive. Your father, at least, would listen when I had advice to offer. Generally about the placement of people within the businesses and holdings of the Moon Shadows."

"Then how did you know he had dealings with Stoddard?"

"The young believe that they own all the secrets. Older eyes often choose not to tell everything they know. Until there is a time for revealing those secrets." Ea-Han paused. "Perhaps I have waited too long to tell you what I know."

"No. There is still a lot I do not know."

"I know your brother sold Pei-Ling Bao."

"I have discovered that."

Ea-Han nodded. "You were always alert and attentive, daughter. If Syn-Tek had relied more on you instead of trying to do so much himself, he might be alive today."

"Or we could both be dead."

"Perhaps. But I don't believe that is true. You were always more clever than your brother. He was like your father—a man of convictions who would never back down. His failing, again like his father's, was that he had difficulty admitting when he made a mistake."

"I have made the same mistake. I have trusted Stoddard, as well."

Ea-Han gazed at her. "Have you then, Saengkeo? Have you truly?"

Saengkeo took in the air, then pushed out her breath. "No. I have made things difficult for Stoddard."

"You sought only to honor the arrangement your brother made with the CIA man."

"Stoddard is also the only man who can help our family, Uncle."

Ea-Han smiled. "See? Again, you are so young in your ways despite your thoughts that you are grown."

"What do you mean?"

"Today," Ea-Han said, "you only see Stoddard as the means of the Moon Shadow's salvation. At the most, that was only true of yesterday. Yesterday is gone, never to be returned. Today falls about your ears. You can only plan for tomorrow."

The statement was one that Ea-Han had told her several times during the years she had spent with him. "Why was Syn-Tek suspicious of Stoddard?"

"Your brother believed that Stoddard had opened negotiations with Duk Mok Dahn."

"The Jade Mantis triad?" At first, Saengkeo didn't believe it, but as the thought aged in her mind, the possibility made sense. The Americans never committed totally to one path; they always had backup plans and alternate routes to achieve whatever success they desired. In some ways, the overplanning was their greatest strength, and yet it was also their greatest weakness.

"Yes," Ea-Han replied. "Your brother was trying to ascertain that fact only a few days before he was killed."

"He never told me."

Ea-Han looked at her. "You had your own life, daughter. And Syn-Tek was a man. No matter that you were his sister, he would still see you as a woman first."

Despite how much she loved her brother and knew that he loved her, Saengkeo knew the old man's words were true. "Did Syn-Tek tell Johnny Kwan of his suspicions?"

"I don't know."

Saengkeo considered that. Had Johnny Kwan known of Syn-Tek's distrust? She didn't know. Thinking of Syn-Tek's silence, and Johnny Kwan's own ideas of what she should have done at different points, she thought of the man in black.

She looked at the old man. "How do you know when you can trust someone, Uncle?"

Quietly, Ea-Han returned her stare full measure. "Do you trust me?"

Saengkeo didn't hesitate. "Of course."

"That is how."

"But I've known you all my life."

"Yes."

Saengkeo thought of the man in black. "The man that I am thinking of, Uncle, I have only met once."

Ea-Han was quiet for a time. "Do you think you can trust him?"

"Perhaps."

"Do you distrust him, then?"

"No."

"Then if you do not do one, you must do the other."

"I don't want to trust him."

"Yet you don't want to distrust him."

Saengkeo made a face. "That is no answer."

Ea-Han smiled, then reached out and put his thin hands over hers. Saengkeo felt the coldness of his flesh and thought of how few years had to remain to him. I will miss you so much, Uncle, when you are gone.

"That," the old man said, "is the answer to everything in life. There is no one true answer. That is yin and yang. No matter which way life pulls you, there is always a piece of the other path within it."

"Trusting this man could be a mistake," Saengkeo warned.

"Trusting me could be a mistake," Ea-Han said.

"No," Saengkeo replied, squeezing the old man's hand reassuringly, "trusting you could never be a mistake."

"But if I did break trust with you, trusting me would have been a mistake. You will have just spent years making the mistake instead of making it in an instant. The good a person does is measured in lifetimes, Saengkeo, but even Buddha lived his life in moments. Each moment is a fork in the road, each choice a new journey. But most people, I have found, end up where they are supposed to no matter what they do."

"Perhaps I will never need to trust this man."

"But you are considering the possibility."

"I have to. He is still involved in the business I have before me."

Ea-Han considered for a moment. "What do you know of him?"

"He tried to kill me."

"Ah."

"Then a few days later, he spared my life when he could have killed me."

"I see."

"That is why I don't know what to do with him if he turns up in this situation again."

Ea-Han patted her hand with his. "Follow your heart. During all the years I have known you, you have always shown good instincts. You have never long stayed blinded by what you want. You have always paid attention to what is real."

Saengkeo reflected on her friendship with Pei-Ling, how she had protected the other woman only to have Pei-Ling lie to her. In the end, confronted by Pei-Ling's omission, Saengkeo had broken trust with that friendship herself. Or redefined it, she amended.

"Your life will never be easy as head of the Moon Shadow triad. You will have to accept that or walk away from this family."

Saengkeo bowed her head and touched it to the back of the old man's hand. "I could never walk away from my family, Uncle."

"Then you must accept the weight of your responsibilities."

Saengkeo clung to the old man, feeling once more like the young girl she had been. Memories of fishing boats, strolling through the market districts of Kowloon and quiet dinners shared with Ea-Han during birthdays and holidays filled her thoughts. She wished that she could once more be that child, so innocent of the ways of the world, so sheltered from all the hurts she had experienced.

But that was not to be so. Her brother was dead, killed by an unknown murderer. And she had to make decisions and alliances that would forever affect her family.

Just as sleep was about to return to her, just as she was about to forget the way that Ea-Han's hand felt like a sack of small sticks that quivered slightly in her grip, the cell phone in her coat pocket shrilled. She pulled the device from her pocket and flipped it open. "Saengkeo," she answered.

"We know what he knows," Johnny Kwan said without preamble.

Saengkeo sat up, squeezed Ea-Han's hand reassuringly and asked Kwan, "Where do we meet?"

"KELSO KNOWS about the nuclear weapons."

Masked by the thick shadows clinging to the port area, Saengkeo walked with Johnny Kwan toward one of the warehouses that faced the bay. Her body thrummed from fatigue and excitement.

"What did you do with Kelso?" she asked.

"He still lives," Kwan replied. "He is being cared for. When the time is right, he will be released from our custody. Or not."

"No," Saengkeo said. "I want him released. Without further harm." She made it a point not to ask how much the CIA agent had been hurt during the interrogation, and she tried to distance herself from her role in whatever had been done to him.

"Kelso knows we took him. We have little deniability in the matter after the manner in which you insisted he be taken. Leaving him alive with that knowledge will endanger our chances of continuing to get help from the American government." Kwan's tone indicated that killing the CIA agent would have been no problem.

"No. Letting Kelso live and speak freely about what happened to him—what we did to him—will only let us know more certainly how much the United States Central Intelligence Agency wants our assistance. If they want us, they will have to accept what we have done to protect ourselves." Saengkeo climbed the wooden steps at the warehouse's side.

"Kelso will lie about the information he had regarding Stoddard's activities."

"And we will tell the truth. One thing I know about the American spy agencies—they do not even trust their own people. Kelso's lies will be found out."

"If they are not, we will be in even worse trouble."

"Worse trouble than denying that we killed an agent they know we did? Worse trouble than having the American intelligence agencies believe we know where the missing nuclear weapon is?" Saengkeo hoped there was only the one left unaccounted for.

Kwan looked at her from behind his sunglasses. "You're playing a very dangerous game, Miss Zhao."

"We've been playing a very dangerous game," Saengkeo responded. "Only now I choose to play as dangerously as everyone else." She had come to terms with what she had to do during the drive from the school after bidding Ea-Han farewell. "You said Kelso knew about the nuclear weapons."

"Yes."

"As a CIA agent, as one of Stoddard's elite agents, Kelso should have known about the weapons."

"Only he and Stoddard knew about those weapons. And they knew about them before they were officially told by their agency."

Saengkeo considered that. The fact dovetailed with her belief that Jacy Corbin knew nothing of the theft of *Kursk*'s deadly payload at the time, and still didn't know about Syn-Tek's or Stoddard's involvement in the matter. "The CIA didn't know they knew about the weapons."

"No. Their agency told them the weapons had been taken from *Jadviga*. That was the first they were supposed to know of them."

"And the theft from *Jadviga* was supposed to have been perpetrated by my brother?"

"No. According to the reports Stoddard and Kelso got, unidentified Chinese pirates took the weapons from *Jadviga*."

"Weapons? You're sure Kelso said *weapons?*"

"Yes. Kelso knew that Stoddard had enlisted Syn-Tek to investigate the possibility of the weapons. They were working on information they had received themselves through sources of their own."

"Who?"

Kwan shook his head. "Kelso didn't know. Stoddard came to him with the information. They ran a visual surveillance of Syn-Tek's attack on the Russian ship by putting short-range digital cameras on one of Syn-Tek's men."

"That's a lie," Saengkeo said with conviction. "My brother would never have allowed such a thing."

Kwan nodded. "There is only one way one of Syn-Tek's men carried a camera on him."

"Stoddard bribed one of my brother's men."

"Yes."

Saengkeo entered the top of the warehouse where Johnny Kwan had staged the assault team. The warehouse's interior was dark. Kwan's men stood at the other end of the building facing the warehouse they had under surveillance. They wore black clothing and military combat harnesses. All of them were equipped with night-vision goggles.

"Stoddard told us that Syn-Tek found only one of the weapons on board *Jadviga*," Saengkeo said.

Kwan's voice was flat and hard. "Stoddard lied. Syn-Tek's suspicions that Stoddard was lying caused him to try to keep the weapons. During the initial confrontation, one of the weapons was lost overboard. Syn-Tek got away. But only for the moment. There was another team lying in wait."

"The Jade Mantis triad," Saengkeo said, remembering everything that Pei-Ling had told her about Sebastian Cain and Duk Mok Dahn.

Johnny Kwan nodded. "Stoddard has film footage of Syn-Tek and his group taking the nuclear weapons from *Jadviga*. Stoddard was planning to use that footage later."

"For what?"

"Kelso doesn't know."

Saengkeo looked at Kwan's black-lensed stare. If she trusted Johnny Kwan, then Kelso didn't know. But if Johnny Kwan had his own reasons for hiding the truth...

Suddenly, her head swam in sick pain. Belief was so strong, yet so weak once it started to buckle. She had no reason to believe Kwan. He hadn't even been there the night her brother had been killed.

As if reading her mind, Kwan said, "Syn-Tek ordered me not to go with him, Miss Zhao. You know me. You know that was the only reason that I was not at his side. There could have been only one reason for that."

"Syn-Tek wanted vengeance," Saengkeo said. "He knew that if Stoddard double-crossed him, that if something went wrong, you would kill whoever killed him."

Slowly, Johnny Kwan shook his head. "That wasn't the reason. If your brother were thinking like that, he would have put me close to Stoddard. He couldn't be sure who would betray him, or what danger his family would be in. Syn-Tek left me behind to protect you, Miss Zhao."

Saengkeo clung to the certainty of that. If Kwan still thought that way, then he was still loyal, still someone she could count on. Thinking anything else—believing anything else—put her on the road straight to madness.

She stood at the observation point Johnny Kwan had chosen to spy on their quarry. She still wore the black clothes and duster she had worn when they had taken Kelso in Kowloon. "Are you certain that Stoddard is inside the building?"

"Yes." Kwan stepped to her side. "I have had a team on him since your brother's death. After we decided in Vancouver to come back here, I had them stay more closely to him. They have not failed." He nodded at the warehouse. "Stoddard is inside that building."

Saengkeo took off her duster. "Is anyone else?"

"The female agent, Jacy Corbin."

Taking a deep breath, knowing that she was choosing to believe in someone else solely because she chose not to disbelieve them, a pure illustration of the yin and yang of life Ea-Han was talking about, Saengkeo nodded. "I do not want her hurt, Johnny."

Kwan said nothing, only kept staring at the target building.

"I think she could be an ally," Saengkeo said. "We need at least one of those within the CIA group."

"As you wish, Miss Zhao."

"Pass the word," Saengkeo instructed. "We're going to take this building."

16

"Where's Kelso?"

Stoddard heard the suspicion and paranoia in Jacy Corbin's voice and had to restrain himself from smiling. During their time together in Hong Kong, the young woman had always been so smug, so certain of herself.

Checking Corbin's reflection in the side glass, limned green from the instrument panel, Stoddard said, "We're supposed to meet the agents bringing the body in here."

"He's dead?"

Stoddard nodded.

"Who killed him?"

"I was told the Moon Shadows killed him."

"By who?"

"By McElway."

"Where did he find Kelso's body?"

"Someone dumped it in front of one of the brothels near Temple Street Night Market." Stoddard felt her eyes on him.

"You don't seem to be very broken up about the fact one of your men is dead," she said.

"Kelso isn't the first agent under my command who's been lost." Stoddard kept his voice flat because she would expect that from him. In truth, adrenaline surged through his system. He was about to be free from all the chess playing, all the layers of duplicity.

And he was going to be incredibly rich.

Corbin reached across the seat and dropped her hand to his crotch. At first, Stoddard's immediate impulse was to push her away from him, but he mastered that reflexive action because he knew that behavior would escalate her suspicions of him.

The woman slid across the console between the sedan's bucket seats. Her hand squeezed Stoddard's crotch almost enough to be painful. But the pressure was at once familiar and welcome, as was the tingle of fear that ran through him.

"How long is McElway going to be?" Corbin's voice was heavy with lust.

Stoddard made himself more comfortable in his seat. "I don't know." He honestly didn't, but was certain that it would only be a matter of minutes. Still, minutes had been enough time between them in the past.

Corbin smiled lasciviously. "Working against an unknown deadline." Her agile fingers found the zipper to his pants and dragged it down. "I've always found that stimulating." Her hands snaked through the opening in his pants and past his underwear. In seconds, she held his erection in her palm. She leaned forward and kissed him, and her breath tasted sweetly alcoholic.

Stoddard returned the kiss, surprised at the woman's reaction. They seldom kissed. Usually, Corbin got down to business quickly, sating her own needs, as well as his. To his surprise, she bit his lip just as one of her nails bit into his erection. He tasted his own blood, and he was afraid to push her off because she might bite through his lip. He cursed as best he could and seized one of her breasts, feeling the Kevlar vest beneath his fingertips. Before he could squeeze, if that was possible through the bulletproof vest, she pulled back and laughed at him.

Blotting his bleeding lip with the back of his hand, Stoddard checked the rearview mirror and saw the cuts in his flesh. "What the hell were you doing?"

"Putting an edge on things," Corbin replied. "You're not ready to give up, are you?"

Before Stoddard could reply, while he was considering killing the woman in that moment, his cell phone rang. He kept his right hand between them while he brought out his phone with his left. "Yes," he answered.

"It's getting boring out here, Stoddard. My cameraman and I have been sitting in position for damn near four hours. Are we going to get a story or not?"

The voice belonged to a British freelance international reporter who regularly reported political and crime news out of Hong Kong. Stoddard didn't know how the reporter had gotten his cell phone number, but he wasn't surprised. Milo Watson was dangerously good at what he did.

The reporter had been fired from several major networks because he liked to run things his own way. He had put two news directors in the hospital, one in England and the other in Australia.

Watson was also a man Stoddard had used a few select times in the past with a great deal of success, feeding the reporter stories that put pressure on key events that he needed to shape and push.

"Yes," Stoddard said. "We're minutes away from delivery."

"I don't feel like staying out here another damn minute," Watson said. "There's a drink, a woman and a bed somewhere calling my name."

"Then I'd go," Stoddard said, knowing full well that Watson wouldn't. The CIA section chief had already told the man the story involved the missing nuclear weapons from *Kursk*.

"I'll wait a little while longer," Watson grumbled.

"Do that," Stoddard replied. "And stay off this line." He closed the cell phone with a snap and put the device away.

Corbin cocked an inquiring eyebrow at him.

Stoddard still wanted to smash her face with his fist, but he resisted the impulse. Her presence there could add to the credibility of the scene, but damage he did to her could show up in a later forensic investigation. He didn't want any questions.

"McElway," Stoddard said, feeling certain that the answer had to be true and that the men they were waiting on would arrive.

Hardly had the word left his mouth than stone grated. Then a light appeared in a hole in the warehouse floor as a section shifted to one side. A man scrambled up into the warehouse, quickly followed by a half-dozen others.

Stoddard closed his eyes and opened the car door, avoiding the sudden glare of the dome light and knowing the brightness would temporarily wreck Jacy's night vision. However, there was no hiding the fact that the arriving men were crawling up through the floor instead of driving through the warehouse doors.

Jacy Corbin slid out of the car, her hand already seeking her pistol.

By that time, Stoddard already had his SIG-Sauer P226 in his fist. Then his finger curled around the trigger, and he pulled it three times in quick succession.

He hated that he had to shoot her, but thought that maybe gunshots would be easier for a coroner to figure—if anything was left—than fresh bruises to her face. He didn't have time to make the damage look as if it had been done during an interrogation, and only a few blows to the face would definitely indicate that she had been hit by someone she had trusted.

The .40-caliber boattails slammed into the woman, driving her sideways from the car. She went down.

The men who had crawled from the smuggler's tunnel that ran under the warehouse produced weapons.

Stoddard spoke in Chinese. "Duk Mok Dahn, have your men put their weapons away before they alert the Moon Shadows." He knew that gunners from the Zhao family triad had followed him to the warehouse. He had been noticing them in his back-trail for hours, hoping they wouldn't choose to make their move too soon. Kidnapping Kelso was one thing, but moving against him was too big to be done without further proof, and Kelso hadn't known enough to hurt him.

One of the shadows stepped forward, allowing himself to be touched by the yellow light from the sedan.

Stoddard recognized the Jade Mantis triad leader at once.

Duk Mok Dahn gazed down at the woman lying at the side of the car. Stoddard joined the man, gazing down at Jacy Corbin's crumpled body. Blood spilled freely across the stone floor from the wound along her lower jaw and the back of her head. Stoddard guessed that she had turned in the end, had suspected him and turned to face him. And she'd caught a bullet in the mouth that had exited the back of her skull for her trouble.

"Who is this?" Dahn demanded.

Stoddard nudged Jacy's body. "Someone I used to know," the CIA section chief answered. "Get her body into the car. We'll leave her, too."

Dahn instructed his men to put the woman's body into the car. Two of them came forward and did that. They also deposited the body of a bound man behind the driver's seat. When the triad members had the man strapped in, Stoddard raised the SIG-Sauer and put three rounds into the man, two for the body and one for the head.

Seconds after that, Dahn's men expertly wired explosives to the sedan. When they were finished, Stoddard joined them in the roughly square four-foot-high smuggler's tunnel. In years past, small rail tracks had been bolted to the bedrock so handcarts could be used to smuggle in goods from the ships in port.

A hundred yards away from under the warehouse, Stoddard paused. Dahn handed him the remote-control detonator and a pair of earplugs. Stoddard put in the earplugs, watching as the rest of the triad members did the same. Then he opened his mouth to keep the pressure equalized in his ears and depressed the remote control button.

THE EXPLOSION RIPPED the warehouse's roof to shreds but left the walls standing. Caught off guard, Saengkeo turned to Kwan.

Johnny Kwan shook his head, letting her know he had nothing to do with the explosion.

"The Hong Kong police will be here in minutes," Saengkeo said, sprinting toward the door. "If there is anything left to see there, we must go now." Her mind raced, trying desperately to figure out how Rance Stoddard and Jacy Corbin had come to meet their fiery deaths. She was certain that nothing human could have lived through the blast, nor the blazing pyre that had been left of the destroyed building.

"We shouldn't go there at all," Johnny Kwan said. His movements were still a little slow from the injuries he had received in Vancouver. "We should leave."

"Who killed Stoddard?"

"The man had other enemies."

Saengkeo reached the bottom of the stairs leading from the warehouse. "The people that set the explosives inside that building got past your men?"

"No. That is not possible."

Turning toward the blazing building, seeing the reflection of the flames against the dark water in the harbor, Saengkeo ran toward the warehouse.

"The explosives could have been put there earlier," Kwan said. "Stoddard was meeting someone here."

As she neared the warehouse, the heat from the twisting yellow-and-red flames nearly seared Saengkeo's skin. The blast had torn open the double doors at the front of the warehouse. She peered inside, having difficulty seeing anything. The only thing that she saw for sure was the twisted hulk of the sedan in the center of the warehouse. The top had been blown away, the glass broken out, and flames chewed into the rubber tires. Behind the steering wheel, a man's figure sat wreathed in fire.

Stoddard? Saengkeo couldn't tell. She took a few steps forward, then knew no one would be able to brave the fire that would claim the building in only a few short moments. The fire rescue units wouldn't be able to hope to do anything but contain the blaze.

Then, incredibly, a figure lurched through the haze of flames and curling smoke. At Saengkeo's side, Johnny Kwan raised his pistols.

Even backlit by the warehouse fire, Saengkeo recognized Jacy Corbin. "Don't shoot," Saengkeo ordered. She holstered her own weapons, yanked her duster up to protect her face from the intense heat and ran forward to help the CIA agent.

Embers seeded the woman's clothing and pitted her exposed flesh. Third-degree burns showed charred skin and her hair had been burned, her eyebrows singed from her face. Stripping out of her duster, Saengkeo used the heavy material to smother the embers. Only then did Saengkeo see the flattened bullets against the Kevlar body armor Jacy wore beneath her shirt and the terrible wound along her jaw that ran to the back of her neck. She had only just avoided being shot in the face.

The CIA agent coughed and wheezed, then cursed and shivered. Saengkeo knew the pain had to have been horrible, and that the woman had somehow found the strength and presence of mind to walk out of the warehouse required nothing less than superhuman effort. Yet the ability to be that focused and ignore that much pain was exactly what Saengkeo would have expected from the woman.

"Saengkeo," she croaked, then coughed again. "That man in there...isn't Stoddard. He's faked—faked his own...death." She smiled through blistered lips. "He doesn't know it, but—but I have him." She coughed. "He's always so—so damn sure of himself, so certain...that he's one step ahead. But—but I have him. I got him by the balls...this time." Her eyes searched Saengkeo's. "And I'm giving him—him to you, Saengkeo, because that—that bastard betrayed us both. You can find him. And...when you do, kill him."

"CHINA IS a looming threat many people fail to properly recognize because the United States government doesn't make those people aware of how dangerous that country is. Many of those leaders—and I use the term loosely—who are supposed to make us aware of geopolitical situations that endanger our lives sit in the Senate and in the House. Just as they sat there when the United States was so callously attacked at the World Trade Center, supposedly caught off guard because they didn't act on information they already had. Something should be done about those people, but the situation will have to be addressed at the same time."

Seated in the safehouse Barbara Price had arranged in Hong Kong, Bolan studied the media clips that he had retrieved from the FTP site the mission controller had set up. The safehouse was near Exchange Square, hidden away in property owned by international investors.

The man on the notebook computer monitor was Sebastian Cain, a billionaire who had lobbied extensively against China the past few years. The interview on the screen was one of the few that Cain had performed himself. Usually he used the army of lobbyists he hired to do the same thing. The speech on the screen had been delivered ten months ago at a private meeting of European developers and investors in London.

Sebastian Cain was tall and robust, his dark hair neatly clipped, his jaw square and resolute. He wore a midnight-blue tuxedo and oozed authority and charm. His charisma was that of a box-office leading man.

"China has already surpassed the United States and Europe in the number of cell phones they use," Cain said. "Ten years ago, no one expected that to happen. Today's China embraces technology and consumerism on levels that would have never before been believed. The nation has changed from the old guard, and is rapidly becoming a nation of demanding consumers that today's production levels can't satisfy. Whatever we allow to happen to Taiwan is going to happen to other, weaker nations around China. They'll be swallowed up by a Communist nation no longer afraid of throwing her weight around." Cain took a moment to survey his audience.

"Of course," Jack Grimaldi said, "Cain isn't mentioning all the factories and businesses that he owns in Taiwan, or that their loss is one of his main concerns."

Bolan paused the MPEG file. "Taiwan isn't the main issue," the soldier said. He had gotten the files through satellite feed while Grimaldi had flown the plane from Moscow to Kowloon. For the time being, he was waiting to find out where Saengkeo Zhao was. Price's information was coming in steadily, but the Moon Shadow triad leader was staying on the move. "Cain's main concern is oil."

"Oil?"

Bolan nodded. "Twenty-seven percent of Cain's business portfolio depends on oil that comes through the Middle East." He played the video footage again, fast-forwarding the section to one of the places he had bookmarked.

"Most people don't realize how vulnerable the United States' oil supply is," Cain said, continuing his address. "China has become a major oil consumer. By 2010, estimates show that the nation will be using more oil than the United States. The Middle East reserves aren't enough to meet the increased demands of the Western world and the gluttony China will exhibit."

"Now there's a real neutral view," Grimaldi commented.

"The consumption figures are right, though," Bolan said. "Barbara and Aaron have verified them, and pointed out several industrialists, economists and military leaders who are concerned with the upcoming oil shortage. Many of them have banded with Cain in the lobbying activities. Some of them are on the list of investors that Barbara and Aaron have turned up from Torvitch's files." He started the video clip again.

"You don't hear much about the coming oil problem in the news," Cain said. "That's because most of those people in Washington don't want to rock the international boat, and they don't want to think about how vulnerable they have made this country with their shortsightedness. What they don't realize, or rather—as I believe—choose to ignore, is that the boat is going to get rocked anyway. And when it comes down to that, I want to be one of the ones doing the rocking. China is going to be our fiercest competitor for Middle Eastern oil. Thinking of the situation any other way is stupid."

Bolan watched Cain, studying the man, knowing that his was the true face of the enemy and that bringing him down or removing him from a position to do further harm would be difficult. Price and Kurtzman had confirmed that Cain's money had been used to bankroll the nuclear-arms purchase in Russia through Torvitch. There were other names connected with the accounts, other people who had helped raise invisible capital. The Stony Man teams were still in the process of ferreting them all out, and some of the names known and guessed at were surprising.

"While the United States has made its presence known in the Middle East after September 11," Cain said, "while my country has buckled on her weapons and once more sent her young men to foreign shores to shed their life blood to maintain world peace by declaring war on terrorism, China has been making overtures to Afghanistan and gaining the popular support and empathy of the rest of the Middle East. The Chinese intend to usurp Western holdings in the Middle Eastern oil fields by allying themselves with many of those Middle Eastern oil-producing nations. China points to the United States' staunch willingness to take a stand against terrorism at any cost, even to the point of invading known terrorist-friendly nations, and says that the United States is the Great Satan so many of those nations have feared. My country makes war on terrorism, and China has set herself up to reap the rewards."

On the computer screen, the audience applauded enthusiastically. They would, though, Bolan thought. Cain wasn't just making a patriotic speech; he was outlining a plan to put profits into the pockets of the listeners.

"Beyond that," Cain went on, "much of the oil shipping comes through sections of the ocean that China has faster and stronger access to. If China chooses to, and if war should come to pass between her and the Western world, the Chinese navy may well be able to shut down those shipments and none of us will be able to protect them."

"The man makes a persuasive case for his cause," Grimaldi said. "If you cut the legs out from under the oil imports to the United States, or even seriously raise the price of crude, at the very least the economy will be rocked even worse than after September 11."

Bolan nodded. All of it was true. "Those oil shipments haven't been lost yet. Cain may be jumping the gun."

"Maybe he isn't," the pilot replied. "You take away the oil, Sarge, you're shutting down truckers, airlines and personal freedom. Not to mention the impact, like Cain points out, to the American economy, which is still in seriously questionable shape."

"That hasn't happened yet, Jack."

Grimaldi sighed and paced the floor of the small apartment. "I know, but I can't help thinking there were people who didn't believe September 11 would happen until the World Trade Center was leveled."

"Yeah. I know."

"So what do you think Cain wants with a nuclear weapon?" the pilot asked.

"Barbara and Aaron have confirmed the tie between Cain and the Jade Mantis triad," Bolan said. "The triad provides protection and labor enforcement in several of Cain's holdings in Taiwan, just as they help protect and care for the businesses of other people Cain has rallied to the arms buy."

"So much for the issue of personal freedom for the Taiwanese people," Grimaldi growled. "They're just a labor pool to be fought over. Cain states that Taiwan would suffer a lot if they allowed themselves to be completely taken back into the fold by China."

"There's some truth to that, as well," Bolan said. "Other nations wanted Taiwan free to provide a military staging area to launch attacks against China if world politics ever came to that.

"The first thing that comes to mind is a blackmail threat," Grimaldi said. "We've got the bomb—we'll use it. That kind of thing."

"By who?" Bolan asked, playing devil's advocate.

"Cain. Or one of the people he controls."

"Anyone connected with Cain or one of the other investors we've uncovered would trigger an international incident. Sooner or later, once the warhead was revealed, it would have to be used. Or the threat would be ignored because Cain's people won't do it."

"What about the Taiwan government? Would Cain give them the bomb?"

Bolan shook his head. "Everything about Cain screams control freak. He wouldn't go to the trouble of purchasing nuclear weapons, buying off a CIA agent and exposing himself only to hand over control to someone else. I don't think he would simply keep the warhead lying around, either."

The realization of what Bolan was saying hit Grimaldi like a physical blow. "You think Cain intends to use the nuke?"

"Yeah," Bolan said.

"Against China?"

Bolan nodded and stood. He and Price had talked during the flight while Grimaldi handled the plane through turbulent weather. "Using the nuke, Jack, is the only thing that makes sense."

"Against China?"

"Yeah." Bolan rubbed his stubbled chin, feeling the long, hard miles that had brought him to Hong Kong. "Looking back over Sebastian Cain's history, one fact always comes out—the man never leaves an option unplayed, never a tool unused. During his career of corporate takeovers, mergers and buyouts, Cain has always leveraged everything he could get his hands on to achieve what he wants."

Grimaldi looked at the man's face frozen on the computer monitor. "So what does Cain want?"

"A weaker China."

Grimaldi grimaced. "Just add nuclear weapon."

Bolan studied the man, as well. "It's the only thing that makes sense, Jack."

The sat phone on the small table next to the notebook computer chimed for attention. Bolan answered before the second ring.

"There's something you should see," Price said. "I'm sending a live feed through the network connection, but you can probably pick up the story on the local television news service."

Bolan pulled up the live-feed connection that had been packed onto the notebook computer. Even as the screen cleared, he crossed the room to the television and turned on the set. The view showed a warehouse going up in flames.

"What am I looking at?" Bolan gazed at the image of the burning building on the television.

"The murder scene of Rance Stoddard, CIA section chief of Hong Kong, China," Price answered. "Milo Watson, a freelance reporter, broke the story just now. He said Stoddard called him to the warehouse minutes before the warehouse exploded and went up in flames."

"What was Stoddard doing there?"

"Watson says Stoddard went there to bargain for the life of one of his agents."

"Kelso."

"Yes."

"Did he?"

"I don't know, Striker," Price admitted. "I do know that Kelso turned up at a CIA safehouse only minutes after the warehouse—and presumably Stoddard—was blown up."

"Kelso was used as bait in the end?"

"That's the way it looks. He says he was being held by the Moon Shadows."

"Were the Moon Shadows involved in the warehouse explosion?" Bolan's mind raced, flipping the implications around like puzzle pieces, trying to make sense of the way the play had broken down.

"Take a look at the computer monitor. The television footage will probably play back through in a few minutes, but we've captured the footage broadcast and enhanced it to remove the shadows."

As Bolan watched the monitor screen, the camera view switched from the warehouse, focused on a group of running figures dressed all in black, then zoomed in to reveal Saengkeo Zhao with a pistol in her fist. She stood in front of the burning building. The Executioner thought that the triad leader looked surprised by the turn of events, as if she had not been expecting it.

"The reporter suggests strongly that the Moon Shadows are responsible for the destruction of the warehouse and Stoddard's death," Price said.

"Stoddard is dead?"

"It hasn't been confirmed yet. Watson says that he saw Stoddard enter the building. Hong Kong police report that one body has been removed from the warehouse."

On the computer screen, a figure ran from the warehouse. Saengkeo ran forward and wrapped her duster around the figure, tripping the other woman and taking her to the ground in an effort to extinguish the flames clinging to her.

"What about the woman?" Bolan asked.

"We don't know who she is," Price said. "If Stoddard was there, it stands to reason that the woman was Jacy Corbin, the only female CIA agent operating in Hong Kong at the moment."

"Has she turned up?"

"Not yet. Aaron and I are scouring the hospital records in Hong Kong and Kowloon."

On the screen, Saengkeo stepped back while two of Johnny Kwan's soldiers picked up the injured woman. A moment later, they loaded her into a black van and disappeared down the street. The camera view remained on the burning warehouse.

"Milo Watson paints the picture like the Moon Shadows lured Stoddard there to kill him," Price said.

"What does Kelso say?"

"He says the Moon Shadows released him."

Bolan looked back at the television screen. The reporter stood in the foreground while fire rescue units pulled to a stop before the burning warehouse. Water streams slapped the twisting fire but had little effect.

"Letting Kelso go makes no sense," the Executioner said. "If

Saengkeo Zhao wanted to make a statement, she would have killed all the CIA agents."

"I agree," Price said, sounding distracted. "Hold on. Something else has just been released. You're going to want to see this."

Bolan walked back to the computer and watched the monitor. The screen momentarily turned blue, then took up another live feed. He checked the television but saw that the footage was different.

On the monitor, footage started rolling featuring a ship at sea being boarded by crew from a cigarette boat. When the focus tightened on one of the men, Bolan recognized Syn-Tek Zhao.

"What you're seeing here," a smooth British voice stated, "is footage from the pirate attack on *Jadviga,* the Russian freighter that transported nuclear weapons from Russia that were to be sold to Middle Eastern terrorists." A slug line appeared on the screen, announcing Special Correspondent, Milo Watson, Reporting Live, Hong Kong, China.

"I got these video files only hours ago from an informant and was working to determine their veracity. Shortly before his tragic death tonight, CIA Section Chief Rance Stoddard reviewed these documents with me, saying that he suspected someone within his own organization of betraying him and his operation. He was called away to negotiate the release of Special Agent David Kelso. As you now know, Agent Stoddard met his death while trying to see to the safety of one of his agents."

"Is the video real?" Bolan asked.

"We're working on it now," Price replied. "But from everything we've seen so far, it's the real thing. We're checking what we have for digital alterations."

"The group you're seeing in these shots," Watson said, "is a Chinese triad group—a crime family, if you will—called the Moon Shadows. At this time, Syn-Tek Zhao, the hereditary leader of the Moon Shadows, was leading them. Later this same day, Syn-Tek Zhao's body turned up in Hong Kong. As you'll see, he is shot down during the exchange of gunfire with the crew of *Jadviga.*"

Bolan watched in silence, feeling the tension ratchet up inside him as the fuse on the op became shorter. "The local Chinese networks aren't carrying the story?"

"Not yet," Price confirmed. "The police are searching for Watson now. If they catch him, they'll shut him down."

Glancing back at the television footage of the burning warehouse, which had started to cycle through again, Bolan watched the emergency units continuing to battle the blazing warehouse. "Who killed Stoddard?" the soldier asked.

"You don't believe Saengkeo Zhao did?" Price asked.

"No. Why use a bomb? If she had him in her sights, why not put a bullet through his head?"

"Deniability?"

"If Saengkeo was trying to put a layer of deniability into place, she wouldn't have been caught on the scene as she was. She wouldn't have taken Agent Kelso so publicly. She took Kelso to make a statement to Stoddard. Why kill Stoddard only minutes after releasing Kelso? There's more to it than what we're seeing, Barb. Too many pieces don't fit."

"Tonight," Milo Watson said as the news channel pumped through, "the political bodies in China have to be asking themselves what the Moon Shadow triad has done with the last nuclear weapon that was removed from *Kursk*."

"Gonna be open season on Moon Shadows after tonight," Grimaldi stated.

Bolan knew that was true. The Moon Shadows would be ostracized in Hong Kong, driven out, then hunted down by the police, military and other triads. "Stoddard has been one step ahead of everyone so far," the soldier said. "You have to ask yourself how he managed to get killed so easily tonight."

"He was believed to be negotiating for the return of Kelso," Price said.

"No. After everything she's been through, Saengkeo wouldn't negotiate with Stoddard if she knew he was behind her brother's death. And she wouldn't kill him with a bomb. Not from a distance. It would be up close and personal."

"You don't think Stoddard is dead," Price said.

Bolan looked at the warehouse, seeing the building as it had been before the explosives inside had destroyed it. "No," he said. "I don't."

"I've got another phone call Aaron is pushing through."

Bolan waited, wondering where he should start looking for Saengkeo Zhao or Stoddard or Sebastian Cain or the nuclear weapon. Eventually, he was certain, all of those trails would cross, all meet. But which one to follow now was the question that most needed—

"Striker," Price said, "Saengkeo Zhao is on the other line. She wants to speak to you."

"Patch her through," Bolan said.

A series of clicks followed, then Saengkeo's voice came over the line. "Mr. Belasko."

"Yes," Bolan replied.

She hesitated a moment. "You said I could trust you."

"You can." Bolan knew how hard it was for her to ask, knew also how trapped and desperate she had to be feeling. And some of those feelings resonated within him because he was operating against an unknown timetable with a nuclear weapon on the loose.

"Then," Saengkeo said, "I'm going to have to ask you to trust me, as well."

THE MAN STOOD ALONE in front of the club. Neon lights reflected red, blue, purple and green against the long black leather duster he wore. His face was crisp, fresh shaved, his jawline as hard as granite. Foot traffic along the corner and auto traffic in the street remained brisk. It was just past 1:00 a.m., and late-night Hong Kong was very much alive.

The man looked, Saengkeo was acutely aware, like a warrior at post. She watched him from down the block, from where she was seated in the back of a sleek black limousine owned by a holding company that existed independently of all Moon Shadow business. He was a man who was solid, of the earth, but wielded lightning-quick death in his hands.

"What are you going to do?" Johnny Kwan asked from the seat beside her.

"I'm going to talk to him."

"This could be a trap."

Saengkeo looked at the man waiting for her. "Not with this man. If anyone else had been here to meet me, I would think that." She remembered how he had looked when she had seen him in her hotel room in Vancouver.

"He might not be the only man here," Kwan pointed out.

"Then your men have failed at the reconnaissance you assigned them to do after I told you not to do it."

Kwan looked at her.

"I know you had your men do that," Saengkeo said, "in the same fashion that I know I can trust that man. Both of you run true to your natures, Johnny Kwan. As I must run true to mine and do everything I can to save my family." Bloody purges against the Moon Shadows had already begun. Her people had gone into hiding, but many would be lost. The school had already been surrounded and everyone in it restricted to the building.

She leaned forward and told the driver to pull up and stop a few feet from the corner.

As the limousine glided to a halt at the curb, the man turned to face her as if drawn by radar. No emotion showed on his features. He moved his hands away from his body slightly, rotating his hands to show that they were empty.

Saengkeo stepped out of the limousine, aware even without looking that Johnny Kwan had his pistols out. She wore a black turtleneck and black jeans. Her clothing was tight enough to reveal that she had nothing hidden beneath, but it was also tight enough to reveal her figure to its best, and she knew that, too.

"Miss Zhao," the man said, giving a small nod of respect and unexpected gallantry.

Sacngkco stoppcd in front of him, looking up at him, feeling small against his height and breadth. If she fully trusted him, she knew that proximity to him would make her feel safe. It was a safety, though, that she didn't require. She had spent her whole life learning to be secure all on her own. The problem now was that she had no way of securing her family from the predators that gathered in the night as the news stories about Stoddard's "murder" and her guilt continued to air on the television and radio stations. She needed his help for that.

"Mr. Belasko," she said politely.

He didn't look around and kept his eyes locked on her. He gave the impression that he could wait forever.

"Rance Stoddard faked his own death," Saengkeo said. "Neither I nor any of my people had anything to do with the warehouse explosion."

"The people I work with," Bolan said, "are going to tell me that's easy to say."

Saengkeo nodded, accepting his rebuttal. "They won't say that once they learn that Stoddard is still alive."

"You know that for a fact?"

"Yes."

"How?"

"Jacy Corbin told me."

Bolan nodded. "All right."

"Jacy had been getting suspicious of Stoddard," Saengkeo explained. "At first she believed he was having a relationship with me." Unbelievably, she felt her cheeks flame in embarrassment. What was it about this man that made her feel so much like a girl again? She didn't know, and she didn't want to think about it because it only made the situation worse and those feelings stronger.

Steeling herself, she remembered what she had been faced with, the challenges she had met, the men she had killed and the way she had beaten the truth from Pei-Ling Bao. She had paid a high price to get where she was this night, and if she didn't get things in hand, the price was going to be even dearer.

"That wasn't what was going on," Bolan stated.

"No. Tonight, Stoddard found Jacy waiting for him. She was confrontational. Evidently, he was unwilling to ditch her and brought her with him to the warehouse. Duk Mok Dahn arrived there instead of the agent Jacy had been told would arrive. Do you know who Dahn is?"

"The leader of the Jade Mantis triad. Stoddard has been using them."

Saengkeo wasn't surprised by everything the man in black knew. She was counting on his knowing even more. "Jacy knew something was wrong and tried to get away. Stoddard shot her and she was knocked out. They must have believed she was dead. When she woke, she found she had been placed inside Stoddard's car with a fresh corpse that had the same height and build as Stoddard."

"Where is Jacy Corbin?"

"Safe. She's being well cared for. Her injuries are extensive, but she can be made whole again. When I am ready, when I believe it safe to do so, when all of Stoddard's coconspirators within that agency are known, she will be returned to the CIA."

"All right."

A group of laughing people walked out of the bar behind them, offering a sharp counterpoint to what had brought them there.

"I am here," Saengkeo said, "to offer you a deal."

The man in black said nothing, waiting quietly.

"I know how Stoddard can be found," Saengkeo said. "But I'm going to need your help to find him. If you're able."

Bolan nodded.

"However, there is a price," Saengkeo warned. "Once I tell you how to find Stoddard, you have to stay with me. I don't want an

American military force involved as long as this remains something the Moon Shadows can do. After you know what I know, you will not be allowed to leave. If you try, my men will kill you."

A faint feral grin twisted the big man's lips. "I can live with that," he replied.

"I SEE THE REPORTS of your death have been greatly exaggerated."

Rance Stoddard cradled the satellite phone to his ear as he stood at the railing that ringed the freighter's cargo area. The freighter, *Aristotle's Star,* was a cargo handler registered out of Cyprus. He gazed down into the cargo area where the specialty team worked on the third nuclear weapon that had been purchased from the Russian *mafiya.*

During the past hour, a storm had risen at sea that raised the waves and filled the air with rain that came so hard and so fast it was blinding. Stoddard had been abovedecks for only a short time and still felt the preternatural cold that had slammed into him.

Down in the cargo area, the team finished assembling and testing the specialized computer consoles that could detonate the nuke by remote control and started bringing the weapon systems online for quick use. The plan was to detonate the nuke as soon as the freighter was out of the danger zone.

The warhead remained in Hong Kong, quietly waiting in a shipping warehouse where it lay in storage. Stoddard still hadn't given the techs the arming codes. He didn't put it past Sebastian Cain to have the warhead detonated while he'd still been within Hong Kong. Cain was a zealot and a man who was driven to feed his own desires no matter what the cost to others. Once they were past what was known to be ground zero for the blast, and all chance of fallout, Stoddard would give the team the arming codes. During the purchase, he had controlled that information himself.

"I can't wait to see how the eulogy will go," Stoddard said. "If I don't get a nice send-off for dying a hero's death in the performance of service for my country, I'm going to be pissed."

At the other end of the sat-phone connection, Sebastian Cain laughed. "Don't worry, my man. I've got you covered. When your funeral is conducted, you're going to have a nice turnout from Washington, D.C. After all, you're the hero who tried to keep the Moon Shadows in check while they betrayed a very generous United States government by plotting to sell captured nuclear arms to Middle Eastern terrorists. Milo Watson is doing justice to you even now as we speak."

"I'll have to take a look at that. Maybe send Watson a congratulatory note."

Cain's voice turned cold but maintained the light easiness that was one of his trademarks. "If I knew you weren't kidding, my man, I'd make certain you never left that ship alive."

In those words, Stoddard remembered how vulnerable he was. He had hired most of the crew aboard the freighter. They were men he had used during some of the shadow operations that had been kept off the books even from the CIA. Ex-CIA agents, like the ones he had used in New York in an attempt to stop the investigation triggered by the De Luca Family, also sprinkled the crew. All of them were hardcases, men who were used to killing.

"If we're going to work together," Stoddard said, imitating the coldness and the easy tone, "then you're going to have to get used to my sense of humor."

"I don't have to get used to much. I usually change the things I don't like."

"I'll have reasons to make you like me." Stoddard had put together packages of information regarding the whole operation in Hong Kong—from the capture of *Jadviga*'s illegal cargo, his own betrayal of Syn-Tek and faking his death—in safe-deposit boxes in banks around the world.

Even if Cain's people found some of them, and Stoddard knew Cain had people who were exemplary at their jobs, they wouldn't find them all. The packages would be mailed to dozens of media networks. All of that would be triggered by Stoddard's failure to call in with a password once a month. Cain knew the condition existed and hadn't been happy with it.

"I'm sure you'll find new reasons to make me happy," Cain said.

Under the new identity Cain had helped him create, Stoddard would take a position with the billionaire's corporation. The identity was already in existence and had a history that was bulletproof. Cain created a handful of such identities twenty years ago, knowing that hiring people who could no longer afford to be themselves—or keeping people who could no longer afford to be themselves—would be a necessity. Others had already done that. Stoddard had met one of the men and one of the women early on in their negotiations, though he didn't know the names they currently wore. Just as they wouldn't know the new name or new face that he would be given.

Stoddard glanced at the new watch he wore. After leaving Hong Kong, he'd divested himself of everything that had been part of his old life. He'd even taken care that the dead man he'd left to take his place in the exploding car matched his Agency medical reports. That had been one of the more demanding aspects of faking his death. But those files matched the dead man to a T. Remembering the blaze that had run rampant through the warehouse, Stoddard doubted much of the man would remain. But what there was would match those files exactly.

"I'll give you new reasons to like me," Stoddard agreed. "And we're going to start with a big one seven minutes from now."

The DC-3 was a World War II troop transport plane, but she was vintage and Jack Grimaldi handled the aircraft as if he'd been doing it a lifetime. Barbara Price had provided the plane, just as she was now providing the satellite tracking for the quarry they pursued.

At present, the plane flew east into the teeth of a savage storm that raked the ocean. Miniature typhoons whipped up from the black water, crested with white foam that seemed to glow in the sudden stabbing glare of the jagged lightning that burned through the clouds. Rain drummed against the DC-3's metallic hide like machine-gun bullets.

Dressed in combat black, Bolan sat in the copilot's chair and studied the digital transmission coming in from the Stony Man signal. The monitor light bathed the cockpit, the greenish hue created by the light-amplification software Price scanned through the satellite relay.

On the screen, *Aristotle's Star* cruised sedately through the rolling waves of the ocean.

Bolan tapped keys, taking command of the transmission and

focusing on the men posted around the freighter's deck. Out at sea now, the men openly carried assault rifles. He scanned the deck, raking the ship from prow to stern.

Although Bolan didn't know the particulars of the situation, Saengkeo had told him that Jacy Corbin had tagged Stoddard with a subcutaneous tracking device. Kurtzman had ripped through CIA files to find Jacy Corbin's private files and access the tracking frequency, something that Saengkeo's computer hackers might have been able to do given time. But time was something they all knew they were out of. Saengkeo had gambled that Bolan's support team would already have access to the CIA files on some level. Kurtzman had located and locked on to the special frequency within minutes, discovering that Stoddard had already put out to sea.

Clearance for the mission had come straight from the White House. Initially, the Man had wanted to use his CIA teams, but Hal Brognola had gone to bat for Bolan, reiterating the fact that none of them knew the kind of loyalty Stoddard might still have within the Agency, or if he was still tapped into the communications network. If they had any chance at all, the action had to take place now, and come from a source that Stoddard couldn't expect. Jacy Corbin's act had given them the thinnest of edges.

And part of the reason the Man had acquiesced, Bolan knew, was the deniability factor the Moon Shadow triad brought to the picnic. If something went wrong, if the nuclear device somehow ended up wreaking havoc in China, the Moon Shadows were there to be blamed.

"Striker," Price called over the headset, "you're three minutes out from your target."

Bolan glanced up from the notebook computer. The residual light from the monitor ruined his night vision for the moment, but he knew it would quickly return. Lightning scored the sky again, bursting white-hot against the plane's windows. Rain turned the scene blurry. "Visual?" he asked Grimaldi.

The pilot shook his head. "Not yet. I'm flying by the lady's instructions."

"Let me know."

"Bet on it."

Bolan closed and put away the notebook computer. He glanced at Saengkeo, who sat in the navigator's chair. "Ready?"

"Yes."

Bolan stood and led the way to the rear of the plane. The throbbing engines filled the cavernous cargo bay with hammering noise that sounded almost like the deep basso boom of the rolling thunder that shivered through the plane.

Johnny Kwan sat on one of the narrow benches that lined the sides of the plane. More men sat on the floor in the open cargo area. All of them wore black Kevlar and looked deadly as they held assault rifles and other weapons. The men, the Executioner knew, were all veterans of violence, trained by Johnny Kwan.

"The ship?" Kwan asked.

"Below us," Bolan replied. "We're less than two minutes out." He took a parachute from the rack on the wall and pulled into it. The other men were already equipped, having gotten into their gear twenty minutes earlier.

Kwan stood, and his men stood with him. "Have you confirmed that Stoddard is onboard?"

"No," Bolan said.

Kwan made a face. It had been obvious from the start that he hadn't liked the idea of Bolan being made part of the assault team, and had even talked to Saengkeo back in Hong Kong about leaving him behind. That hadn't become an issue because Saengkeo had stated that Bolan would be coming along from the beginning.

"Then we don't know if Stoddard is there," Kwan said.

"If Jacy Corbin told the truth," Bolan said in a flat voice, "then Stoddard is down there."

Kwan remained silent.

Saengkeo stepped between them, facing Kwan. "I am the reason we are here," she said. "I believed the woman. Whatever mistake was made, if there was one, is mine."

Kwan nodded. "Then he is down there and we will find him."

"Alive," Bolan said. At present, Price and Kurtzman were rifling through all the electronic data they could on Stoddard's operations in Hong Kong, trying desperately to find out where the warhead was if it wasn't on board *Aristotle's Star.*

Kwan silently agreed.

The radio headset crackled in Bolan's ear. "I've got visual," Grimaldi said. "I'm staying high enough that they shouldn't notice me. With the storm shoving rain straight down at them, I doubt they'll see us even if lightning strikes us."

"Affirmative, Mustang. We'll move on your go." Bolan walked to the end of the plane. He tripped the control that lowered the plane's tail section and switched out the lights inside the cargo hold.

The hatch yawned open, revealing the storm's fury. Lightning flashed with blinding intensity, followed immediately by a sonic boom that vibrated through Bolan. He pulled on a Kevlar helmet and slid goggles into place. Saengkeo hadn't stinted in supplying her troops.

"Mustang, make the shift to the open channel." Bolan switched his headset to the frequency he'd chosen to run the assault team from.

"Affirmative, Striker. Making shift."

Bolan had Kwan cycle through his lieutenants, making certain each man's headset worked.

"Drop zone in fifteen," Grimaldi announced.

"Count it down," Bolan instructed, he cradling the M-16/M-203 combo he carried. The Desert Eagle was holstered at his right hip and the Beretta 93-R under his left arm. The combat harness carrying grenades and extra rounds sat over his Kevlar armor. A video camera relay was affixed to his chest, sending images back to Stony Man Farm.

At zero, Bolan sprinted down the tail section and leaped out into the storm winds that swirled through the black night. He twisted, made sure he'd cleared the plane, then surveyed the raging sea beneath him. *Aristotle's Star* was a dark, hard finger lying in the ocean southeast of his position.

"I have the target," he announced. Then, after quickly checking his wrist compass, he added the heading.

A chorus of confirmations came from the Moon Shadow warriors as they dropped from the DC-3.

Bolan popped silk. The black canopy spread overhead, blocking some of the driving rain that knifed into his lower face. Kevlar and thermal wear covered everything else. Using the control lines, he adjusted his glide path, streaking through the night toward the freighter.

SAENGKEO PULLED the elevators and shot through the air close on the American's heels. Kwan would command the ground troops as they took the freighter, and she would follow the American. The old skills she'd developed while sport diving came back to her automatically although it had been years since she had done any serious diving.

She studied the freighter, knowing all of the men who had jumped from the DC-3 were risking their lives. If they missed the ship, and some of them probably would, the cruel, dark sea waited to gather them in. Only the American pilot above, with a skeleton group of men, might save them by dropping inflatable rafts near their positions. The woman, whoever it was that coordinated the satellite reconnaissance, had a team standing by on a rescue channel that would guide those unfortunates to the nearest raft. But the number of the assault team would dwindle with every miss.

Then, in the space of a few seconds, the American landed on the freighter's deck, coming down like a big black bird of prey. One of the freighter's guards turned and saw him. Yellow muzzle-flashes winked against the darkness.

Throwing himself flat, the American pushed the assault rifle forward and caught his attacker with a 3-round burst that snapped the man's head backward and knocked him back over the railing into the sea.

Saengkeo concentrated on her own survival as she swept in toward the ship. Too late, she saw that the freighter rose up on a high wave and her latest adjustment was going to bring her in too low to make the deck. She threw her arms forward, just managing to grab on to the railing.

Her parachute came down behind her, then filled with air and tried to rip her from the side of the ship. Her feet couldn't find purchase on the wet steel. Her arms ached from the effort expended just to hang on, and she lacked the strength to haul herself up against gravity and the treacherous pull of the parachute.

Ahead of her, toward the stern, one of the Moon Shadow warriors slammed into the ship's side, as well. He never moved. Unconscious or dead, the man was yanked away by the parachute.

Saengkeo couldn't even turn to see what became of him. "Mustang," she called, "there is a man down on the port side of the ship."

"We've got him," the pilot's calm voice reassured her. "You're with a first-class op, lady. No sparrow falls without being counted."

Arms burning, knowing she wasn't going to be able to hang on much longer, Saengkeo thought of how her ancestor Chi-Kan Zhao had started the family into the life of crime that had held them trapped for almost two hundred years by an act of piracy. And here she was, a pirate taking a ship at sea, and she was going to fail.

Suddenly, a man's face took shape over the side of the railing. Rain smashing into her goggles made her vision blurry, but she knew in an instant that the man was white and he wasn't the American.

The man lifted his AK-47 and aimed down at her. Blood erupted from his face as a bullet crunched through the back of his head. Even as the dead man fell, the American stepped into her view.

He slung his rifle, then reached down with both hands. He caught her Kevlar vest in his right hand and pulled her up as he released her parachute with his left. The parachute blew away in the wind. With his help, she scrambled onto the deck.

"Are you okay?" he asked.

"Yes." Saengkeo's body ached from the collision against with the ship.

The American slid the M-16 from his shoulder. "Then let's move."

Saengkeo pulled her assault rifle from her shoulder and swept the freighter's deck with her gaze. Muzzle-flashes winked against the wet ship's deck, sliced jagged holes in the darkness and freeze-framed raindrops as pocket battles raged the length of the ship.

The American was already in motion.

Pushing herself up, Saengkeo followed him to the ship's aft hatch.

BOLAN RAN, the M-16 up. He took advantage of the ship's superstructure, the abovedecks machine shop and the control station for the cargo boom arm to make his way to *Aristotle Star*'s stern.

"Kwan," Bolan spoke into the headset.

One of the freighter's guards stepped out in front of Bolan, obviously seeking cover. The Executioner stroked his weapon's trigger and tracked a burst up from the man's sternum to his face, knocking him backward. Without breaking stride, the warrior raced over the corpse. He felt Saengkeo at his back, matching his speed and flowing over the heaving deck with fluid grace.

"Yes," Kwan radioed back.

"Are your teams in place?"

"A moment more. We lost three men who were part of those teams. They are being replaced."

Bolan switched over to the frequency that gave him a private channel to Stony Man Farm. "Base, do you read?"

"Base reads, Striker."

"Can you get a lock on the signal transmissions coming from

this ship?" Bolan flattened himself against the stern corner of the boom arm operations building built onto the ship's deck near the mizzenmast. *Aristotle's Star* was a motor sailer, capable of wind power or—as now—powered by diesel engines. He glanced up into the rigging, tightly folded against the storm's wrath.

A handful of Kwan's troops occupied the rigging and used them as sniper nests. The M-24s they carried cracked intermittently.

"Not yet," Price replied. "We don't have signal lock, and there aren't any transmissions towers to work with to triangulate the signal."

"Understood, Base." Bolan peered around the building's corner, spotting a knot of men who held their positions among three lifeboats and prevented the stern team from taking the area. He changed channels again. "Kwan, I need a sniper team assigned to the rear deck. Your team there is pinned down."

Kwan barked orders to the snipers.

Looking aloft, Bolan watched as two men made their way through the rigging. They settled into position, then fired into the freighter's gunmen holding the stern section. Splinters ripped from the lifeboats, then two bodies hit the deck.

A man stepped from hiding with an AK-47 and unleashed a blast of withering fire into the rigging. One of the snipers fell, disappearing into the black water over the ship's side.

Snapping the M-16 to his shoulder, Bolan fired, coring three rounds through the gunner's head and neck, pitching him back against the lifeboats. Gambling that the survivors' attention was focused on the last sniper, the Executioner threw himself forward. He skidded on the Kevlar armor, hydroplaning across the wet deck, then rolled and came to his knees, bringing up the M-16.

Saengkeo slid into position beside him, adding her firepower to his. The 5.56 mm rounds chopped into the four gunmen that had taken cover behind the lifeboats. Living, breathing men turned to face the Executioner and the triad warlord, but corpses hit the deck.

"Stern crew," Bolan barked. "Move in now." He shucked the assault rifle's empty magazine and shoved in a fresh one. His mind scanned through the schematics of the ship that Price had forwarded through the computer links. There were three hatches, forward, amidships and stern. All of them opened to the main cargo hold that had been partitioned off below. In addition to

Stoddard and possibly the warhead, the Greek ship also carried conventional cargo.

Four Moon Shadow fighters raced forward and set up around the aft hatch. The hatch measured eight feet by eight feet and wasn't the monster that the amidships hatch was. The forward hatch measured the same as the aft.

Bolan joined the four men, hunkered down in front of them to meet any of the ship's crew who might be driven back toward them. The men worked quickly, affixing shaped charges to the corners of the locked hatch. The Executioner locked a rappelling line to the lifeboat rack bolted to the ship's deck. He tested the grappling hook and found that it had seated.

"Done," Saengkeo said, in position beside the soldier.

"Kwan," Bolan said, "we're done here."

"Forward team is ready," a man said.

"Amidships hatch is ready," Kwan added.

"On my go," Bolan said. "In sequence and by the numbers."

Grimaldi brought the DC-3 down from the dark heavens. Even in the distance the Executioner saw an inflatable raft pitched from the rear of the plane as it cut low over the heaving waves.

"Forward hatch," Bolan ordered.

Almost immediately, the forward hatch blew, a small explosion of light that cut through the night and reflected against the sea as the ship heaved to port.

"Stern," Bolan ordered, throwing himself prone on the rocking ship's deck.

The four explosions came so fast they sounded like a single, prolonged blast. Burning embers bounced against the ship's deck but quickly extinguished. The aft hatch blew into the air, then came down on the lifeboats only a few feet away.

"Amidships," Bolan said, gathering himself.

The explosion that ripped the amidships hatch away was the loudest. The hatch blew fifty feet into the air, tore through the ship's rigging and ended up sailing out of sight over the starboard side.

"Flash-bangs are going in," Kwan announced.

Bolan gripped the rappelling line and stood at the edge of the aft hatch. He listened to the muffled detonations beneath the ship's deck, almost lost in the fury of the storm. For a moment, light filled the cargo below, squirting out the aft hatch in a white-hot blast.

When the light dimmed, Bolan stepped over the side of the

aft hold and dropped like a stone. He plummeted face forward in an Australian style descent, controlling his fall with his left hand while he held the M-16 in his right hand. Several of the freighter's gunmen had been below, taking shelter from the rain and killing time in crew's quarters. After the initial battle had been joined, they'd come roaring out and set up skirmish lines, obviously intent on letting their unknown enemies come to them while their comrades died abovedecks.

The flash-bangs Kwan had thrown into the mix had disoriented the gunners with the blasts of color and noise. Bolan marked their positions as he dropped, noting the catwalk around the outside of the cargo hold. He sprayed 5.56 mm rounds into the biggest clusters of men, leaving wounded and dead in his wake.

As the ship rolled from side to side across the waves, Bolan swung wildly. He arched his body out, slung the assault rifle over his shoulder and reached for the catwalk railing on the port side.

Before Bolan reached the catwalk, a gunman popped up from cover, his AK-47 spitting death. One of the rounds caromed from Bolan's Kevlar vest, sending the warrior spinning like a top at the end of the rappelling line.

Even as he reached the apex of his swing and started back, the Executioner drew the Desert Eagle and snapped off a round. The .44 Magnum boattail round caught the gunner in the forehead and drove him backward against the hull. Leathering the pistol, Bolan swung toward the catwalk again and caught the railing. He pulled himself over the side and unlimbered the M-16, dropping the empty magazine and ramming a new one home.

Whirling, the Executioner mapped out the battlefield in his mind, picking out targets even before he went prone. He kept the M-16 on single-shot fire, pulling the trigger through, riding out the recoil and moving on to his next target as smoothly as drawing a breath.

Other Moon Shadow fighters dropped into the hold with rappelling lines. Not all of them made it, picked off by hostile fire, but they didn't stop coming. A few made it to the catwalk as Bolan had, but most of the rest dropped all the way to the cargo deck. All of the crates and containers packed below made a deadly maze.

A moment later, Saengkeo made the same swing and drop that Bolan had, managing to arch up over the railing and drop onto the catwalk. She took up a position near him, blasting across him to take out an enemy gunner who had appeared at the other end of the catwalk.

The dead man toppled over the catwalk's side and yelled all the way down to the cargo floor thirty feet below. The impact cut him off and he sprawled, arms and legs moving only to the pitch and yaw of the ship as she made her way across the ocean.

"Striker," Price called over the headset.

"Go, Base," Bolan said, changing out magazines again. Gunfire raked the catwalk. Metallic screams echoed overhead as sparks sprayed into the air.

"I need a private."

Immediately, Bolan switched frequencies. "I'm here."

"We need a closer look at the computers in the lower cargo hold."

Rolling over, Bolan took the video camera from his combat harness and panned it over the smoking debris of the computers. The machines had taken several hits.

"What you're looking at there," Price told him, "is a modular remote-control arrangement."

"Can it set off the missing nuclear weapon from *Kursk*?" Bolan asked. He was immediately conscious of Saengkeo's attention, but she never broke pace on the deadly sniping she was doing against the remnants of the freighter's crew.

"That apparatus configures a remote-control detonator," Price explained. "Once it ties in the signal to the freighter's communications systems, the bomb can be set off by the detonator."

"Where's the detonator?"

"I don't know. The device is portable. Once the weapon has been activated with the arming code, the remote control can set it off."

"Understood, Base." Bolan switched back to the team channel. Before he could say anything else, the freighter's PA systems fired to life.

"Attention!" Rance Stoddard's harsh voice bellowed. "The nuclear weapon you people are looking for isn't on this ship. The weapon is back in Hong Kong."

Bolan considered his options, a desperate plan forming. Stony Man still didn't have a lock on the freighter's communications system. He glanced at Saengkeo. "Order your men to cease fire." He felt certain they wouldn't take the order from him.

Saengkeo looked back at Bolan. Hurt surprise registered in her eyes. "The weapon is back in Hong Kong?"

"We expected that," Bolan told her.

"You expected it? Damn you!"

"I told you these people weren't to be trusted," Johnny Kwan said over the headset.

"The weapon has to be here," Saengkeo said. "Stoddard was planning on selling it to the highest bidder, right?"

"No," Bolan said quietly, understanding only then that they hadn't talked about all the reasons Stoddard had taken the weapons. They had only discussed how they were going to stop him. "We've made a tentative assessment that Stoddard was hired by Sebastian Cain."

"I know of Cain," she said.

"We believe Cain wants the device detonated in China and he was planning to frame the Moon Shadows for the detonation. It would have looked like the Moon Shadows accidentally triggered the device while keeping it in hiding and waiting on a buyer."

"That's why the footage of Syn-Tek taking the cargo from *Jadviga* has been released." Once she had been pointed in the right direction, Saengkeo had no problems catching up.

"Cain is afraid of China's growth right now," Bolan said. "A lot of countries are."

"The same way those countries are afraid of your nation's desire to seemingly bring world peace at gunpoint."

Bolan chose not to argue the perspective. "Cain believes that a nuclear incident wiping out a significant portion of China's population and industry will hold your country in check."

"I have a remote-control detonator that will explode that nuclear weapon," Stoddard warned over the PA system. "If you don't surrender immediately, I'm going to detonate that warhead."

Bolan looked into Saengkeo's eyes. "I need you to trust me."

"Trust you?" Anger flared in Saengkeo's eyes. "If I had known the warhead was back in Hong Kong, our time could have been better spent there searching for it."

"Even if you'd found it, you'd have had the Hong Kong police and every triad in the city gunning for you," Bolan said. "You'd have never gotten clear of the city, and the warhead might not have been taken out of Hong Kong in time. It may even have been booby-trapped." He paused. "The warhead is being searched for, Saengkeo. The people that I'm working with are going through everything they can find that Stoddard touched. They'll find it."

"In time?"

"I don't know." Bolan nodded toward the smoking computer systems. "Right now already seems too late." He paused. "Right now, Saengkeo, this is the only chance we have. I need you to trust me."

"You can't," Johnny Kwan said.

Saengkeo's eyes searched Bolan's, seeking something in his gaze that she couldn't find.

"If you can't trust me," Bolan said, "know that I'm going to trust you. Because I have to. And because I think I can." He stood, raising his arms and letting the M-16 hang from his shoulder. "Stoddard, we need to discuss the terms of our surrender." He was consciously aware that several of the enemy gunmen had him in their sights.

"Hold your fire," Stoddard ordered.

"Cease fire," Saengkeo commanded over the headset.

Tense silence filled the cargo hold, marred only by the sound of the savage storm raging abovedeck.

"Stoddard," Bolan called again. He switched his headset to the private frequency.

"I'm here," Price called tensely.

"Patch Mustang in," Bolan whispered. "Patch Saengkeo in, as well."

"Well, well," Stoddard said. "Our mystery man. I'm really not surprised to see you here. Come on down to the cargo deck."

Moving easily, Bolan walked along the catwalk and went down the ladder. He walked to the center of the cargo area near the smoldering remains of the computers.

"Over here," Stoddard called. This time he didn't use the PA system.

Looking to the left, Bolan spotted the rogue CIA agent standing with his back to a scarred and rusted container nearly as big as an 18-wheeler.

"Stop right there," Stoddard ordered. He pointed the SIG-Sauer in his fist at Bolan's head from less than twenty feet away. He held an electronic detonator in his left hand. "Drop your weapons. Slowly."

Moving carefully, Bolan slid the M-16 off his shoulder and laid the assault rifle on the cargo deck. He emptied his holsters of the Desert Eagle and the Beretta 93-R. Then he unlaced the combat harness containing the grenades and Cold Steel Tanto knife and left it on the deck.

"Come over here," Stoddard said.

"Mustang," Bolan said.

The open amidships hatch allowed the sounds of the storm and the bitter cold rain into the cargo area. Water already sluiced back and forth along the deck, rocking with the motion of the freighter.

"Mustang reads you, Striker," Grimaldi replied.

"That signal can't be sent," Bolan said. "I need you to take out the antenna array."

"Copy, Striker. It's gonna be dicey with that ship rising and falling in the ocean like she is."

"I've always counted on you, Mustang."

"You still can," Grimaldi said grimly. "On your go."

"Go," Bolan ordered. The DC-3 didn't carry any armament. The only choice Grimaldi had was to use the plane as his attack weapon. "Saengkeo, do you read?"

"Yes," she answered simply.

"It's all a matter of trust," Bolan said. "It goes both ways."

Stoddard glared at the Executioner. "What are you saying?" the CIA man demanded.

"My prayers," Bolan replied, aware that Saengkeo was in motion, tracking along the catwalk until she was directly in back of the soldier.

"Give me that damn headset," Stoddard ordered.

Without a word, Bolan took off the headset and extended it.

"Throw it over here," Stoddard demanded.

Bolan threw the headset onto the deck in front of the CIA man. The Executioner could no longer see Saengkeo, but he could feel her behind him in his mind. Inside the cargo hold, with the way the ship rolled and in the uncertain light, a shot would be difficult.

Stoddard pointed his own weapon at Bolan's head from nearly point-blank range as the soldier stopped in front of him.

"You weren't counting on this, were you?" Stoddard snarled.

"You weren't counting on getting caught up with."

Stoddard gestured with the remote control. "Looks like I'm still holding the top card here."

"We have control of the ship," Bolan said. "If you blow that warhead, I won't be able to keep the Moon Shadows off you."

"Looks like we've got a stand-off, then."

"Maybe," Bolan agreed.

"This ship goes where I want it to," Stoddard said. "And I say it goes to Macao."

"Cain's got people there who can take care of you," Bolan said.

Stoddard grinned. He remained up against the container, keeping himself under cover as much as possible. "So you know about that, too."

"Yeah," Bolan agreed. "We pretty much have it all. Even if you explode that warhead, the Chinese government is going to know who caused it."

"There'll still be a lot of dead people, though, won't there?" Stoddard kept his pistol level.

Bolan heard the DC-3's engines coming closer. "No," the Executioner said, "but there will be at least one more."

Stoddard started to say something, then he heard the engines, too, and looked up.

From where he stood, Bolan saw the open area of the amidships hatch. The lights strobed through the falling rain, and the DC-3 was a gray ghost that flashed through the night and smashed through the communications tower in a shower of sparks.

Sudden understanding filled Stoddard's face. He dropped his thumb over the detonator and pressed the button as Bolan dodged to one side. Stoddard shifted the pistol, tracking the soldier's head.

Then Stoddard jerked backward, struck by two bullets from Saengkeo's rifle. Another bullet glanced from the container wall behind the rogue CIA agent. Hit but not dead, Stoddard surged forward, his breath rasping from a sucking chest wound. He was dead on his feet and refused to give in.

Moving quickly, Bolan stepped forward, caught the man's extended hand, broke his elbow and placed the SIG-Sauer's barrel under Stoddard's chin. The Executioner slid his finger over Stoddard's and pulled the trigger.

Stoddard fell backward.

The Executioner plucked the pistol from the dead man's hand and spun, bringing the SIG-Sauer up in a Weaver stance. "Anyone who wants to live," he said in a graveyard voice, "drops their weapons now."

Only a heartbeat passed before the freighter's gunmen surrendered.

Bolan retrieved his headset. "Base."

"Here, Striker."

"What about Hong Kong?" Bolan looked up at Saengkeo, seeing the tension in her face.

"It's still there, too."

Epilogue

Bolan sat at an outside table of a café in Exchange Square and gazed out at the emerald waters of Victoria Harbour. Farther down the beach, Star Ferry disgorged another group of tourists. The breeze felt good, cooling him even beneath the turtleneck, khakis and black bomber jacket.

The events aboard the Greek freighter were thirty-three hours in the past. Five hours earlier, the missing warhead had been found by CIA agents using information Price and Kurtzman had given them and quietly taken away.

Restlessly, Bolan checked his watch.

"Didn't you know, Mr. Belasko, that it is a woman's prerogative to be late?"

Turning at the sound of Saengkeo Zhao's voice, Bolan saw the woman moving across the plaza behind him. She was dressed in sea-foam green stretch pants, a white shirt that showed the barest hint of the golden skin of her stomach, and a sea-foam green jacket with the sleeves rolled up to midforearm. Sunglasses hid her eyes.

Bolan stood and offered her a chair. "It was worth the wait," he told her.

A thin eyebrow arched above the sunglasses as he took his seat opposite her. "Flattery?"

"Appreciation," Bolan replied. Despite the business they had to conduct, he had to admit she was a hell of a good-looking woman.

"I hope this place is good for you."

"Yes."

"After meeting as we did on *Charity's Smile* and in my hotel room, I thought perhaps a different atmosphere might be in the offing."

"Yeah," Bolan said. "I didn't recognize you at first without the pistol pointed at my head."

She smiled. "A sense of humor?"

"Seldom used," Bolan agreed.

"Neither one of us are in the business for it."

"No," the soldier agreed. "Though it appears you may be something of a hero."

With Hal Brognola's help, most of the true story behind the theft of the nuclear weapons from *Jadviga* had been told to the Chinese government. Repercussions from the situation were still forthcoming, but they were left up to the diplomats to take and give trade concessions for a period of time.

However, Sebastian Cain was going to find himself in trouble in China and in the United States. Triads had descended on his businesses in the Far East, and the IRS was paying particular attention to his business dealings in the United States. At the moment, no one knew where the billionaire was, but his life wasn't going to be a good one.

The Moon Shadow triad's efforts in taking down *Aristotle's Star* had been played up. The suspicions that had been formed that the triad had been allying itself with the CIA had been offset by the fact that a case could be made that Stoddard was setting them up.

"Things here are going to be...difficult," Saengkeo acknowledged, "but we'll make do. My family always has."

The waiter came and took their orders. Saengkeo requested a glass of white wine, and Bolan took a beer.

"I don't understand why you wanted this meeting," Saengkeo said.

"Because," Bolan answered, "I wanted to make you an offer."

Settling back in her chair, the humor left Saengkeo's face. She wrapped her arms around herself. "I'm not interested in further dealing with your government."

Bolan let her words hang in the air between them for a time. "You're a good woman, Saengkeo. What you're trying to do—getting your family out of the business it has been in—is a good thing to do. But you're not going to be able to do it for a very long time without help."

"Then it will be left for my descendants to do."

Bolan nodded. "You could do that. But you could lose a lot of people between now and then. You can cut that time down."

"And this is where I'm supposed to ask how."

Despite the situation, Bolan grinned. He liked the woman. It would have been interesting to meet her under different circumstances; if things were different for her and things were different for him. He still remembered how she had looked dressed in steam in the hotel shower.

"There's a man I can hook you up with," Bolan said. "He's a good man. His name is Harold Brognola, and he can go to bat for you with my government. He can help you place more of your family outside Hong Kong, continue moving them from the triad life as you have done."

"What do I have to do?"

"The same thing you've been doing. Just feed Brognola information about the triads and the Chinese governments."

"Be a spy? That doesn't sound very noble."

"You say spy. I say you're someone who's risking her life to help her family. These same people you'll be spying on are the people you're trying to save your family from."

"I'm not interested," Saengkeo said. "I've had enough of trusting people."

"Brognola is a good man," Bolan repeated. "You can trust him."

She remained silent.

"Saengkeo, I know about the school where you spend time. I know how you feel about those kids. Brognola can help you get them and their families out of this life."

Pain touched Saengkeo's eyes. "You make it sound so easy. It's not that easy."

"I know it's not that easy." Bolan shifted in his seat. "I don't like asking you to do this."

"Then why are you?"

"Because I know you," the soldier said. "I know you'll continue trying to help your family and risking your life. This is the best way I know to help you, the best way I know to keep your risks at a minimum and maximize your efforts and time."

For a moment, she sat as silent as stone. He thought she was going to walk away from him. But she remained seated and she looked at him.

"Do you know this Brognola?" she asked.

"He's my friend," Bolan answered.

"Do you trust him?"

"With my life."

Saengkeo looked away from him. "Trust is so hard, you know."

"I know," Bolan agreed. "It's like faith and belief. Once you know something is true, you no longer have to believe in it. Once you know someone will always be there for you, it's no longer trust. It's not belief anymore. It's a fact."

"Which would you rather have? Facts or belief?"

Bolan thought about that for a moment. "Belief changes more lives, allows more people to change themselves, than facts ever did. I'll take belief. And the day I quit believing in what I'm doing is the day that I no longer know how to be true to myself."

Saengkeo sipped her wine. "Do you know where you are going after this?"

"Not yet."

"Or when you're leaving?"

"When I'm ready."

"You know," she said, "I could make you an offer, too. My organization, I can afford to be very generous."

Bolan shook his head. "My path doesn't lie in that direction. Money doesn't mean anything to me."

"But you prize family."

"Yes."

"I could offer you another family."

"I already have one."

"You know, it's been a very long time since I relaxed and enjoyed some of the things this island has to offer. Perhaps you would agree to join me. We could discuss your friend Brognola."

Bolan didn't hesitate. Grimaldi was looking for another plane to replace the DC-3 he'd sunk out in the ocean, and after everything they had been through in the past few days, they both had a little downtime coming. If something came up, Stony Man would be in touch.

"I'd like that," he told the lady.

DEATH LANDS®

Bloodfire

*Available in December 2003
at your favorite retail outlet.*

Hearing a rumor that The Trader, his old teacher and friend, is still alive, Ryan and his warrior group struggle across the Texas desert to find the truth. But an enemy with a score to settle is in hot pursuit—and so is the elusive Trader. And so the stage is set for a showdown between mortal enemies, where the scales of revenge and death will be balanced with brutal finality.